Wick stopped dancing, a sort of primal anger running through his veins. What sort of woman would cheat her own niece out of her fortune? And treat her like less than a servant in the meantime?

"Believe me, Lady Louisa," he said, breathing hard as he pulled her closer to him. Until their bodies met fully together. His hardness to her softness. Their curves perfectly matching the other's dips. "You are the most beautiful woman I have ever seen and you will be surrounded in London by suitors—and not just because of your fortune and title."

Lady Louisa's eyes were still focused on the folds of his cravat. "Will you be one of them?"

"You won't need me," he assured her, stepping back. Touching her was too tempting. "There are plenty of other eligible young men who will appreciate your charms. But first, we must take you to your uncle. There will be less gossip if you are staying with a family member, and he should know who your trustees are and how to reach them. Surely, they cannot be aware how you are being treated by your aunt. No man or woman of conscience would have allowed it."

"Will...will you help me?"

He knew better than to give rash promises, but her countenance was so open and trusting that he couldn't help himself. "I will."

Author Note

I am delighted to introduce you to the Marquess of Cheswick and the Stringham family. They are quite the most delightful and quirky bunch of characters that I have ever penned. They live in Hampford Castle and have an animal menagerie. The story is set in 1810 before there were formal zoos in England.

The menagerie was inspired by the animals kept at Chiswick House by the sixth Duke of Devonshire, William Cavendish (1790–1858). It is believed from archive receipts that his menagerie included an elephant, a giraffe (called a "camel leopard"), cockatoos, gold and silver pheasants, a monkey, a llama, elks, emus, kangaroos, ostriches, a Neapolitan pig, goats, an Indian bull and his spouse, a coatimundi and a blood-sucking ichneumon.

The Marchioness of Hastings asked the Duke of Devonshire what animal he would like her to send from India. Cavendish reportedly quipped, "Nothing smaller than an elephant." And she did. On May 17, 1828, Sir Walter Scott wrote in his diary that "the scene was dignified by the presence of an immense elephant, who under the charge of a groom wandered up and down, giving an air of Asiatic pageantry to the entertainment." Sadi the elephant also performed a number of parlor tricks according to *The London Saturday Journal* (November 1839): taking her cape off a peg and putting it on, kneeling down and giving rides, and cleaning her own house with a broom or scrubbing brush.

The animals in the menagerie are tame compared to the Stringham sisters!

SAMANTHA HASTINGS

—

The Marquess and the Runaway Lady

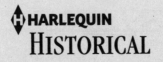

HARLEQUIN®
HISTORICAL™

Recycling programs for this product may not exist in your area.

ISBN-13: 978-1-335-72376-5

The Marquess and the Runaway Lady

Copyright © 2023 by Samantha Hastings

For questions and comments about the quality of this book, please contact us at CustomerService@Harlequin.com.

Harlequin Enterprises ULC
22 Adelaide St. West, 41st Floor
Toronto, Ontario M5H 4E3, Canada
www.Harlequin.com

Printed in U.S.A.

Samantha Hastings met her husband in a turkey sandwich line. They live in Salt Lake City, Utah, where she spends most of her time reading, having tea parties and chasing her kids. She has degrees from Brigham Young University, University of North Texas and University of Reading (UK). She's the author of *The Last Word*, *The Invention of Sophie Carter*, *A Royal Christmas Quandary*, *The Girl with the Golden Eyes*, *Jane Austen Trivia*, *The Duchess Contract*, *Secret of the Sonnets* and *A Novel Disguise*. She also writes cozy murder mysteries under Samantha Larsen.

Learn more at her website: SamanthaHastings.com

Connect with Samantha on social media:
Twitter: @HastingSamantha
Instagram: @SamanthaHastingsAuthor
Facebook: SamanthaHastingsAuthor

The Marquess and the Runaway Lady
is Samantha Hastings's debut title
for Harlequin Historical.

Look out for more books from Samantha Hastings
coming soon.

Visit the Author Profile page
at Harlequin.com.

To Violet

Acknowledgments

First and foremost, I want to thank my family for all of their support: Jon, Andrew, Alivia, Isaac and Violet. I am so blessed to have parents who tell everyone they meet about my books. I am grateful for my sisters, Michelle Martin and Stacy Moon. They are always my first readers and loudest cheerleaders. I owe a huge thanks to my agent, Jen Nadol. She tirelessly champions both me and my work. And finally, to the incredible publishing staff who created this beautiful final product. I was lucky enough not to have one but two editors! Thank you so much, Bryony Green and Soraya Bouazzaoui, for helping me make my book the best it can be.

Chapter One

England, 1810

Louisa didn't expect gifts on her twenty-first birthday. Her aunt and uncle had never given her a present in the ten and a half years she had been their ward. If she ever complained about her threadbare dresses, or the lack of fire in her room, Aunt Rockingham would explain that it was all *her* fault.

Lady Louisa Bracken was the only child of the Fourth and deceased Earl of Rockingham. His younger brother, Alfred, had become the Fifth Earl of Rockingham and had brought with him his wife and four sons. She had been left in their care, and her mother's fortune, which Louisa was to inherit, had been entrusted to three trustees. A yearly stipend was paid to her uncle for Louisa's upkeep.

Aunt Rockingham protested that this allowance barely kept her niece in gloves, and would rage for days at a time at Louisa's selfish father, who hadn't trusted his only brother to care for the financial interests of his niece. Strangely enough, Aunt Rockingham herself dressed in the finest of silks and muslins. And had a pair of gloves dyed to match every gown. She also never missed a London season, claiming that she must be there for Uncle Rockingham to take his seat in Parliament.

Every time Louisa begged to go her aunt claimed that there simply wasn't enough money for such an expensive endeavour.

Pulling on her stocking, Louisa felt her big toe go straight through. With a humourless laugh, she thought that she had to be the poorest heiress in all of England. She didn't even have a maid to help her dress. And the maids had finer clothing than she did. Louisa had never once seen a darn in a servant's stocking, or a tear in their clothing.

She took out the needle that she always kept stuck in the hem of her skirt and deftly repaired the new hole in her stocking.

It was all going to change today. Louisa was finally one-and-twenty years of age and she could now take possession of her fortune. Buttoning up her gown, she determined she would no longer be under her aunt's thumb. With her inheritance she would go to London, be presented to the Queen—as her mother had been—and find a suitable match of her own.

She wouldn't even miss her home, Greystone Hall. She had loved it as a child, but in the last few years it had begun to feel like a prison. Her aunt would only let her attend church, never the local assemblies. Not that it mattered… Louisa didn't know how to dance. Her aunt had insisted that she could not afford to employ a governess for Louisa, let alone a dancing master. She'd dismissed Louisa's former governess the day after her father's funeral.

Pulling on boots that were too small and pinched, Louisa sighed. What sort of match would she make when she didn't even know how to behave like a young lady?

Louisa found her aunt in the newly refurbished blue drawing room, writing letters at her desk. Her aunt was a formidable woman of middling years. She had a distinguished face with a black mole on the side of her cheek. Today, she was wearing a lovely day gown of jaconet, with a necklace of three strands of pearls. Her cap did not fully hide her greying black hair.

How long Louisa had wished to please this woman! To change her behaviour and earn her aunt's elusive approval. But it didn't matter how agreeable, effacing or obedient she was, Aunt Rockingham did not love her. Nor even like her. There must be something wrong with her, thought Louisa, that not even her closest relatives could abide her.

'Hello, Aunt,' Louisa began, feeling the blood rushing to her face. 'I was hoping to talk to you today.'

Her aunt's countenance tightened into an expression of annoyance. 'I am very busy writing letters at this moment. Perhaps I will be able to find time for you later this morning.'

'Today I am of age,' Louisa continued, clutching the sides of her gown with both hands to steel her courage. 'Now that I am possessed of my inheritance I wish to go to London. Immediately.'

Her aunt snorted, shaking her head. 'Oh, you silly girl. You couldn't possibly go to London without me. Poor Barnabas has lost a fortune, due to unscrupulous card sharps, so there's no money for you to go. Besides, a young lady of birth must have a chaperone to attend parties, and I find that I am much too weary this year to take you. You will simply have to wait until next year. Or perhaps the year after.'

Louisa's shoulders drooped, but she was not going to give up yet. 'I am sure one of my trustees has a wife who could be my chaperone and present me to the Queen.'

'But they are not your guardians.'

'I am one-and-twenty, ma'am. I do not need a guardian any longer.'

Aunt Rockingham set down her pen. Her mouth pinched into a fine line. 'I agree that you are quite old enough to make your own choices. But your late father's will does not allow you to touch your inheritance until you are five-and-twenty years old or married to someone with your guardian's approval.'

Four more years?

Louisa's stomach dropped in dismay. She could have lain on the floor and thrown a tantrum like a small child—kicking and screaming. She could not endure being locked up in her own home for four more years, with an aunt who didn't like her and an uncle who ignored her very existence.

'But I am already old to be a debutante. Most young ladies are presented at court when they are seventeen. I fear I am losing all my chances.'

'I hadn't wanted to mention this to you,' her aunt said, frowning. 'But you are an ill-favoured, extremely freckled young woman. It would be highly unlikely, even if I did take you to London, for you to find a suitable husband. It would be a waste of time and money.'

Touching her hot cheeks, Louisa felt her heart drop as she wondered if her aunt's words could be true. Her hair was like the red of leaves in autumn. Her eyes the same green as moss. But her face and arms *were* covered in freckles. Tiny reddish-brown blemishes.

Glancing down, she knew that she was tall and skinny. At least compared to her aunt. What if she was ugly? Was her unprepossessing appearance the reason why her aunt could never feel affection for her?

Louisa gulped, trying to hold in the tears that threatened to spill down her cheeks. 'Then I am to stay home for another four years?'

'Let me be frank with you, Louisa,' her aunt said, giving her niece a withering stare. 'I had hoped that Barnabas could be brought up to scratch before now. But he insists that he is too young to marry yet, and there are his debts that must be repaid. So you'll have to wait another year or two. Then you will be married. After the ceremony you will be presented to the Queen of England as Barnabas's wife.'

Barnabas was her eldest cousin and heir to the earldom. He was a stocky and sullen young man who was several inches shorter than her. Like his mother, he had a distinguished black mole on his face, but it was on his chin. His only notable accomplishments so far were being sent down from both Eton and Oxford. Barnabas ate too much. Drank too much. Gambled too much. If the maids were to be believed—and Louisa thought they were—he had a lascivious eye and wandering hands. He was five years her senior and the last man in the world she would ever want to marry. Her entire body shivered in revulsion from just thinking of it. She could not be his wife.

Louisa shook her head slowly, her heart sinking further. 'I don't blame my cousin for not wishing to marry me. I don't want to marry him either.'

'Of course Barnabas wishes to marry you,' her aunt said in a scolding tone. 'He simply isn't ready to do so yet.'

'But Aunt—'

'Louisa!' she said, in a high shrill voice. 'I am done with discussing the matter. You had best go and see if Mrs Barker has any mending for you to do. I can't have you underneath my feet all day. You've already wasted half of my morning, and I have important correspondence to write.'

Shoulders slumped, Louisa left the parlour and went to the kitchens to find the housekeeper. When she opened the door, she saw the entire staff were lined up They all began to wish her a happy birthday and the cook, Mrs Hatch, held out a small cake that was decorated with a delicate white swan on top.

Louisa couldn't help but smile as tears fell down her cheeks. Mrs Barker and the rest of the staff had not forgotten her birthday. They loved her even if she was ugly.

'Thank you! Oh, thank you!' Louisa said, accepting the cake from the cook. 'I have never seen a more beautifully decorated cake. I am the luckiest young lady in the world! Come, we must all have a piece of it together.'

'We can't eat with you, my lady,' the butler, Mr Meadows, insisted. 'It wouldn't be proper.'

She sniffed and wiped at her eyes. 'Oh, please do join me. Or I shall have to eat this marvellous cake by myself, and that would be such a sad thing on my birthday.'

Mrs Hatch had a merry red face and she cut the cake into perfectly even slices and gave Louisa the first one. Louisa took a bite and it was like tasting heaven—sweet, buttery and light. Her aunt rarely let her partake of anything sweet. She insisted that it was to preserve Louisa's figure.

She took another bite of cake, but this time it tasted like ash. She forced herself to swallow it and then played with her fork, unable to eat any more.

'Am I truly ugly?' she blurted out.

Mrs Hatch dropped the knife she was holding and it clattered on the table top. 'Why would ye ask such a thing, my lady?'

'Of course not,' Mrs Barker said, patting Louisa's shoulder with her bony hand. She was an extremely slender elderly woman, with fine features and soft white hair. 'You're a beauty, just like your mother was.'

Louisa could feel a blush coming on. Her red hair and light complexion were unfortunately prone to blushes.

She glanced down at the slice of cake on her plate. 'My aunt said that I was ill-favoured and would not be able to find a suitable husband. She insists that I marry my cousin Barnabas. Only he doesn't want to marry me yet…so I have to wait a few more years.'

'Don't marry that lecher, my lady!' said Lily, a pretty blonde maid a year or two younger than Louisa. She squeezed Louisa's wrist. 'He ain't worthy of you.'

'The old witch just wants your fortune for her son,' said Goodman. He was a bald, gruff elderly man who had been head groom under her father, but now was relegated to a lowlier position in the stables.

Louisa clutched at her throat. It felt as hot as her face. She had no family who loved her or would help her.

'I don't want to marry Barnabas. He's a dreadful person. Only, I don't know what to do. Or who to ask for help. I don't even know the names of my trustees. My mother's only brother is a vicar in Somerset, but I've never been in contact with their family... And look at me. No one would believe I was a lady or an heiress.'

'Right,' said Mrs Barker, pointing a bony finger at her. 'First things first. You'll need a new dress. There's a bit of material left from the curtains in the blue parlour.'

'I can sew it. But I'll need new boots,' Louisa added. Her toes were starting to feel numb in her too-tight ones.

'Mine have grown too small, if you don't mind having second-hand,' Lily offered. 'Mrs Barker has already purchased a new pair for me.'

Louisa patted the maid's hand. 'I would be most grateful.'

Mrs Hatch touched the end of Louisa's nose. 'And I've trimmed a straw bonnet that would look very fetching on ye.'

'Lady Rockingham has so many pairs of gloves she wouldn't notice if one went astray,' offered Miss Talley. She was her aunt's lady's maid, and a handsome middle-aged woman with a trim figure and lovely auburn hair.

Goodman cleared his throat. 'I could take the gig and drive you to your uncle's vicarage in Somerset, my lady. I'm not allowed to drive the carriage any more... Me not being fancy enough for the Countess.'

Hope filled Louisa's chest for the first time in years, but she didn't want to hurt these servants who had been kinder to her than her family...who had loved her when no one else did.

'But won't you all get into trouble?'

'For what?' the butler said in his snobbish tones. Meadows was more polished than a duke, and looked like one with his dark hair and aquiline nose.

He gazed haughtily down that same aristocratic nose

now, as he added, 'I don't know what you are talking about. I will certainly never say I saw Lady Louisa leave.'

'And neither did I,' Mrs Hatch said with a merry wink. 'And you can take this month's leftover housekeeping money.'

Louisa listened as one by one they all vowed to claim no knowledge of her plans or whereabouts. Wiping happy tears from her eyes, she thanked them with all her heart. Maybe she wasn't completely ugly and unlovable…

Chapter Two

Lord Simon Anthony Peregrine Stringham, the Marquess of Cheswick, known to his family as 'Wick', was head of the family whilst his parents, the Duke and Duchess of Hampford, were travelling in Africa to return animals to the wild. They would be gone for about a year, and he'd been tasked to keep an eye on his five younger siblings.

It was enough to put a fellow into a permanent cold sweat.

Wick had been forced to leave his best friend the Duke of Sunderland's shooting party early, for he feared the mayhem that his family would cause during his absence. Or, worse, that scarlet fever would strike again, as it had the last time his parents had gone to Africa, nearly ten years ago. His youngest sister Becca had only been three years old at the time.

After travelling to London, he had at least reassured himself of his brother's health and wellness. Lord Matthew Stringham was living in bachelor's rooms and working with their maternal grandfather, Mr Stubbs. Like their grandfather, Matthew had a head for legal affairs and was busy building his own fortune in business. He'd laughed at his elder brother's concern.

Wick had also checked on his married sister Mantheria, the Duchess of Glastonbury, and her three-year-old son, Andrew. He'd taken them on a drive around the park in his phaeton and then to Gunter's for ices, carefully cementing his position as favourite uncle.

His two middle sisters, Lady Frederica and Lady Helen, were safely at a school in Bath run by the eminently respectable Miss Victoria Cluess. And his youngest sister, Lady Rebecca—Becca—hadn't liked the school, so he had hired her a governess—Miss Young, a niece of the Reverend Robertson, the vicar from the village near the castle.

He hadn't actually met the woman, but she'd come highly recommended. He'd written for her to take up the position at Hampford Castle immediately. Becca was a darling, and his favourite sister, but left to her own devices she could be quite a handful…and she was unfortunately fond of making rodents her pets.

Lifting his whip, he snapped it above his greys' heads. The horses immediately increased their pace. As if they, too, knew how close they were to being home.

Now all he had to do was check on the Hampford estate and the new governess and all his worries for his family would be put to rest.

Wrinkling his nose, Wick manoeuvred his horses through the south gate of Hampford Castle. To the average viewer the old place was large, dark and forbidding. But to Wick this stone pile with its many towers and parapets was home.

Handing his reins to a groom, Wick jumped out of the phaeton in time to be caught in a tight embrace. His little sister Becca's head barely reached his shoulders, but at the moment she was pushing it most painfully into his stomach. He gently took her arms and pushed her away from him, so that he might see her face.

Becca had the same brown hair as he did, but instead of brown eyes she had bright blue ones that sparkled with mischief. Today, however, her eyes were full of tears. There was a new line of freckles on her nose, and her dress and apron were covered in mud—not an unusual occurrence.

'What's the matter, Becca, my heart?'

She sniffed and rubbed a dirty finger under her nose, smudging dirt on her face. 'Wick, it wasn't my fault. Truly!'

'What wasn't your fault, love?'

Becca blinked and grabbed the end of her untidy plait. She fingered it as her eyes focused on his feet. 'Miss Young has left.'

It took Wick a moment or two to remember who the blazes Miss Young was—the governess who had come so highly recommended by the vicar and his wife.

A trickle of worry ran down his neck like a bead of sweat. 'What happened? What did you do?'

His littlest sister took in a deep breath. 'Mademoiselle Jaune wouldn't stop calling her a tasty tart.'

Wick was torn between a desire to yell in frustration and another to laugh.

Their yellow macaw with a missing claw was known for her bawdy language. Papa had purchased her from a one-eyed man in a rookery. He had been keeping her in a small, dirty cage. His father had tried to free the bird, but Mademoiselle Jaune had always come back to the castle. Papa had explained that some animals, particularly those born in captivity, became too domesticated ever to go back in the wild. They did not know how to hunt or how to take care of themselves.

'She left because of the bird?'

Becca bit her lower lip and looked even younger than her thirteen years. 'Miss Young said that either she or the bird had to go. Then Frederica said that we infinitely preferred Mademoiselle Jaune's company to hers. Miss Young left in a huff on foot over an hour ago. She didn't even take her things with her.'

'Wait a minute,' Wick said, holding up a hand and trying to take it all in. A frisson of fear was crawling down his spine and his left eye had started to twitch. 'What is Frederica doing home? She's supposed to be at school. The summer holidays aren't for another two months.'

Two more *glorious* months of relative peace and quiet.

Becca's honest little face went red. 'Well, Helen and Frederica being sent home from finishing school *is* my fault.'

A dozen curses ran through his mind and he had to grind his teeth together to keep them from coming out in front of his sister.

He shook his head. 'How could it be your fault, Becca? You weren't there.'

She sniffed and her chin quivered. 'I told Frederica the name of the girl who had bullied me at school and called me stupid…and Frederica cut off all her hair while she was sleeping. So the headmistress sent her home.'

Wick was torn between pride and disapproval. He'd been more angry than fire when Becca had written to him asking to come home because of a girl who had mercilessly teased and excluded her. He had removed Becca from Bath, but there hadn't been much else he could do to make it better. Now, he couldn't help but feel a tiny bit satisfied that the nasty girl had got her due.

'And what did Helen do to get sent home from school?'

'Nothing much.'

'Becca…' He said her name this time without the usual added endearment. His left eye was twitching again.

His little sister grabbed the end of her plait again—a nervous habit. 'Helen put a snake in the bed of every girl my age who had not befriended me. They weren't poisonous, though! Just simple grass snakes.'

Wick could only close his eyes and moan. How long had his sisters planned their revenge that they'd been able to find enough snakes?

'So now I have all three of you home and no governess?'

Becca nodded and his two other sisters popped out from behind the main double doors of the castle. Frederica looked smug, but Helen gave him a tremulous smile.

Frederica, his second to eldest sister, could usually slither her way out of trouble—but not this time. She had been blessed with the same brown hair and buxom figure as their mother; at nearly seventeen, she should have known better than to participate in schoolgirl pranks.

Helen was younger by two years and did not look like either sister. She was small and slight, almost waif-like. Her hair was flaxen-yellow and her blue eyes seemed to take up most of her face. Helen was a naturalist, like their father, with an unfortunate affinity to snakes.

Taking off his hat, Wick raked one hand through his hair. He could have used an entire dictionary of curses. Twice. 'I cannot believe you two! This is beyond anything you've ever done before.'

'We are really sorry to have upset you, Wick,' Helen

said, holding her clasped hands together beseechingly. 'Truly.'

'But you aren't sorry for what you've done?'

Frederica snorted, folding her arms across her chest. 'Of course not. Those little beasts deserved everything that they got and more.'

Wick swallowed; his throat felt dry and scratchy. 'Mama will be furious. You two are supposed to be at school, preparing for your debuts, not behaving like hoydens. This little stunt might have ruined your chances of ever finding a suitable match and harmed Becca's.'

Becca was practically chewing off her lower lip. Helen sniffed, and one theatrical tear fell from her eye and slid down her cheek. She could cry on command—a useful talent that she'd used to weasel her way out of trouble more than once. Frederica merely snorted again, and gave him a glare very similar to their mother's stare.

'We're *Stringhams*, Wick,' Frederica said, unimpressed by his threats. 'We could parade down the street in our small clothes and every blasted peer would still beg to marry us.'

'We might get even *more* offers!' Helen said with a high giggle.

Before he knew it, all three of his little sisters were laughing. Wick experienced a full-body shiver. His sisters were wild and stubborn enough to do anything. And he'd learned from the last time he'd been in charge that he could not do it alone.

He had to get that governess back *now*.

He wouldn't fail his family this time.

Chapter Three

Louisa sewed through the night to finish the dress. It was a simple high-necked gown with a small puff at the top of long sleeves that tightened at her wrists. Miss Talley, her aunt's lady's maid, had pilfered not only a pair of white gloves, but stockings without holes. They felt amazingly soft on Louisa's feet.

Mrs Hatch put the new bonnet on Louisa's head and tied the ribbons. The cook must have spent hours adding the artificial flowers and ribbons, but instead of keeping it for herself, she was giving it to Louisa. A few tears escaped Louisa's eyes as she hugged Mrs Hatch and thanked her. Mrs Hatch squeezed her back tightly. She had always given the best embraces. Ever since Louisa was little the cook had chased her around the kitchen and when she'd caught her kissed the top of Louisa's head.

Mrs Hatch had always made her feel safe and loved. Unlike her aunt, who had continually reminded her niece that she was an unwanted encumbrance.

Lily brought her the old boots, which fitted much better than Louisa's own and were much nicer and newly polished. The only thing that Louisa was missing was a spencer or a shawl, but that did not matter. She was in a new dress, hat, gloves, stockings, and even boots. The leftover housekeeping coins jiggled against each other in her pocket.

Then Mrs Barker came up behind her and wrapped a beautiful lace shawl around her shoulders. 'I tatted it myself. I always planned to give it to you on your wedding day, but needs must.'

Delicately fingering the lace, Louisa thought that the shawl was the loveliest piece of clothing she had ever seen. Not even Aunt Rockingham had anything so fine. Oh, the hours it must have taken Mrs Barker to make it!

Tears filled Louisa's eyes as she hugged the bony woman for the first time. She wasn't soft and cuddly, like Mrs Hatch, but she returned the hug.

'I will take great care of it,' Louisa promised her. 'And when I marry I shall wear it around my shoulders. I promise you.'

'We'd best hurry, my lady,' said Goodman in his usual gruff voice. 'Daylight is coming and it would be best for us to be out of sight.'

Swallowing her emotions, Louisa shook hands with him and thanked everyone again, before following Goodman out into the cold and wet dawn. He had already hooked the old gig to a pair of horses. They weren't the flashy ones that her uncle drove his curricle with, but strong, reliable work horses from the farm. She accepted his hand up into the carriage and sat beside him.

He flicked the reins. 'Giddy up.'

The Greystone Hall estate's circumference was over ten miles. Louisa had not been off it in over a decade. Still, she wanted to memorise every detail. Each tree. The paths. The valley. Because she never intended to come back. She planned to have a London season and marry a man she loved, just as her mother had. Even as a child she had known that her parents loved each other. And they had loved her dearly. That knowledge had often been the only thing that had helped Louisa through all her monotonous days stuck at Greystone Hall.

Yawning, Louisa found it harder and harder to keep her eyes open. Her late-night sewing was catching up with her, and the jolts and bumps of the carriage were gentle. She fought to keep her eyelids open, but eventually the struggle was too great.

When Louisa woke up, a few hours later, her neck was sore from sleeping while sitting, and her stomach growled with hunger. She moved her hand to her nape and rubbed it gently.

'Almost there, my lady,' Goodman said, pointing to a lonely house further down the road, nestled by a church.

She picked up her small bag from the floor and clutched it to her stomach. What if her uncle refused to help her? What if he sent her back to Aunt Rockingham? Her aunt was shrewd enough to put a watch on her to make sure that she never escaped again. She did not like to be crossed. This was Louisa's only chance for freedom. She prayed that she hadn't made a foolish choice.

Goodman stopped the gig on the road, a few dozen yards away from the vicarage in Frome. ''Tis best if I leave you here.'

Holding his hand, she stepped out of the carriage. Her knees were shaky. 'Thank you, Goodman. I appreciate your assistance more than I can say.'

He touched his hat to her and then clicked his tongue. The horses moved forward and she watched him turn the vehicle on the small pike road and return in the same direction he had come. The poor man had a long carriage ride in front of him.

Taking a deep breath, Louisa forced her quaking limbs to walk down the gravel drive. She paused as she reached the house. Should she go to the front door or the back? She wanted her aunt and uncle's first impression of her to be the best possible. Glancing down, she saw her new blue dress was covered in dust from the drive. Even her lovely new shawl would need to be soaked in vinegar and washed. She hardly looked like the respectable daughter of an earl. She'd best go to the servants' entrance.

Louisa knocked sharply on the door.

A middle-aged woman with white hair pulled severely back, wearing a white cap and apron, answered it. 'What can I help you with, miss?'

Louisa jumped, felt her mouth dry. 'I am here to see the Reverend Laybourne.'

The woman shook her head and harrumphed. 'He's not here, miss.'

Lowering her chin, Louisa felt her confidence receding. 'When will he be back?'

'Never. He was promoted to Canon of Sherborne and now he and his family live in a fine house there. The new man, Reverend Nance, kept me on as housekeeper. But he ain't married so it wouldn't be proper for you to stay.'

Her heart sank in her chest. 'How far is the town of Sherborne from here?'

The woman scratched her arm. 'Thirty miles, I'd say.'

Louisa felt dizzy and her limbs tingled with fatigue. She kneaded her chest with the heel of her hand, trying to soothe the pain there. Such a distance was unfathomable, but what choice did she have?

'Which way?'

The housekeeper stepped out of the vicarage and Louisa trudged behind her. The woman pointed down the path. 'Just head south through the town and continue down the road. You can't miss it. But first come in my kitchen for a cup of tea and something to eat, miss. Can't have you setting off on an empty stomach.'

'Thank you.'

Louisa was grateful for the meal as she walked and walked until she thought that her feet had more blisters than skin. She feared that by the time she reached her uncle's house that she would give her relatives a bad first impression. She was dusty, sweaty, and her once tidy hair blown about.

She dimly recalled her Uncle Laybourne from her mother's funeral. He'd seemed solemn and had not spoken a word to her. His wife had wrapped her thin arms around Louisa and promised to invite her for a visit to meet all her cousins. Louisa had longed to go home with her. But she had not realised how serious her aunt's perpetual cough was until she'd died not long after, of consumption. Her uncle had remarried, but his new wife had never attempted to make contact with Louisa.

What if they rejected her, like Uncle and Aunt Rockingham?

What if she wasn't good enough for them either?

She swallowed; her throat was parched and her stomach continued to make loud noises of hunger. Wiping off her brow, she gazed further down the road and saw a lone rider coming towards her. The hairs on her arms stood up and her pulse quickened. She was all alone. No family. No friends.

Could he mean her harm?

Chapter Four

There was nothing for it. He would have to find the erstwhile governess and offer her more money. His sisters needed constant supervision and he was not able to give it to them whilst he took care of the affairs of the estate.

Wick heaved a sigh filled with exhaustion and frustration. He pointed his finger at his three youngest sisters. 'Don't get into any mischief while I'm gone.'

'We won't,' Helen assured him with her most charming smile.

It set him on his guard. His usually sweet sister was like the snakes she carried around; you never knew when she was going to strike with her strongest venom.

'Don't count on it!' Frederica said.

At least she was always honest.

'Where are you going, Wick?' Becca asked, taking his hand and pulling on it. 'You have only just got home.'

'To find your blasted governess. No thanks to any of *you*,' he said gruffly.

Wick called for the groom to harness a horse to the curricle. His greys were already spent from the drive to Hampford. Shoving on his hat, he climbed up into the driver's seat. He was dusty, tired and abominably thirsty, but there was nothing else to be done.

'Which way did she go, Becca?'

His little sister hesitantly pointed to the north gate— a direction he usually avoided. It was the opposite way from the village and the vicarage where Miss Young's aunt and uncle lived. The foolish governess had headed in the wrong direction.

Wick flicked the reins to urge his horse forward. The north gate was not used as often as the south. Both still had the wrought-iron pulleys of another age, but the gates were rarely closed in these modern days. The only time he remembered them being shut had been when Papa had lost control of his emu and contained it by closing the iron gates.

Wick only wished that he could have kept the governess in the same way.

His heartbeat was irregular as he passed Animal Island, the animal sanctuary where his father kept those creatures too domesticated to be freed. The island was close to the family crypt, where those they'd loved were buried. The grief had not lessened over time. If anything, it had become more keen and painful.

Wick felt an overall feeling of weakness, but it was growing dark now. He had to find Miss Young and make sure that she was safe.

He drove for another five miles, his headache increasing with each furlong.

Where could the blasted woman be? She clearly had no sense of direction or she would have long before realised that the village was in the opposite direction and much closer to the castle. She should have been at her uncle's vicarage long before now.

Wick had nearly given up hope of locating the governess when he saw a woman trudging down the road. She was coming his way. He rocked back and forth in his seat in relief. Perhaps the governess had finally realised that she was heading in the wrong direction. Or that it had been foolish to walk away without her belongings.

Urging the horse on, he sped towards her. The woman wore a blue dress that was liberally covered in dirt from the knees down. She clutched a small bag in her hands as if it possessed her entire fortune. Mayhap the woman wasn't as careless as Becca had said, and hadn't left all her money and belongings at the castle.

As he got closer to her the woman looked up at him. He'd been expecting a plain governess with sensible hair, a no-nonsense stern mouth, and hands like cricket bats. The young woman before him had none of those things. She was tall and slender, but with gentle curves. Her hair was a riot of red curls, completely untamed. Her pale skin was covered in hundreds of sweet freckles. Wick had the most unaccountable thought that it would be lovely to kiss every single one.

The young woman smiled at him, but it was fearful. Her expression was like his little sister Becca's when she was in trouble.

Wick felt the hardening in his stomach lessen. The poor woman was already scared—he didn't need to bite her head off. Though he dearly wished to.

'It would appear that you are in need of a lift, miss.'

She tipped her head up to look at him. Her eyes were a bright green that sparkled like emeralds in her face. There was a freckle just above her lips—that was the one he'd kiss first. If he kissed any of them. Which he wouldn't. Because she was the governess, and such things weren't done. And, frankly, he'd never been tempted to kiss his own governess. Miss Nix hadn't inspired affection or physical admiration. She'd been an old battle-axe, who had retired after Mantheria's debut four years before.

'I should not wish to put you out, sir,' the lady said in a soft tone, and well-spoken accent. It was no wonder that his sisters had ridden roughshod over her. They were wild animals compared to this gentle woman.

Wick held out his gloved hand to her. 'You can sit by me.'

The young woman looked down at her feet. Her shoulders were tight. Presumably with embarrassment.

'There is no need to be missish,' he said, a little of his frustration coming out in his tone. 'It's already dusk and you don't want to be alone on the road.'

'Where are you going to take me?'

'Hampford Castle, of course.'

'But I don't want to go there.'

Wick huffed, gritting his teeth. 'It's too late to go anywhere else. And I promise that my sisters will be on their best behaviour. We can discuss where you want to go tomorrow. I will send you anywhere you wish to go in a blasted carriage.'

If he couldn't convince her to stay. At least until he could find a suitable replacement. It was clear that this shy miss was too young, too pretty and too sweet to be anyone's governess. Certainly not wild hellions like his sisters.

He offered his hand again and this time she took it. Wick pulled her up beside him. They were too close, their bodies lined up next to each other. Her wild curls were in his face and she smelled of vanilla. It was his favourite scent. Breathing her in once more, Wick resolved to be as impersonal as possible. He scooted over on the seat so that they were no longer touching and urged the horse into a brisk trot. He forced himself not to think of her lovely shape, or of the fact that she was sitting next to him.

The young woman said not a word. Which was good—for Wick had no idea how to speak to a governess. Particularly a recalcitrant one who was attracting him against his will.

His mouth was dry when they finally reached the north gate. The courtyard was full of lanterns and torches. He drove to where a groom stood waiting to take care of the curricle and horse.

'Time to get down, miss,' he said, jumping out of the vehicle.

Without waiting for her to respond, he lifted her down. Her soft form rubbed against him and he felt another wave of desire for the woman. He released his hold on her waist as if she was a hot potato, burning his hand. The heir to a dukedom did not court a governess, and Wick had no intention of paying his addresses to any woman. No matter her rank. He was perfectly happy to remain a bachelor and he already had enough responsibilities.

Wick strode towards the house.

Glancing over his shoulder, he saw that the young woman was still standing where he had put her. 'Why aren't you coming?'

She pointed at herself with her thumb. 'Me?'

'Yes, you,' he said impatiently, beckoning her with his hand. 'Come. I'll put you in the capable hands of the housekeeper and you can get dressed for dinner. I'm dashed thirsty and starving.'

The governess took a few shaky steps towards him. 'I am to eat with you?'

'And my sisters, of course,' he said, taking off his hat and running his hand through his sweaty hair. 'Unless you'd prefer to eat alone? Then a tray will be sent to your room.'

'I should like to eat with your sisters,' she said, taking the last few steps until she was at his side.

Blast it! Did a marquess offer his arm to a governess? He was too tired to care. He squashed his hat back on his head and grabbed her hand, pulling her into the house where Mrs May, the housekeeper, stood waiting. She was a thin, middle-aged woman, with dark hair and eyes, a hooked nose, and a smile that could melt butter. Except she wasn't smiling now and her gaze was dull and flat.

'Please show her to the governess's room and give her any assistance she needs to dress for dinner,' Wick said, dropping the young woman's hand. He'd liked holding it all too well. 'I should like to eat dinner in no more than a half an hour. Please ensure that my sisters join me.'

'Yes, my lord,' Mrs May said with a sharp curtsy.

Wick felt a pain in the back of his throat. He shouldn't have been so curt with the housekeeper. She'd been his ally since he was a boy in small coats.

Striding to his father's study, he pulled out the best whisky and poured himself a glass, knocking it back with one large swallow. How quickly he'd lost control of his sisters. He dared not leave them unattended again. The alcohol burned out the dryness and pain in his throat. He wanted a second glass, but he didn't dare before dinner and on an empty stomach. He couldn't afford to be incapacitated with his sisters at home. Who knew what trouble they would concoct?

Wick found his valet in his room, already laying out his dinner clothes. He was only too happy to change out of his dusty riding coat. Giving himself a sponge bath, he wiped away the grime of his trip from London and his second outing to find the governess. His valet handed him his clothes, lastly his dark green double-breasted tailcoat of superfine with gilt brass buttons. Then he arranged his hair in the style of the Brutus and Wick went down to the breakfast room.

The family rarely used the formal dining room for dinner, unless they had company. It could hold over fifty people. It was also farther from the kitchens, which caused the food to be a bit cold. He passed the large painting of Charles II on a horse that took up an entire wall. The dead King with his long black locks leered down at him and did nothing to improve Wick's mood.

His sisters entered the room together. They all looked cleaner and in the best of spirits. There was no mud to be found on their faces or skirts, but Helen's four-foot-long pet African snake was draped around her neck and shoulders like a wrap.

'No reptiles at the table,' he snapped.

'No one is here but us,' Helen protested, patting her snake as most people might stroke a dog. 'Besides, Theodosia is family.'

Wick would be boiled in his own pudding before he ate his supper with a snake named Theodosia. 'Your governess is back and I don't want you to scare her away again with your reptile friends.'

'Go on, Helen,' Frederica said with a wave of her hand. 'Your snake deserves somewhere warmer…like Wick's bed.'

'If I find that blasted snake in my bed, I'll throw it in the fire,' he said, massaging the back of his neck. His patience was long gone.

Helen covered her mouth with her hand. 'You wouldn't!'

'I would.'

Becca placed a hand on Helen's arm, near the snake's tail. 'He won't. Wick wouldn't harm a fly. Let alone a lovely creature like Theodosia.'

Helen gave her brother a withering stare and left the room with a sniff.

The door opened again shortly after, and it wasn't his sister, but the pretty governess. The cream dress she wore was clean, but it seemed to have been made for another woman. It was six inches too short and showed her lovely ankles. The bodice seemed to hang on her slim frame, showing the gentle swell of flesh at the top of her chest. He felt his body tighten again.

The governess's wild curls had been mostly tamed into a bun at the back of her head, but a few tendrils escaped from it. Both of his hands itched to touch her hair, to pull out the pins that contained it. He had to resist the animal attraction that he felt for her. It was improper. Unseemly. And dashed inconvenient.

Shaking his head to clear it, he pointed to his sister. 'Frederica, apologise to the governess.'

His sister blinked, and then glanced from the young woman to Wick and back again. It wasn't like Frederica to be silent on any occasion. Her mouth hung open.

'Wick,' Becca said, tugging on the sleeve of his coat. 'You've brought home the wrong governess.'

His mind had difficulty processing her words. He pointed stupidly at the redheaded young woman. 'This isn't Miss Young?'

The not-governess's cheeks flushed a pretty pink. 'I am not.'

'She is not,' his sisters said, at the same time as the unknown lady.

Wick gulped. Could this day get any worse? 'Then who the devil *are* you?'

The young woman shook her head and a few more red curls escaped. His hands twitched.

'I am afraid I cannot tell you,' she said.

Wick groaned and brought a fist to his forehead. 'There is no need to play coy, miss. Tell us your name and we will see that you are taken home safely.'

Her green eyes watched him mournfully. 'I would tell you my name if I could…only I can't. Because I do not wish to go home.'

The young woman spoke and acted like a lady, but why had she been all alone on the road? Could she have run away from home? Did she live in a vicarage? A manor? His teeth clenched. The last thing he needed was another wild young woman on his hands. He already had three. He had no intention of taking on more responsibility.

Frederica clapped her hands together. 'Ooh! A lady travelling incognito. I *knew* coming home from school would not be dull.'

'It will be dull as soon as we return this young woman to her home,' Wick threatened. 'Now, no more games, miss. What is your name? And where is your home?'

She looked at him with luminous green eyes. They were filled with unshed tears. 'Please, sir. I cannot tell you.'

He raked his hands through his hair and took a deep breath, trying to rein in his impatience and failing. 'Cannot or will not, miss?'

The young woman pulled her shawl up around her

shoulders. It appeared to very fine—like something his mother would have worn. Perhaps she wasn't from the middle class, but the upper one. But if that were the case surely he would know of her family?

She shook her head resolutely, but her chin quivered. 'I have worked too hard to escape. I will not go back home. I should be grateful to spend the night here, but I will not tell you my name.'

Wick sighed. A string of the foulest curses went through his mind. He had mistaken a runaway for his governess. If he wasn't careful he'd end up in hot water. He needed to find out who she was and return her home as quickly as possible. In the meantime, Mrs May would have to be chaperone. He didn't want to put himself in a compromising position and be forced to marry her if she was indeed a lady.

'Does she look like anyone you know?' Becca asked her sister, in a loud whisper that everyone in the room could hear.

'I'm afraid not,' Frederica said loudly, not even attempting to be discreet. She turned back to look at the not-governess. 'Your hair is entirely gorgeous, and I am sure that if I had ever seen this particular shade before I would remember. I'm Frederica, by the way. If you want to be formal and tedious my name is Lady Frederica Stringham. And this is Lady Rebecca. But we all call her Becca.'

The young woman bowed her head. She certainly had good manners, whatever her real name and situation. 'It is an honour to make your acquaintance.'

Becca took the young woman's hand—a sign of her approval. 'And that's our eldest brother, Wick. His real name is Simon, but no one calls him that because his courtesy title is the Marquess of Cheswick—one of our father's other titles. Our brother Matthew is in London. As is our elder sister Mantheria... What would you like us to call you if you can't tell us your name?'

Wick had to bite his lower lip to keep himself from saying something caustic. Trust his sisters to take the young runaway into the bosom of the family like a stray animal...

Chapter Five

Louisa opened her mouth stupidly. She didn't know what to say. Nor could she believe her luck. She had somehow landed in a castle with a handsome marquess and his two little sisters.

She only had her male cousins to compare him with, but this man named Wick was nothing at all like them. His clothing fitted his frame as if it had been sewn onto his skin. Louisa longed to run her hands over the seams of his sleeves and the darts on the back of his coat. The garments showed that Wick was a muscular man. Not at all like Barnabas. Even his knee breeches were snug on his frame, and showed his calves and what was above them to be perfectly toned.

But it was his face that caused her to feel wobbly in the knees. His brown hair was thick and curly and exactly the same shade as his eyes, as if they had been embroidered with the same thread. He had a square jaw, with lips that were not too small, nor too large for his face. She found herself looking at his mouth again, blushing.

'You're not Miss Young,' a voice said from behind her. Turning, she realised that there were three sisters. The third sister did not at all look like the others, who were brown-haired, sturdy and powerful-looking. This one was a slight young woman with the palest blonde hair Louisa had ever seen. She could tell that even though Lady Becca was younger, she was already taller than this sister.

'She can't tell us her name,' Lady Frederica said, grinning like a cat with a bowl of cream. 'Isn't that the most delicious mystery? She could be a lost princess. Or hiding from pirates or vagabonds. And Wick is positively boiling.'

'There is definitely something nefarious going on,' said the handsome Marquess named Wick, his lovely kissable lips tightening into a straight line.

Did he think that she had tricked him on purpose? That she was trying to catch his title by compromising him? The very thought made Louisa blush all over. What a scrape she was in.

'I know what we will call her!' the youngest sister shouted. 'We can call her Miss Nemo—because *nemo* means *no one* in Latin.'

Louisa attempted a smile, her heart beating rapidly. 'That would be perfect. You must be a very clever young lady to know Latin.'

Lady Becca grinned up at her, looking part little girl and part young woman. On the cusp of changing.

'Oh, I say we keep Miss Nemo,' Lady Helen said, taking a seat beside Louisa. 'I already like her so much better than Miss Young.'

Louisa's heart and spirits lifted. She would love to stay with such a charming family—even for only a little while.

The Marquess cleared his throat. 'You can't just take

a young woman in like a stray cat. She must be returned to her home.'

'Anyone would be preferrable to Miss Young,' Lady Frederica added, ignoring her brother and picking up her napkin.

Louisa heart fell back down in her chest. It would be too much to hope that these young ladies and their handsome elder brother would *like* an uneducated and unprepossessing young woman like herself. They would respect her, but only if they knew she was a titled lady with a fortune. Aunt Rockingham had been right.

Lord Cheswick hit his fist on the table. 'Be that as it may, I have to find your cursed governess. She is my responsibility. I can't have her toiling alone down the wrong road. Blast! I'll have to go out again and find her.'

He strode to the door, as if to leave, but the eldest sister said, 'There's no need for you to be a hero, Wick. I'm sure the horrendous Miss Young is happily drinking tea at the vicarage now, and telling all sorts of unflattering stories about us to her cousins.'

Lord Cheswick shook his head. 'The vicarage is south. Becca said that she went north.'

The littlest sister buried her head in Frederica's shoulder. Obviously not wanting to face her furious brother. 'I lied.'

The Marquess came towards them both and knelt down by his standing sisters. 'Becca, my heart, why did you lie to me?'

Lady Becca said something, but it was mumbled. Louisa couldn't quite hear her.

'I can't understand you,' said the Marquess.

Becca released Lady Frederica and turned to face her brother. Her round face was completely red. 'Miss Young said I was slow in the head and that she would have more success trying to tutor a cow. I didn't want you to bring her back, so I told you to go in the wrong direction on purpose. I'm sorry that I lied to you, Wick.'

Louisa thought that she had seen the Marquess angry before, but the expression on his face now was positively murderous. His hands were clenched again into tight fists. She watched him get to his feet, breathing heavily.

'Frederica, take Miss Nemo up to your rooms and find her a suitable gown. Then have a maid pack Miss Young's things. A groom will take them to the vicarage this very night. That *woman* will never enter our home again, and if she asks for a letter of recommendation I will write such a blistering reply that not even the devil will hire her.'

Lady Becca all but jumped into her brother's arms.

His face softened. 'Come, Becca. Let's get your former governess's wages and send them with her trunk. Once she is paid, we will never have anything to do with her again.'

'If you'll come with me, Miss Nemo?' Lady Frederica said, walking to the door.

Nodding, she followed the young woman out of the room. They were quiet until they reached a bedchamber at the top of the stairs. It was an opulently furnished room, with a grand four-poster bed with scarlet hangings. One wall held a large tapestry and the floor was carpeted. A fire burned in the hearth. Such luxury Louisa had never experienced.

'I hope you don't mind if I act as your lady's maid?'

Louisa found herself blushing again. Even though she was the daughter of an earl. 'Oh, I couldn't allow that, Lady Frederica.'

The young woman began to unbutton the back of the too-large gown. 'We're only formal when there's company. Not to say that we don't consider *you* company… Do you think you could stay on and be our governess? I agree with Helen. I already like you better than Miss Young.'

Louisa stepped out of the dress. 'You—you don't even know who I am.'

Lady Frederica shrugged. 'Becca likes you. That's enough for us.'

'And the Marquess?'

'Wick?' Lady Frederica laughed. 'You'll soon see that Becca's got the big lump wrapped around her little finger.'

Louisa watched the bold young woman take a beautiful emerald silk gown trimmed with golden string out of her bureau. She couldn't help but gasp when she saw it. Not even Aunt Rockingham had a dress so fine. Instinctively, she put her arms up, and Frederica pulled the dress over her head. Like Miss Young's, the dress was a little too large in the bodice. Lady Frederica, although several years Louisa's junior, was already very well endowed.

'And your parents?' Louisa asked. 'Won't they mind?'

She laughed. 'They're in Africa, freeing captive animals back into the wild. By the time they might mind I dare say we will have solved the mystery of your identity and helped you find your rightful place in the world.'

Louisa went still and let her arms hang loosely at her sides. 'Are your parents really in Africa?'

The younger woman laughed again. 'If you are an adventuress, you're also a fantastic actress. Don't you know who we are?'

Louisa could only shake her head, not trusting her tongue to speak.

'My parents are the Duke and Duchess of Hampford,' Lady Frederica said. 'My father is a famous naturalist, who doesn't believe in taking animals from their natural habitats, and my mother owns a world-renowned perfume house on Bond Street in London.'

Louisa knew that her mouth was hanging open. But she couldn't quite believe her luck. She had somehow, by the help of Providence, landed in a loving family like the one she'd always dreamed of. But no doubt such fashionable people would know Aunt and Uncle Rockingham. She briefly considered asking them for a ride to her Uncle Laybourne's home, but thought better of it. If the Marquess knew her true identity, he might try to return her to Greystone Hall and she could not bear it.

She yelped as Frederica stuck her with a pin.

'Sorry! But now you don't look as if you're wearing your older sister's gown.'

Louisa turned and gazed into the full-length mirror. Somehow, with a few pins, Lady Frederica had tucked and pulled the bodice so that it appeared to have been made for her. 'It's beautiful.'

'Come!' Lady Frederica said, laughing. 'But don't eat too much at dinner or you'll get poked.'

Louisa followed her back down the stairs, wondering if she was somehow in a beautiful dream.

Chapter Six

Wick woke up with a pounding hangover. He didn't recall drinking that much the night before, but he'd been dashed thirsty, and so angry that he hadn't been able to see straight. Perhaps it was for the best that he had never met Miss Young. He still wanted to wring her neck. How could a woman who was supposed to be a teacher and a mentor treat a pupil with such callousness? Especially one so winsome as Becca?

He knew that Becca struggled with reading, writing and arithmetic. For her, the numbers and letters didn't stay in their right places. But it didn't mean that she was stupid. Becca had a great memory. Once someone told her something, it was there to stay. Like the Latin word for *no one*. He'd told her that over five years ago, and she had popped out with it as if it were yesterday.

No. His Becca was not stupid. She simply learned differently from most girls, and any governess worth her salt should have realised it.

Unbidden and unwanted, the image of Miss Nemo in that emerald gown the night before filled his mind. She had looked magnificent. He had almost believed his sister's opinion that the young woman must be a missing princess. He had never seen a more vibrant and beautiful woman in his life. His hands had twitched throughout the entire meal. He'd wanted so badly to touch her again. To feel her slender body against his. To kiss her senseless.

He shook his head to clear away the image. For all he knew she might be already married. They didn't know her name, her family, or where she was from. Her manners suggested that she was well born, but perhaps she'd been a servant in a grand house. Or the base-born daughter of an aristocrat. He'd always been glad that his own father wasn't like that. Papa didn't have a mistress, and nor was he unfaithful to his wife. A smile grew on Wick's lips. Not that Mama would have stood for it. She'd probably have poisoned Papa if he'd tried.

His parents weren't at all alike, but there was a deep and abiding love between them. A love that they freely shared with their children. Growing up, Wick had always wanted to find a similar match for himself—but that had been before he had buried two of his siblings in the cold family crypt. Before he'd learned that love wasn't always enough.

Rubbing his eyes, he caught a whiff of vanilla from his soap. Again Miss Nemo's face and shy smile filled his mind. She had smelled like a vanilla cake that he would like to bite into. Or simply lick.

What was she doing this morning? Did she want to be his sisters' governess? Did he want her to stay? It would be dangerous for him to keep her in the castle. He'd never felt such an overwhelming attraction before. Not to the *ton* debutantes he'd flirted and danced with. Nor to the pretty barmaids he'd kissed. He didn't trust himself to be near her without touching her. The pull towards her was simply too great.

No. She would have to go. He would give her some money and send her anywhere she wanted in the carriage. As long as it was away from him.

He pulled the cord for a servant. The butler came into the room. He was a portly fellow with a distinctly snobbish air and never a hair out of place. Wick had always respected Mr Harper, and secretly attempted to copy his dignified manners.

The butler bowed. 'You called, my lord?'

'Harper, I should like to speak to my sisters.'

'I am afraid the young ladies have already gone.'

Fear gripped his chest. He wanted to see Miss Nemo again. At least once. He had to touch her hand as he bowed over it.

'Gone?'

'Gone to see the new baby camel leopard, my lord,' the butler intoned. 'Mrs May has accompanied them to act as chaperone.'

Wick bowed his head in relief and said a prayer of thanks for the housekeeper. His little sisters were going to be the death of him.

'That will be all, Harper.'

'Very good, my lord.'

Yawning, Wick returned to the estate's books. Unlike his father, he had a natural flair for estate management—one he'd inherited from his mother and maternal grandfather. Ever since he'd graduated from Oxford he'd been handling the estate. The Duke, frankly, was not interested, and his mother, who had previously overseen the estate's finances, was already busier than she needed to be with her perfume company.

He'd also found that whilst Mama was excellent with numbers, she was less focused on the needs of their tenants. She wasn't unfeeling—she was simply a businesswoman. Wick, however, liked to spend time with the farmers and learn their methods. He planned to farm the home fields next year. He would also replace the roofs on all the cottages instead of taking the less expensive option of continuing to patch them.

After completing his work on the books, Wick had the less pleasant job of riding over to Animal Island to find his sisters.

He should stop at the family crypt and pay his respects. He hadn't visited it in nearly a year. He liked to suppose that if he didn't go there, maybe his little brother Charles and his little sister Elizabeth would still be alive. He liked to imagine that they were away at school. He tried not to remember that they had died when *he* was in charge...whilst his parents were in Africa.

Wick had been only sixteen years old at the time—too young for the responsibility of watching over his younger siblings. Matthew had been fourteen and Charles only twelve when they had brought home scarlet fever from school and all five of their younger sisters had caught it. But none so badly as Elizabeth, Mantheria's identical twin.

They'd been ten years old at the time, and Elizabeth had been slim and frail even before she had contracted the disease. Papa had called her his Little Songbird. She'd never walked when she could skip, nor talked when she could sing. Elizabeth must have made up hundreds of songs for she'd rarely sung the same song twice.

After she'd died, none of his sisters had ever sung again.

He had been powerless to help those he'd loved the most. He had failed his little siblings and his parents. It had been the hardest time of his life.

Now, after riding to the edge of the cemetery, he tried to force himself to get off his horse and go into the family crypt. But his body wouldn't move.

He was a coward.

Turning his horse, Wick rode through a field of sheep and across the bridge that connected Animal Island to the land.

'Lord Cheswick,' said Mr Merrell, doffing his hat. 'Good to see ye.'

Swinging out of the saddle, Wick held out his hand to the brawny man. 'And you, sir. Everything appears to be in excellent order.'

Merrell laughed heartily. 'Ye haven't even seen the animals yet, my lord. How would ye know?'

Wick wrinkled his nose. 'My sense of smell tells me all I need to know.'

The head animal keeper barked another loud laugh. 'Too right. Ye never cared much for any of the creatures. Not like wee Charles. Now, he would've made a right fine naturalist. Poor Sadie still misses him.'

'We all do,' Wick said quietly.

Sadie was an Indian elephant that the Marchioness of Hastings had sent to Charles who, at the age of seven, had already been a budding naturalist. Before she'd gone to India, the Marchioness had asked Charles what he would like as a pet.

'Oh, nothing smaller than an elephant,' he had said.

Little had Charles or his parents expected a beautiful female of the species to be delivered to their home several months later.

Papa had been remorseful, wishing that his son's ill-timed remark had not resulted in the captivity of such a majestic creature. Wick had been too young to understand his father's moral objections to keeping an elephant as a pet. He'd loved Sadie from the first time he saw her. Almost as much as Charles.

Wick had even helped his father build Sadie a large house on Animal Island. It was well ventilated, with every particular arranged for Sadie's comfort. Nor was she kept in a paddock. She was free to roam all around Animal Island as far as the iron gate before the bridge. But Sadie preferred her house, which Charles had taught her to clean herself. The clever elephant would take up a bucket of fresh water from the river and then, using a broom or scrubbing brush, begin to wash her home.

Merrell cleared his throat, recalling Wick from his memories.

'Is there anything you need, or something you would like to bring to my attention?' Wick asked.

'Naught, my lord. All is as it should be. Your sisters are in the camel leopard enclosure.'

'Inside?'

The horror that Wick felt must have shown on his face, for Merrell clapped him hard on the back. 'Don't worry, my lord. Them's gentle creatures who wouldn't hurt a fly.'

'I assume you mean the camel leopards? For I can assure you that my sisters most certainly are anything but gentle.'

Merrell laughed again, but Wick had not been joking. He tipped his hat to the head keeper and tied his horse to the bridge. He'd learned at an early age that horses did not get along with the creatures on the island.

Crossing the bridge, he unlocked the fence on the other side and stepped onto the river island.

He saw the llama, which stood by the elks. The kangaroo bounded towards him but didn't kick. His luminous eyes seemed to say he remembered Wick. Next, he passed the emus and ostriches—impressive flightless birds. They were rather mean creatures, though, so they had to be kept apart from the cockatoo, peacocks and the gold and silver pheasants. Then came the paddocks for the Neapolitan pig, the coatimundi, the different varieties of goats and the Indian bull.

He saw the elephant's house ahead of him, but he didn't have it in him to go there either. It reminded him too much of Charles. Turning to the left, he went to the camel leopard enclosure. There were two long-necked creatures there, that were nearly eighteen feet high. Between them was a baby which was six feet tall and had been nearly four stones at birth. It swayed on its thin legs.

Frederica, Helen and Becca were stroking the baby calf. Dear Mrs May was next to them, as fearless as his sisters. Miss Nemo stood near the gate of the enclosure, her face pale. She was wearing the same dress he'd found her in the day before, except it was no longer dusty from travel. Mrs May must have had a maid tidy it up.

Wick opened the gate. 'Good morning, miss.'

He tipped his hat to Miss Nemo. A beautiful flush formed in her freckled cheeks and she gave him a glittering smile. Heat spread throughout his body. The woman was too fetching for her own good, and her temperament even sweeter.

'Good morning, my lord,' she said, in a low, sultry voice.

Wick swallowed down his desire.

She had to go.

Immediately.

'I will have a carriage take you wherever you wish to go, and provide enough money for you to start again elsewhere. But it is time for you to leave, Miss Nemo.'

The young woman lowered her head. 'I understand, my lord. I will go immediately. I have an uncle who might help me.'

'His name?'

She sniffed. 'I would like to retain my anonymity. Your driver may drop me off in the city of Sherborne. I can make my way from there.'

He saw that her hands were shaking and felt a pang of guilt. But he was not like his parents. He did not take in strays. His only responsibility was to ensure she was returned to her family.

'Oh, stuff it, Wick,' Frederica said, walking up to them and taking Miss Nemo's arm. 'She's staying with us until we solve the mystery of who she is and why she has run away.'

Helen took Miss Nemo's other arm. 'And we need a governess anyway.'

Since both of Miss Nemo's arms had already been taken, Becca leaned on his. 'Please, oh, please, Wick. Miss Nemo will make an excellent governess. She has already taught me so many things on our walk here, and she has promised to show me how to do an embroidery stitch called a French knot.'

Breathing heavily, Mrs May reached them. Both her hands rested on her slender hips. 'My lord, stitching is hardly as important as arithmetic or literature, but it *is* part of a female's education. I don't think it would hurt for the young woman to stay a little longer. It might even encourage your sisters to try new things. And I will watch them all very carefully.'

It seemed Miss Nemo had somehow bewitched his housekeeper—a typically stern, but loving woman.

However, someone to distract his sisters and keep them out of trouble until he found a new governess was not a bad thing. Obviously she couldn't stay with them indefinitely. But what harm could a few more days do? Besides, he might be able to discover her true identity and therefore make sure she safely arrived with her relatives, instead of leaving her alone in the town square.

'That sounds very promising,' he said, 'but I shall need to give Miss Nemo a proper interview.'

Becca stood on her tiptoes and kissed Wick on the cheek. Then she whirled around. 'Come, Miss Nemo. You can show us that French embroidery knot that you promised to teach us.'

Still holding Miss Nemo's arms, his sisters began to walk away, without a look at him. Miss Nemo's emerald eyes glanced back at him, softening his hard heart. She appeared so young. So vulnerable. He could hardly throw her to the wolves yet. But she couldn't stay with his sisters for long. With him…

'Wick isn't normally this bad,' Frederica said loftily, loudly enough for him to hear. 'But he's taken his position as temporary head of the family a little too seriously.'

'He's been worse than a rattlesnake without its rattle,' Helen added.

'Wick means well,' Becca put in. 'But he's a man. Mother says they are all a bit stupid. It's in their nature. They cannot help themselves.'

A wiser man would have retired from the lists, but Wick wasn't about to let his headstrong sisters win. He offered Mrs May the support of his arm and they trailed behind them. He meant to interview Miss Nemo to find out who she truly was. And he would do it even if his three sisters pestered him the entire time.

Chapter Seven

Louisa felt dazed as the Stringham sisters led her to their mother's favourite parlour. It was not even midday and she'd already had the best day of her life. She'd been warmly welcomed into the family and taken to see the most extraordinary baby calf that was taller than all of them! The camel leopard's two parents had towered above them with long necks and made not a sound. Louisa had felt safest near the fence, but she'd enjoyed every minute of it.

Even when Lord Cheswick had come. He clearly disapproved of her presence, but he allowed his sisters a great deal of freedom. More than Louisa had ever known.

Now, Lord Cheswick and Mrs May followed them into the room and watched as Louisa tried to teach the Stringham sisters the complicated French knot, but when Louisa realised that the young ladies couldn't even thread a needle, she had to start on basic stitches. She taught the girls how to do a backstitch and a running stitch. They were the two easiest.

Lady Helen shrugged, pulling her needle through. 'I've never been any good at my stitches. All I ever do is prick myself and bleed on the material.'

Louisa smiled and showed her how to always point the needle away from herself. Her housekeeper at Greystone Hall, Mrs Barker, did not approve of bleeding on material, and had made sure that Louisa never did. Once all three girls were doing a running stitch, she turned to glance at Mrs May and the handsome Marquess on the other side of the room.

He beckoned her with one hand. Lowering her head, she moved towards him.

'Will you not sit down? I have some questions about your qualifications for being a governess to my sisters.'

Louisa took a seat on the sofa next to Mrs May and the woman briefly patted her hand before folding her arms. Louisa was grateful for the encouragement.

Touching her hot cheeks, Louisa opened her mouth to say, 'Sewing and embroidery are my only talents, my lord.'

Lord Cheswick cleared his throat. 'Do you sew your own clothing, Miss Nemo?'

'I have sewn my wardrobe for the last ten years.'

'And before that?' Mrs May asked.

She felt more blood rush to her face and internally cursed her fair complexion. 'No. There was no need to make my own clothes when my father was alive.'

'I knew she was an orphan!' Lady Frederica shouted from the other side of the room.

Lord Cheswick scoffed. 'How?'

'All the heroines in novels are,' his sister answered smugly.

The Marquess turned his attention back to Louisa. 'Do you like to read novels, Miss Nemo?'

Louisa shrugged and ducked her head, embarrassed by his scrutiny and afraid that the Stringhams would no longer like her when they knew how ignorant she was. 'I have never had the opportunity. My aunt is not a great reader, and the only books at the hall are of a scientific or mathematical nature.'

Lord Cheswick's lips twitched. 'Our first clue to your true identity.'

Startled, Louisa jumped in her seat. 'What do you mean?'

'You said that you lived in a hall, which means that you grew up in an aristocratic household,' he said, tapping his fingers on his knees. 'There are probably only five or six such homes within a day's journey of Hampford. I will send a groom to each one with a description of you.'

Louisa's hands flew to her face. 'Oh, no, please! I do not wish to go back to my aunt.'

'I bet her aunt is wicked,' Lady Helen added from across the room, stabbing her needle through the counterpoint.

Louisa swallowed in surprise and coughed. 'How—how do you know that?'

'Why else would you run away from home?' Lady Frederica said, glancing up from her stitching. 'Your aunt is clearly a horrid woman who has made your life a misery. Why else would your shift be little more than strings? Mrs May was shocked by the state of it.'

As she slid down in her chair, Louisa's thoughts were muddied. She was embarrassed that they'd seen and spoken of her poor clothing. Perhaps even more embarrassed that she had not received a proper education or upbringing underneath her aunt. She was unfit to join fine society.

'Stick to your sewing and stop making up stories

about Miss Nemo,' Lord Cheswick said, holding up a hand. 'This is supposed to be a proper interview. We need real information, not guesses.'

Ignoring him, Lady Helen set down her embroidery on the table. 'And your aunt must be jealous of your beauty, or she would have had someone teach your maid how to arrange your hair attractively.'

Self-consciously, Louisa touched her hair. The wild red curls had already escaped her attempt at a chignon. She remembered her aunt's words: *'You are an ill-favoured, extremely freckled young woman.'* Did Lord Cheswick think she was ugly? Such a handsome man with a title had probably met all the most beautiful London debutantes. Stealing a glance at him, she saw that he watched her closely.

Lady Becca plonked her feet on the table in front of her. 'Don't listen to them, Miss Nemo. I think your hair is positively beautiful. I've never seen a shade like it before. It's like the pelt of a fox.'

Louisa felt herself flush as red as a fox at the young girl's compliment. She stole another glance and saw that Lord Cheswick's tawny eyes were still on her.

'It is,' Lady Helen said, brandishing a needle like a sword at her little sister. 'Which is why with a little bit of skill it could be perfect.'

'Now, now…' Lord Cheswick said, holding up both hands. 'Either be quiet during the interview or leave the room.'

Lady Frederica stuck her tongue out at her brother but didn't say anything.

Mrs May cleared her throat. 'Now, where were we, my lord?'

Lord Cheswick cleared his throat. 'Miss Nemo, did you attend school or have a governess?'

Louisa flushed under their open scrutiny and her palms felt sweaty. 'I had a governess until I was ten, but when my father died she was dismissed.'

Mrs May wore a sympathetic look and shook her head, but Lord Cheswick's expression was unreadable as he asked, 'Then your formal education ended at the age of ten?'

Louisa brought a hand to her forehead, feeling rather faint. 'Yes, my lord. I had already learned to read, but I do not play any musical instruments. Our housekeeper taught me arithmetic, sewing, embroidery, and how to run a household. But I have never been taught to speak French or Italian, nor deportment or how to dance. I am afraid that I am a poor candidate to be anyone's governess.'

She took a hitching breath, shame covering her like a shawl. She could no longer meet the handsome man's gaze. She was not worthy of being his little sisters' friend let alone their governess. They would probably despise her now for her ignorance, just like Aunt Rockingham.

Louisa felt a slender hand on her shoulder and glanced up to see Lady Helen. 'Don't worry, Miss Nemo. I cannot play a musical instrument either. The only one of my sisters who does is Frederica. The rest of us are abysmal at the pianoforte, and Papa says that our harp-playing sounds like a rhinoceros in mating season.'

'I thought that was your attempts at the violin?' Lady Becca said, cupping her hands as she called out from the opposite side of the room.

Lady Helen scowled at her little sister. 'You're wrong. He compared my violin music to a hissing hyena.'

Louisa's heart lifted a little and Lord Cheswick laughed—a low, attractive sound.

'And your flute-playing to a dying dodo bird.'

Louisa felt her lips twitch upwards almost into a smile as the other four in the room broke out into raucous laughter. Even Mrs May chortled. They did not seem to think less of her for not being an accomplished musician.

'You know more than I do, Miss Nemo,' Lady Becca said, walking closer to them and fidgeting with her hands. 'I cannot read very well. The words won't stay still. They dance about on the page.'

Her brother grunted, sitting up in his chair. 'Don't let Becca disparage herself. She's one of the cleverest people I know. Never forgets a thing you tell her.'

Louisa saw his little sister turn pink with pleasure from the compliment. She couldn't help but be impressed that Lord Cheswick had stood up for his sister, despite her educational shortcomings. Aunt Rockingham would never have done the same for her.

'And we can teach you deportment and how to dance,' Lady Frederica said, coming over to join the conversation. 'If there's one thing all Stringhams do well, it's dancing.'

'Wick, it would be such fun to be the teacher instead of the student,' Lady Becca suggested shyly.

Uncertain, Louisa swallowed. Her stomach felt tense. Could she accept so much from them? Should she? Would Lord Cheswick let her?

The handsome young Marquess was already in her thoughts more than was proper. She'd stayed up late the night before, wondering how his lips would feel against hers. But she was being unpardonably foolish. Lord Cheswick was wealthy, educated, handsome and titled.

The bride he selected would be both beautiful and accomplished. And Louisa was neither. She didn't even know how to dance. Yet, stitch by stich, he seemed to have woven his way into her mind, no matter how hard she tried to not think about him. Or how badly she longed to earn his approbation.

Louisa's gaze flickered from the young girl to her elder brother. She could tell from his tender expression that he would not refuse her anything. Her opinion of him rose even higher, if that were possible.

'Very well, Becca, my heart,' he said. 'You can teach Miss Nemo to dance and she can stay until we find her proper family.'

Lady Helen's eyes widened. 'But not the wicked aunt?'

Lord Cheswick sighed, noddingly slowly. 'Not the wicked aunt.'

Exhaling, Louisa couldn't hide her relief. The Stringhams were not going to send her back to Aunt Rockingham.

Chapter Eight

Lord Cheswick made Cousin Barnabas and his younger brothers seem even more ordinary. His tall, muscular frame radiated strength and virility. He was patient and kind. Especially with his three sisters, who seemed to live to plague him. Louisa couldn't imagine teasing any of her aunt's sons. Nor speaking as freely as the Stringham sisters did. It would seem that in their home—*castle!*—the daughters were treated the same way as the sons.

She wished that she had grown up with such a large and loving family.

She wished that she had known Wick sooner.

Lady Frederica had lent her another gown, and a maid helped her into it and added several pins. Louisa desperately needed new clothing, which would require money from her inheritance. She needed to find her Uncle Laybourne and ask for his help, but she feared that he would send her back to Aunt Rockingham's care. He had seemed stern and cold at her father's funeral, but perhaps he'd only been mourning as she had.

Lady Helen and Lady Becca were waiting for her outside the door. They each took one of her hands and led her down the stairs to the breakfast room, where it seemed the family dined informally. They passed the butler.

'Harper,' Lady Becca said, 'this is our new friend.'

The butler bowed deeply to Louisa. 'My lady.'

Louisa curtsied in return, and jumped when Lady Helen squealed.

'Miss Nemo is a real lady, Becca. I told you. Now all we have to do is discover your first name.'

Louisa swallowed; her throat felt painfully dry. 'Lady Helen, I don't mean to be taciturn…'

'Do you admit that you are a lady?'

Louisa felt her face go red. She had never been a good liar. 'I never said I wasn't a lady.'

Lady Helen shook her head, smiling widely. 'I meant do you bear the title *Lady* because you are the daughter of a peer? Or do you deny it?'

She swallowed again, and then opened her mouth. 'Yes, I am Lady Lou—' She broke off in confusion. She had nearly given them her entire name.

Nudging her sister with her elbow, Lady Helen grinned in apparent victory. 'Becca, her name starts with *Lou*.'

Lady Becca squeezed Louisa's hand tightly. 'Let me see… There's Louella, Lucetta, Lucille, Lucretia, Louise, Louisa… It's got to be one of those.'

Louisa had involuntarily gasped when the young girl said her name.

Lady Becca beamed up at her. 'I guessed it! You're Lady Louisa.'

There was no point in trying to lie. Louisa's face was hot and no doubt she looked extremely guilty.

'Lady Louisa is much better than Miss Nemo,' Lady Helen said, grabbing both Louisa's and Becca's free hands so they made a circle. 'But now that you are our social equal, and not our governess, we really must insist that you simply call us by our names. Saying "Lady" all the time is a trifle tedious and extremely pretentious.'

'Yes,' Becca agreed, wrinkling her nose at her sister. 'Although you love it when people you dislike have to call you Lady Helen.'

Her sister gave a dignified sniff and chose to ignore her.

Harper opened the door to the breakfast room and Louisa saw that Mrs May and Frederica were already waiting there for dinner. But no handsome marquess who plagued her thoughts more than was seemly.

Becca and Helen tugged her into the room.

'Frederica!' Becca called out loudly. 'Helen and I have solved the mystery.'

Their elder sister snorted and placed a hand on her hip. 'Of why Wick is late for dinner?'

'No, silly,' Helen replied. 'The mystery of Miss N—'

'Oh, there you are Wick!' Becca said in her exuberant voice. 'Where have you been all afternoon?'

The Marquess walked into the room dressed in fine evening clothes, but with his riding coat over the top of them, unbuttoned. He still looked handsome, but Louisa supposed he would be attractive even in a farmer's smock.

'I have been checking on the tenants, of course, and I've found someone who needs a home.'

Lord Cheswick reached into his coat pocket and gently lifted out a black kitten by its neck. He cradled it in his strong hands. She wondered what it would like to be held by such strong, gentle hands.

He placed the small creature into the eager arms of

his youngest sister and Becca brought the small animal against her face and kissed it several times. 'I love him so much!'

Helen narrowed her gaze at her brother, her arms crossed. 'It's a girl, Becca. And why am I not surprised that you gave *her* the kitten, Wick? She's always been your favourite.'

Louisa felt a pang of sympathy for Helen. She had never been the favourite in her home either. Aunt Rockingham only cared for her sons and never brought gifts for her.

'You're right,' Lord Cheswick said, reaching into his opposite coat pocket. 'Alas, Leech only had two other kittens to spare.'

He pulled out two more kittens. One was striped grey and white, and the other an orange ball of fur. Helen was practically climbing his arm to grab the orange kitten from him.

Louisa had misjudged him. Lord Cheswick was not treating his sisters differently.

'Oh, Wick, he's absolutely precious,' Frederica cooed as she took the grey-striped kitten. 'Forget all the nasty things I have ever said about you.'

The Marquess raised his eyebrows as he shrugged himself out of his riding coat and tossed it carelessly on a chair. 'That may take a while. There's been so many.'

His sisters laughed merrily as they cradled and stroked their new kittens. The Marquess watched them fondly and Louisa's chest filled with warmth. He was clearly a loving brother and a thoughtful man.

Mrs May sighed from behind them. 'I suppose you couldn't have waited until after dinner, my lord? Are we to eat with the kittens at the table?'

Lord Cheswick's lips twitched and then he threw back his head and laughed. 'Oh, dear, Mrs May. I didn't intend to bring them now, but one of them behaved badly in my dressing room and Older said that he would resign on the spot if I didn't get rid of them. And I'm afraid that a more superior valet would be hard to find.'

The Marquess had a wonderful laugh, Louisa thought. It made the hairs rise on her nape and arms.

The housekeeper sighed again, appearing resigned. Except Louisa could see that her eyes were smiling. Mrs May was obviously fond of the Stringham family, and Louisa couldn't help but be fond of them too. Even though she knew her time with them was coming to an end.

The Marquess's brown eyes shifted to her and Louisa flushed—again—underneath his scrutiny. She was already breathing hard, but when his eyes were on her she practically panted for air.

So embarrassing.

'Miss Nemo, are you all right?'

Louisa took a deep breath, trying to steady her voice. She wasn't all right. Certainly not when he was near. Her heart beat wildly and her hands felt hot and clammy. And there was a strange sort of pleasant burning in her stomach and a tenderness in her breasts. Sensations that she had never experienced before.

'She's not Miss Nemo any more, Wick,' Becca said, not bothering to look up from her kitten. 'She's Lady Louisa.'

He blinked at Louisa twice, before taking a step towards her. '*You're* Lady Louisa Bracken, daughter of the late Earl of Rockingham of Greystone Hall?'

His tone held scorn and her heart plummeted in her chest. Her title and true name meant something to him.

There was no point in denying the truth. Eventually she would have had to tell the Marquess and his sisters her true name anyway, if they were to help her find her Uncle Laybourne and the trustees named in her father's will. She would need those trustees to access her inheritance and have her London season. Besides, she trusted them. Even Lord Cheswick, who had eyed her with suspicion once he'd realised that she wasn't a governess. And made her feel hot and breathless and full of an unknown want...

'I am... How—how did you know my name?'

His lips turned into a sneer. 'I was unfortunately acquainted with Lord Barnabas Bracken before he was sent down from Oxford because of his gambling debts.'

Louisa touched her hot cheeks. It did not sound as if Wick was fond of her cousin. Not that she liked him either. He was a toad.

Becca cleared her throat. 'The villain enters the scene and the plot thickens!'

'Yes!' Helen's eyes grew wide. 'Is he trying to marry you against your will so that he can steal your fortune?'

'I daresay you're an heiress?' added Frederica.

Louisa swayed on her feet and held a hand against her stomach. She couldn't quite believe that the Stringham sisters had guessed her true circumstances. It was so unlikely. Almost unbelievable.

'How many times do I have to tell you?' Lord Cheswick said dismissively. 'She isn't the heroine in a gothic novel and you should call her Lady Louisa.'

Frederica tickled her kitten under his chin. 'And you should read more of them and then you'd know that a delicately nurtured young lady only flees her family home when she is being forced into a distasteful marriage. And why else would her evil aunt try to make her marry her bad cousin unless she was an heiress?'

'It's entirely obvious,' Helen said, lifting her chin defiantly.

Huffing, Lord Cheswick turned his eyes from his sisters to her. '*Is* it true?'

Louisa felt so mortified that she would have been happily swallowed up by floor. She'd hoped that when she told him the truth of her identity the Marquess would show her the same kindness he demonstrated with his sisters.

'It is.'

'I don't blame you for not wanting to marry Lord Barnabas,' he said, looking at her closely, his voice softening. 'He's a rum touch. But why did you not appeal to your other relatives? Surely there is someone in your family who would help you?'

She wasn't precisely sure what a 'rum touch' was, but by the tone of his voice Louisa was certain that her cousin was one. She rubbed at her forehead. 'I was trying to seek refuge with my uncle, the Canon of Sherborne, when you found me on the road and mistook me for your governess.'

'Then why the secrecy with your name? And why did you not wish to continue to find him this morning? I told you I would have provided you with a carriage and a proper escort.'

Louisa lowered her head, unable to meet his disapproving eyes. 'I am so sorry, my lord,' she whispered, her hands fidgeting against her gown. 'I should have left. Only, I feared being returned to my Aunt and Uncle

Rockingham. The servants at Greystone Hall helped me escape and I don't wish for them to get into trouble.'

'Are Lord and Lady Rockingham your guardians?' he asked.

Still gazing down, she shook her head. 'Not any more. I am turned one-and-twenty. They have never allowed me a season. And in the nearly eleven years they have been my guardians they have only permitted me to leave the estate to attend church. I have so longed for a season, and for an opportunity to be presented to the Queen.'

Chapter Nine

When Lord Barnabas had bragged in his cups about marrying his wealthy and beautiful cousin who was an heiress, Wick had dismissed it as the idle boasting of a gambler whose pockets were always to let. If this Lady Louisa was so fetching, why hadn't she been brought to court and been presented at a come-out ball? Why had she not attended *ton* parties? He'd thought the poor woman must be an antidote or a halfwit.

The fact that she was neither made him almost believe his sister's wild theories about villains. Whatever the case, he couldn't hide nor harbour a runaway. Particularly one of such high birth. It would not look good to the *ton*. And if he wasn't careful he would be forced into marrying her. The last thing he wanted to do.

She would have to go to her uncle's house in the morning.

There was no other option.

Otherwise, by law, she'd have to be returned to her former guardians. Something he could not do after Lady Louisa had worked so hard to escape them. He would have to appeal to her maternal uncle, and hopefully he would help her. It was her uncle's responsibility and not his. Wick had enough on his plate, trying to find a new governess for his wayward sisters. The sooner the better.

'Mrs May and I will escort you to your uncle's home first thing in the morning. There you can explain the situation to him and request his assistance in locating your trustees and arranging a proper come-out and season for you.'

She glanced up at him, her countenance trusting. It touched something in his heart. 'Thank you, my lord.'

'Girls, take the kittens to the kitchen and wash your hands before you return for dinner,' he said, moving to the door and opening it.

They filed out, oldest to youngest.

'Don't say anything interesting without us,' Becca reminded them as she left.

One side of Wick's mouth quirked up into a half-smile. 'I promise we won't.'

His sisters returned shortly after, with clean hands and large appetites. Wick was relieved that they were too busy eating to squabble with each other or him. Conversation passed by amicably, with the help of Mrs May and Lady Louisa. He couldn't help but be impressed by the young lady's excellent manners and thoughtful listening.

Frederica stood up first, tossing her napkin onto her dessert plate. 'It's time for dancing lessons!'

Wick balled up his napkin in his hands. 'I don't have time tonight.'

'Please, Wick,' Becca said, scrunching up her nose at him. 'Helen is a horrible partner. Poor Louisa won't know how to be properly led in the dance.'

This was true. He could only be grateful that Lady

Louisa's personality was neither stubborn nor wilful like his little sisters'.

'I'm a better lead than you,' Helen said.

Becca lifted her chin and sniffed. 'Hardly.'

'Besides, Wick,' Frederica said, 'if she is leaving first thing in the morning we won't have another opportunity to be her teachers.'

'I always enjoy watching a good dance,' Mrs May said, with a twinkle in her smile underneath her cap. 'And it is such good practice for your sisters. As well as keeping them out of mischief.'

The housekeeper is in league with my sisters!

Yet the prospect of dancing with Lady Louisa was not as repugnant to him as it should have been. He liked talking with her, and perhaps holding her in his arms for an hour would cure him of his unwanted desire for her.

He held up his forefinger. 'One hour. I will give you one hour of my time.'

Becca grabbed his arm. 'He said yes!'

Helen took his other arm and his sisters frogmarched him to the blue saloon, Frederica in the lead. She took her spot at the pianoforte. Mrs May sat next to her, ready to turn the pages. Helen partnered Becca, leaving Wick standing by Lady Louisa. He held out his hand to her and she placed her shaking fingers in his. Her eyes were on his cravat, as if she didn't dare look up into his eyes. He hoped that he had not been too terse with her. She was a very comely young woman, and in other circumstances he might have liked her very much, but she was just another responsibility that he did not want, foisted upon him.

Helen folded her arms. Despite being the sister who looked the least like their mother, she had all the same mannerisms. 'The first dance we'll teach you is the Roger de Coverley. It's a very popular country dance. Now, you and Wick will stand across from each other. Becca and I will be the other couple.'

Wick was only half listening to Helen's instructions on how the bottom man and the top lady should advance, link arms, and then weave their way to the end of the group before joining hands and promenading up. He was focused on her shallow breathing and the way it made her chest rise and fall quickly. How her surprisingly dark eyelashes brushed against her freckle-kissed cheeks.

He watched her concentrate on following each of Helen's instructions as she held tightly to his hand and then his arm. Her slender fingers shook. With excitement? Embarrassment? Attraction? Or all of them together?

His eyes kept darting to her lips and the freckle just above them that he longed to kiss. But he wouldn't.

'Very good,' Helen said, dropping Becca's hands. 'Frederica, play us some music and we'll try it again.'

Frederica's nimble fingers began to play a tune. Wick worried that it would be too fast for Lady Louisa's first lesson, but she took his hand. When they released their clasp she turned the wrong way and nearly ran into Becca. His littlest sister burst into giggles, but instead of stopping they kept dancing until Lady Louisa made the figure correctly and they promenaded together at the end.

Becca and Helen clapped their hands.

Wick found that he was reluctant to release his hold on her hand. It felt as if it fitted perfectly inside his own. The weight. The size. The shape. He rubbed his thumb over her knuckles, wishing that they weren't both wearing gloves. That he could feel her skin against his.

Becca placed both of her hands on her hips. 'Wick, you're supposed to let go of her hand.'

Helen sniffed in a superior manner. 'Maybe you need dancing lessons as much as Lady Louisa.'

Dropping her hand, he couldn't help but smile down at her as he clapped. 'It appears that I do.'

'Good,' Frederica said from the pianoforte. 'Because we still need to teach Lady Louisa the waltz. Every fashionable ball has at least one.'

Wick could only be thankful that he managed to miss most 'fashionable balls', which were little better than marriage markets for the wealthy and titled. Not that he didn't like pretty girls—he most certainly did. But matchmaking mamas were to be avoided at all costs. He wasn't interested in marriage, and he knew that his mother was the most determined matchmaker of the lot. She'd already caught a duke for her eldest daughter, and had all but arranged a marriage for Frederica to the heir to another dukedom. He could only be grateful that at present she was on another continent.

Becca cleared her throat. 'Now, you're the one following, so you allow your partner to place his hand on your upper back and you hold his other hand. Like this. Your other hand goes on his shoulder.'

Even though Becca was taller, she was allowing Helen to lead. A rare concession, thought Wick. He used the hand he was holding to pull Lady Louisa closer to him. He let go, but only to place his hand on her narrow waist, holding it just above where it dipped in. He longed to run both hands up and down her back. Instead, he took her other hand and clasped it with his. She tentatively reached out to touch his shoulder. Her fingers were as light as a butterfly perched there. He could barely feel the weight of them through his coat. But he sensed her touch with all his body.

'A waltz is really quite easy,' Helen said, demonstrating the basic step with Becca. 'You're only making a box with your feet.'

Tightening his hold on Lady Louisa's waist, Wick said, 'I step forward with my left foot and you step back with your right.'

Lady Louisa bit her lower lip and gave a slight nod.

Leading her, he performed the first step with accuracy. 'Now, move your left foot sideways and I'll mirror you with my right.'

'All right…' she whispered.

She was a natural dancer, with grace and elegance.

'Next, slide your right foot next to your left, so that they are parallel but not touching.'

Lady Louisa followed him as if she trusted him instinctively—something that none of his sisters would have done. All four of them insisted on leading.

'Then you'll step forward with your left foot and I'll step back with my right,' Wick said as they continued through the movements. 'Now, move back with your right foot and sideways… That's it! The last step is to move your left foot so that your feet are parallel again.'

Still in his arms, she finally looked him in the eyes as she said, 'It is a box. A perfect little box.'

Wick couldn't help but smile down at her. 'Shall we try again?'

Lady Louisa grinned up at him with her kissable lips with that freckle just above their centre that he was so obsessed with.

'Please.'

He tightened his hold and repeated the box step once.

Then twice. And a third time. As they continued to spin around the room together Wick realised that Frederica had begun to play a waltz and he hadn't even noticed the sound. He'd been so intent on gazing at and dancing with Lady Louisa he'd even forgotten Becca and Helen, who were waltzing beside them, both attempting to lead, which was turning the dance into a wrestling match.

Wick turned his attention back to his beautiful partner. 'Did Lady Rockingham give you a reason for not giving you a presentation or a season in London?'

Lady Louisa's ears turned red again and her neck flushed. 'I am afraid that my aunt considers me a burden. I can do nothing to please her. My mother left her private fortune to me, but until I am twenty-five there is only a yearly allowance given from my trustees to my uncle for my keep. Aunt Rockingham says that it is not enough for my maintenance, nor for the hiring of a governess or dancing master. That is why my clothes are little more than rags and why my aunt refused to take me to London. She says that she could not bear the expense.'

Wick snorted in derision, shaking his head. 'According to your pernicious cousin Barnabas, you're the heiress to over one hundred and fifty thousand pounds. Even if your yearly allowance was only the interest, that would be easily over seven thousand pounds a year. More than enough to dress you like a duchess and employ a dozen governesses, dancing masters, and rent a house for the London season.'

'Truly?'

He couldn't help but pull her a little closer on their next turn. She looked so vulnerable. Her body gently brushed his chest and set his pulse racing.

'Your uncle owns your father's house in London and

I've never seen your aunt miss a season. Lady Rockingham is usually drowning in silks and jewels. She must be keeping all your allowance for her own use.'

Lady Louisa's eyes fell again to his cravat. There was a tell-tale pink in her cheeks. 'She said that I am too ugly to take to London and that I'm lucky that my cousin is willing to marry me.'

Wick stopped dancing, feeling a sort of primal anger run through his veins. What sort of woman would cheat her own niece out of her fortune? And treat her like less than a servant in the meantime?

'Believe me, Lady Louisa,' he said, breathing hard as he pulled her closer to him until their full bodies met together, his hardness to her softness. Her curves perfectly matching his dips. 'You are the most beautiful woman I have ever seen. You will be surrounded by suitors in London—and not just because of your fortune and your title.'

Lady Louisa's eyes were still focused on the folds of his cravat. 'Will you be one of them?'

'You won't need me,' he assured her, stepping back. Touching her was too tempting. 'There are plenty of other eligible young men who will appreciate your charms. But first we must take you to your uncle. There will be less gossip if you are staying with a family member, and he will know who your trustees are and how to reach them. Surely they cannot be aware of how you are being treated by your aunt? No man or woman of conscience would allow it.'

'Will—will you help me?'

He knew better than to give rash promises, but her countenance was so open and trusting that he couldn't help himself. 'I will.'

She gave him a shy smile. 'Lady Frederica said that your parents are in Africa—is this their first visit?'

Wick's jaw tightened. 'Their second. The last time was nearly a decade ago.'

'But your sisters would have been so young then... Still in the nursery.'

He nodded sharply. They had all been too young to be left in his care. 'Despite having a menagerie on Animal Island, my father doesn't believe in domesticating wild beasts. He only purchases animals that have already been taken out of their environment by travelling groups or wealthy peers. His trips to Africa, then and now, are to return the poor creatures to the wild. And my mother goes with him. Mostly because they do not like to be parted, but also because she's hoping to find a new plants or herbs to use in her perfumes. She has her own perfume company and a shop on Bond Street. She blends the new scents herself.'

Lady Louisa gave him another dazzling grin. 'I had no idea a lady could have her own business. How very thrilling!'

Wick tried not to return her smile, but his lips kept quirking upwards of their own volition. 'It is not precisely favourable in the eyes of the *ton*, but Mama comes from a trade background. Our maternal grandfather is one of the wealthiest tradesmen in England. There's not a banker or a broker in London who doesn't know his name. Or owe him money. I daresay we would all be shunned by society if Mama wasn't such good friends with the Prince Regent. She blends a cologne just for him, and usually sends him a bottle every month. Before she went to Africa she delivered Prinny a whole case.'

Lady Louisa fluttered her eyelashes and her green

eyes seemed to sparkle in the candlelight. 'What a marvellous family you have, my lord.'

'That's not the exact word I would use to describe it,' he said ruefully.

'Oh, but *I* would,' she said. 'I would...'

And he believed her. Lady Louisa seemed to fit perfectly into his crazy family. Perhaps a little too perfectly. Dancing with her had proved disastrous. Instead of curing him of his obsession with her, it had only stoked his passion. Talking with her... Touching her... He wanted her more than ever. Wanted her breathless and blushing in his arms. He imagined himself kissing her every freckle, one by one.

'I think we had better call it a night,' Mrs May said with a yawn. 'Lady Louisa and I have a journey in the morning.'

Relieved by the housekeeper's distraction, Wick left Lady Louisa's side and offered his hand to Mrs May to help her to her feet.

'You're such a thoughtful man, my lord.'

He was thinking of Lady Louisa entirely too much.

He could hardly wait to be rid of her tomorrow.

Chapter Ten

Despite Lord Cheswick's reassuring words the previous night, Louisa felt anxious about seeing her mother's brother and his family. Her stomach roiled uncomfortably as the Marquess's carriage ambled over the country roads. She patted her curls, hoping that her family would approve of her...that her Aunt and Uncle Laybourne would help her gain her fortune and have the debut her mother had always dreamed of for her.

Lady Frederica, Lady Becca and Lady Helen, with a new, smaller snake, had all offered to accompany her. But Mrs May had been firm, telling them that there was not enough room in the carriage and they must stay at home.

Lord Cheswick sat across from her. He looked awfully handsome. He was so tall, and his build so muscular. The whiskers down the side of his cheeks framed his strong jaw and chiselled cheeks, even when he was frowning. She couldn't help but steal several glances at him. His mere presence gave her both strength and resolve.

She wished he could be one of her potential suitors, but he'd been quite adamant whilst they'd been dancing the night before that he would not. Yet he had pulled her close to him. His body had pressed against hers and everywhere they'd met she had burned with an unknown need. She had longed to touch his skin with her own. His lips with hers.

'Are you quite well?' he asked now.

Louisa could feel a blush growing from her neck into her face. She'd been caught staring at him.

How embarrassing!

'Only a little nervous, my lord,' she said, turning her gaze towards Mrs May. 'I can only hope that my uncle's family is as open and caring as your own.'

Mrs May's eyes seemed to dance. She glanced from Louisa to Lord Cheswick and then back again. The housekeeper was clearly aware of Louisa's attraction to the young Marquess. Louisa could only be glad that the kindly older woman could not see her most intimate thoughts.

'Yes,' he agreed. 'But hopefully without reptiles or camel leopards.'

'Snakes are quite useful in the kitchens and in the cellar, my lord,' Mrs May said matter-of-factly. 'We have no problem with mice, thanks to Lady Helen's pets.'

Lord Cheswick gave a shudder that Louisa assumed was revulsion. Despite adoring Helen, Louisa found she was not fond of snakes either.

Straightening her new gown, Louisa was glad that at least she would not be facing her mother's brother in leftover curtain cloth. Mrs May had found her a gown that had once belonged to the Marquess's oldest sister, the Duchess of Glastonbury, and had altered it cleverly to fit Louisa's frame. The housekeeper had apologised that it was several years out of fashion, but to Louisa it was the finest piece of clothing she'd ever possessed.

The town of Sherborne looked as if it belonged in the medieval past. She loved the stone buildings, white-washed cottages, and the impressive abbey with its pointed windows. Louisa had never been to a large town before, and she hadn't realised how noisy they were. People, animals and carriages...all were going about their business. She was enjoying watching them from the window and was a little dismayed when the carriage came to a stop.

Lord Cheswick opened the door and assisted Louisa and Mrs May out. The Canon of Sherborne's house was large, without being ostentatious, but it was small compared to Hampford Castle. When a servant opened the door, the Marquess handed the man his card. The butler blinked, before opening the door wider and ushering them all into a formal parlour. Louisa assumed that future dukes were not left waiting on the doorstep to see if the family was at home or not.

Mrs May took a chair that faced the front windows, crossing her feet and placing her reticule in her lap. Louisa sat opposite her, next to Lord Cheswick. He was not only handsome, he made her feel safe.

The parlour looked very tidy. The fine chairs appeared as if they had never been sat on. The walls were strangely bare, giving the room an austere feel. Louisa felt unaccountably cold and rubbed her arms with her hands.

Suddenly the housekeeper's reticule moved, and Mrs May jumped in her seat. 'Oh, goodness!' she exclaimed.

Louisa watched as Mrs May took a deep breath and opened her small bag.

She shook her head and held it out for them to see. 'Lady Helen must have put a snake in my reticule because I wouldn't let her come.'

Lord Cheswick groaned and touched his head. 'I am so sorry, Mrs May.'

Louisa couldn't help but think that he was quite sweet and very attractive when he was flustered.

Mrs May closed the strings. 'If I were afraid of snakes, my lord, I couldn't work at the castle. Lady Helen is a veritable snake charmer.'

Louisa had to stifle her laughter. The Stringham sisters were irrepressible. She couldn't help but wish she was more like them. They were strong and fearless. They stood up to their brother in a way that she had never been able to stand up to her aunt. Louisa hoped that Uncle Laybourne's wife would be kinder to her than Aunt Rockingham. Mayhap she could even love Louisa, and help fill the void left by her mother's death.

The door opened and Louisa saw a man with brown, grey-streaked hair and a red beard. His frame was tall and slender, verging on gaunt. He wore unrelieved black, except for his stark white collar. His eyes were green, like hers, but that was the only resemblance between them. His wife was on his arm and she also wore black. Louisa wondered if they were in mourning.

Her Aunt Laybourne was nearly two heads shorter than her husband, and her square frame was not flattered by the high-waisted gown. She wore a white frilly cap, under which her brown hair was scraped back into a tight bun, giving her round face a severe look. Not the warm, maternal expression that Louisa had been hoping for.

Lord Cheswick and Mrs May stood and bowed to her aunt and uncle. Louisa could only stare.

Her Uncle Laybourne brought a handkerchief to his nose, sniffing twice. 'When Lady Rockingham came to see us yesterday, Louisa, claiming you had run away, I was naturally shocked by such disobedient behaviour. I did not think that the daughter of my sister would conduct herself in such a heedless and wanton fashion.'

Louisa felt her eyes fill with tears, and a pain at the back of her throat. She clutched her arms around her middle, hiding her palms. She felt as if she were a child again, standing before Aunt Rockingham and being chided for not being more obedient, for asking too many questions. Desperate to please, but unable to do so.

'Now, see here, sir,' said Lord Cheswick, stepping towards her uncle. They were about the same height, but the Marquess was twice as wide and more intimidating. 'How dare you make assumptions about your niece without even hearing her side of the story?'

Her uncle sniffed again. 'She is in the presence of a notorious young marquess—which is damaging enough without hearing what she has to say.'

Notorious? Louisa could well believe it, for he was achingly handsome and painfully sweet. She could not be the only woman in the world to have noticed it.

She watched Lord Cheswick's hands curl into fists. 'I would hardly compromise a young woman in the company of my three sisters. And my housekeeper, Mrs May, has proved to be a most efficient chaperone.'

'A servant cannot become a chaperone overnight,' her Aunt Laybourne said, touching her husband's arm as if for support.

Louisa could have fainted on the spot. So much for making a favourable first impression on her relatives. She rubbed her face and felt her throat constrict. She feared that after all her scheming and the help of the servants she was going to end up back at the hall, underneath Aunt Rockingham's thumb. She would never enjoy a

London season. She would never see the Marquess or his sisters again.

That thought alone brought tears to her eyes.

'Your home, I believe, is Hampford Castle,' said her Uncle Laybourne. 'Where my niece has spent two nights in your company without a suitable chaperone. You must marry her immediately or return Louisa to her guardians, Lord and Lady Rockingham, for appropriate punishment.'

'Oh, no!' Louisa couldn't help but say it. It would be a poor way to repay his kindness to force Lord Cheswick into a relationship not of his choosing. Even if, for her, marrying him would be a dream come true. 'The Stringhams have been nothing but kind to me. The Marquess should not be forced to do anything.'

Lord Cheswick glanced at her and gave her a reassuring look. 'I have no intention of being browbeaten into marrying anyone. Now, sir, you can listen quietly to your niece's side of the story, or I shall hold you down until you do.'

Her uncle sniffed into his handkerchief once more. 'I would have you know I am a canon and the grandson of a marquess.'

'Well, I *am* a marquess, and heir to a dukedom, with close connections with the royal family,' Lord Cheswick said, stepping menacingly towards him. 'And I won't ask you again.'

Aunt Laybourne whimpered from the seat she had taken on the sofa, but she didn't speak. Uncle Laybourne sat beside her and gave Louisa a cold stare.

She swallowed, and clutched at the sides of her new gown. Her head was lowered in deference, but her voice was clear. 'My aunt, Lady Rockingham, is no longer my guardian. I turned one-and-twenty this week. I asked her for the names of my trustees, for I have never once seen a farthing of my yearly allowance. Aunt Rockingham refused to give me their names and said that my only choice was to marry her son, whenever they could persuade him. My clothes are practically rags. The boots on my feet are second-hand, given by one of the maids. I have no others. I decided to come to you for help. I set off to find you, but I did not know that you were no longer at the Frome vicarage. When I arrived there, I was told that I would find you and your wife here. I began to walk, even though it was getting late. By chance, the Stringhams happened upon me and kindly took me to their home. They even provided this dress that I currently wear. They have been nothing but souls of generosity and goodness. I owe them an irreparable debt.'

'And what do you expect my husband to do?' asked her Aunt Laybourne, her beady eyes narrowing on Louisa.

Louisa slumped a little in her chair. 'I had hoped that my uncle would help me contact my trustees and find someone to present me to the Queen and chaperone me for a season. I wish to find a suitable match and therefore a home of my own.'

Aunt Laybourne's nostrils flared as she turned to address her husband. 'She certainly cannot stay here. We already have nine daughters to find husbands for, without taking in a niece of questionable moral standards with a prodigious number of freckles. She would bring disgrace on our dearest daughters.'

Her freckles again.

Would her blemishes always keep her family from accepting her? Loving her?

'Of course she cannot stay here,' her Uncle Laybourne agreed, clutching his sodden handkerchief. 'And nor do I have time to go to London and see about the legal matter of her inheritance. I know nothing about the trustees named in the late Lord Rockingham's will. Louisa, you would be best served returning to Greystone Hall and begging for your aunt's forgiveness. Perhaps your cousin will refuse to marry you after this escapade—then you'll have no need to vacate the home of your youth. But I can do nothing for you. The scandal of your leaving home is enough to cause damage to my position.'

Louisa opened her mouth and then shut it. The sinking feeling in her stomach was growing with each passing moment. What was she to do now? She could not—*would* not—return to Greystone Hall. Would she have to run away again? Where would she go without any money or friends?

'If you are determined to be derelict in your duties to your niece,' Lord Cheswick said, 'then Mrs May, my sisters and I will take Lady Louisa to London. We won't leave a stone unturned until we find her trustees.'

His words filled the hole in her heart. She stood up to her full height and lifted her chin. Unlike her family, he would not take advantage of her fortune. He would not abandon her. The Stringham sisters didn't expect her to lower herself to earn their approval. Or for her to try and change into someone she was not.

'As you must be already aware,' her uncle said, wiping his running nose with his monogramed handkerchief, 'your servant is hardly an appropriate chaperone.'

Lord Cheswick flexed his arm muscles as he straightened his cuff. It was hardly an appropriate time for her to notice, but he was certainly a powerfully built man.

'But my sister, the Duchess of Glastonbury, is. No one will dare say a word against her chaperonage. Let us take our leave, Lady Louisa… Mrs May.'

Louisa did not have to be told twice. She all but ran for the door to escape her horrible family. Mrs May linked her arm with Louisa's and patted it reassuringly. Louisa felt giddy with relief. Her heart expanded in her chest. Somehow she had been blessed enough to discover true friends at Hampford Castle.

Before she reached the door, Mrs May clutched at her chest theatrically and said, 'Oh, no—is that a snake on the floor?'

From the look of satisfaction on the housekeeper's face, Louisa felt certain that the snake had not been let go from her reticule by accident. Her Aunt Laybourne shrieked even louder than before and her uncle stepped onto a sofa.

'Don't put your feet on the furniture!' Aunt Laybourne yelled at her husband, but then practically jumped on the sofa herself as the snake slithered by her feet. It hissed at her and she shrieked some more.

Lord Cheswick opened the door and they walked out of the room together, leaving her aunt and uncle still standing on top of the furniture.

Mrs May did not laugh until they were all inside the carriage and he had closed the door behind them.

The Marquess grinned at her. 'That was brilliant, Mrs May.'

The housekeeper adjusted her hat on her head. 'Never underestimate a *mere* servant.'

Louisa couldn't help but agree. The servants at Greystone Hall had made her life bearable and helped her escape. She'd been foolish to think that her Uncle Laybourne would help her. Perhaps she didn't deserve his help or his time. It had been wicked of her to demand so much from a stranger. Maybe she really was a selfish as Aunt Rockingham had always said.

'I am so sorry to be a burden to you,' she said now, wringing her hands together, wishing to weep in despair. 'If it is easier, you may return me to Greystone Hall.'

Chapter Eleven

'I have made you a promise, Lady Louisa, and I mean to keep it,' Wick said.

Her head sank even lower, until her chin was touching her chest. 'But I have already been a great inconvenience to you…and you have your three sisters to take care of already. I could not ask you to travel to London. Nor could I presume so much of your sister, Lady Glastonbury, who has never even met me.'

Wick had never before felt such pure anger. His blood twitched in his veins and his pulse was thunderous. He half regretted not punching the sanctimonious clergyman right on his long, skinny and running nose. How anyone could treat Lady Louisa so poorly was beyond his reasoning. This beautiful young woman's actions were nothing but kind and considerate. Her manners were excellent. She hadn't demanded anything much of her relatives; she'd only asked for help in a world that rendered a daughter powerless.

'You needn't worry about Mantheria—she loves to boss people around, and the only person she has now is her three-year-old son. Our sisters have long since stopped obeying her.'

A tear ran down Louisa's cheek and she wiped it away with her gloved hand. 'Your sisters are all very strong young women.'

'It is why they are alive,' he whispered, thinking of poor, frail Elizabeth, who had been unable to fight off scarlet fever. 'Perhaps, in return, you can continue to keep them occupied until I can find them a proper governess.'

'I don't think you can afford to be particular, my lord,' Mrs May said with the same irrepressible twinkle in her eyes. 'You might need to choose an improper one.'

Lady Louisa let out a watery chuckle. 'Proper or improper governess—I should be glad to help you in any way that I am able, my lord.'

Wick clenched his fists tightly until he couldn't feel his fingers. If Lady Louisa's late father hadn't trusted his brother and wife with his daughter's fortune, why in heaven's name had he trusted them with her person? The dead Earl had taken better care of his wife's money than his child… But Wick would change all that.

Several minutes passed before he glanced up to see Lady Louisa's eyes on him. Blushing, she looked down at her hands. He saw that Mrs May had dozed off with her mouth open. The poor woman had probably not got much sleep since his sisters had been sent home. He needed a governess so that the housekeeper wasn't in effect holding two positions at the same time. He knew from personal experience that taking care of his sisters was a thankless and often dangerous task. It was enough to keep a person up late at night and make them rise early the next day.

Lady Louisa peeked up at him again. 'May I ask you about Lady Glastonbury?'

Exhaling, Wick lifted his shoulders and let them fall. 'What would you like to know about my sister?'

She smiled even wider, and he tried not to fix his gaze on the kissable freckle above her lips.

'You have said that she has a little son; does she have any other children?'

'No, only the one—but she's still young. Not even one-and-twenty for another fortnight.'

'She is only twenty and already a duchess?'

Wick shifted in his seat. 'Mantheria was seventeen when she made her debut, and she became engaged to the Duke of Glastonbury after only a few weeks. It was a bit of a whirlwind courtship. They married at the end of the season and left for a wedding trip to France.'

Lady Louisa breathed in and out. 'Oh, I hope that I am as lucky if I get a season of my own.'

'Lucky enough to marry a duke?' he asked sardonically.

She shook her head and a red curl came free of her chignon and fell over her shoulder. He wanted to touch it. Her gorgeous hair looked like liquid flame.

'Oh, no. Or at least not necessarily. It is just that I have always wished to be married and have a family of my own. A home of my own, where I feel I belong. I do not mind if my suitors do not have titles, as long as they have good hearts.'

He had misjudged her aspirations. The sweet young woman wasn't being socially ambitious in her wishes. She merely wanted to have a home of her own and a husband who loved her. Such little things that were often took for granted.

'I suppose most young women wish for marriage and a family.'

A little colour stole into Lady Louisa's cheeks. 'It is what we are taught to look forward to. But ever since my father died I have longed to have a family of my own. Someone to love and someone who loves me.'

That someone would not be him.

Clearing his throat, Wick doggedly continued their conversation. 'I shall send an express message to Mantheria as soon as we get back to the castle. She'll receive it tonight and we can be off first thing in the morning, after I make the arrangements.'

'She won't mind four more guests for the remainder of the season?'

Wick furrowed his brow. 'Four?'

'Myself and your three sisters.'

He could have swallowed his tongue. Of *course* he would have to bring Frederica, Helen and Becca with him. They couldn't be left at the castle without the housekeeper, and Mrs May would have to accompany them to chaperone Louisa until they reached Mantheria's house. Wick couldn't afford even a whiff of indiscretion over the daughter of the late Earl or he'd be forced to marry her.

'Five guests,' he said.

'Will you be staying with your sister as well?'

'Oh, no. I meant Mrs May. I have my own rooms in London,' he explained. 'My parents have a house in Berkley Square, but I prefer the comforts of my bachelor suite.'

The young lady nodded. 'Your sisters mentioned that you have a brother living in London. Do you share accommodations?'

'Matthew's a great gun…but he has his own apartments, closer to the financial district. If anyone can find your trustees and help with your father's will it is he. Matthew makes the pen a dangerous weapon.'

Lady Louisa leaned forward in her seat. 'Do you really think so? Will he be able to help me gain access to my fortune?'

Wick felt himself move towards her, propelled by more than the movements of the carriage…by a need he did not recognise and did not want. 'Yes, Matthew's a legal genius.'

She smiled at him again. 'He is not a naturalist like your father?'

Like Charles.

Wick moved back, folding his arms. His heart was sinking in his chest. 'No, he is not,' he said sharply.

Lady Louisa sat back too, her face looking red, as if someone had slapped her. Wick didn't know how to explain that her words had bruised him but that he hadn't meant to snap at her.

She moved in her seat, bumping into Mrs May, who was startled awake.

'We were talking about governesses?' she said, rubbing her sleepy eyes.

'Yes, Mrs May,' he said.

The housekeeper yawned. 'The sooner the better.'

And the sooner he got rid of Lady Louisa the better. He hadn't meant to tell her so much about his family. It reminded him of Charles and thinking about his little brother was like touching a tender bruise that never healed. He only felt raw pain.

Chapter Twelve

Louisa didn't know what she had said that had made Lord Cheswick so angry, but he'd barely spoken a word to her on their journey home. Perhaps she had been impertinent, asking personal questions about his family. She longed to know him better, but he seemed determined to keep her at arm's length. Her regard for him was clearly not returned. She needed to stop thinking about him so much and focus on her season and the suitors she would meet.

A London season that would take place thanks to *his* kindness.

But ridding her thoughts of him was proving quite impossible.

Mrs May, who was now wide awake, conversed merrily with her about the duties of running a household. Louisa wondered if the housekeeper was quizzing her about her capabilities. Luckily, Mrs Barker had taught her well, and Louisa knew more about managing servants than any feminine accomplishments.

When they arrived at the castle Lord Cheswick helped them out of the carriage and then immediately excused himself to make arrangements for London. Instead of going with them to the house, he went towards the stables.

Louisa spared him one last glance, before Mrs May took her arm and led her inside. The butler opened the door for them and the three Stringham sisters sprang upon them. Literally.

'You're back!' Becca said, hugging Louisa tightly. 'You came back. I am so very glad.'

'What happened?' Frederica demanded, as she patted Louisa on the shoulder. 'Was your family not at home?'

Louisa pulled at her collar, feeling sweat form on her brow. 'They were at home. However, they are not inclined to help me.'

'What fustian!' Frederica said with a growl.

Louisa felt light-headed, and longed to flee rather than tell them the truth. 'Wick… Lord Cheswick…thought that perhaps your sister Lady Glastonbury might let me stay with her whilst he contacts my trustees.'

'So we're all to go to London,' Mrs May said, clapping her hands. 'Now, you'd best stop pestering poor Lady Louisa and start packing.'

'London!' Becca squealed.

Frederica grabbed Helen's hands and they jumped up and down together. 'What fun we will have there.'

'I can feel my hair turning greyer already,' the housekeeper said drily, which sent the Stringham sisters into hysterical laughter.

Sobering after a few moments, Helen cleared her throat and gave Mrs May a sharp look. 'Where is my new snake?'

Mrs May blinked; pretending to be surprised. 'I do not know what you mean, Lady Helen. What snake would that be?'

Louisa had to bite down on her lower lip to keep in her laugh. The housekeeper was not going to let her charge know that her prank had been successful. Nor of her own exploits with the reptile.

The older woman breathed in deeply. 'No more dallying. It's time for you all to go to your rooms and get ready for our trip to London. I'll send up the maids.'

Louisa smiled. Mrs May was more than a match for the young ladies in her charge. She doubted that she could have handled them half so well. Whoever they found for a governess would need a sturdy constitution and a well of patience.

After dinner that night, Frederica declared that they were going to practise curtsying. Louisa was grateful for the help—if a little nervous. She didn't want to embarrass herself or Lord Cheswick in front of his sister the Duchess of Glastonbury the next day. She longed to earn the young woman's good opinion, and it would be entirely lovely to have a friend her own age.

Frederica cleared her throat. 'Place one foot slightly behind the other and then open your hands, bow your head, and slightly bend your knees.'

Helen curtsied to her brother. 'Like this, Louisa.'

'*Lady* Louisa,' Lord Cheswick reminded his sister.

'Oh, I have told your sisters that their calling me just Louisa is fine,' she said, her cheeks warm. 'My lord.'

'*Just Louisa* it is,' Becca said with a giggle. 'You can drop Wick's title as well. If you keep calling in "my lord" he will get terribly toplofty.'

Louisa's face felt as if it was on fire when she turned to look at the Marquess. 'I couldn't…'

'Please,' he said in a low, attractive voice. 'My sisters will tease me abominably if you do not.'

'That's true,' Helen chimed in.

'Louisa, if your rank is beneath theirs, you lower your eyes when you curtsy,' Frederica explained. 'But if it is the same, or higher, you don't have to. *We* only lower our eyes for royalty.'

'Now you try,' Becca said.

Louisa stood in front of Wick—it felt so intimate even to think of him by that name. He bowed to her, one hand on his waist, in a graceful bend. His brown eyes never left hers. Taking a quick breath, Louisa placed one foot behind the other and sank into a deep curtsy. She was too shy to keep eye contact with him when he was smiling at her.

'Too low,' Helen said, shaking her head.

'He's not royal, Louisa,' Frederica said, wagging her finger at her. 'Don't give him any self-aggrandising ideas. You only need to do a slight bend of your knees.'

Her face even redder, Louisa stood up. Her pulse was racing and her heart beating loudly in her chest. Loud enough that she was sure that the Stringhams could hear it.

'Try again?' Becca suggested.

Helen touched the bottom of Louisa's chin. 'And keep your chin up. He's only a *courtesy* marquess. Not even the real thing.'

Wick barked out a laugh and gave Louisa another perfect bow. Biting her lower lip, Louisa kept her eyes and chin up and made a shaky bounce with her knees, barely dipping. Her body felt stiff and unnatural. Aunt Rockingham had been right: Louisa was terribly awkward.

Frederica clicked her tongue and folded her arms

across her chest. 'Not bad, but not good… Louisa, you
need to try again.'

'Why don't you three go and play a game of cards over
at the table near Mrs May?' Wick suggested, clearing his
throat. 'I think having three demanding tutors is rather
overwhelming *Just Louisa*.'

Louisa's lips twitched upwards when he said her name.
'Just Louisa' almost felt like an endearment. But that was
ridiculous. He'd made his lack of interest in her plain.

'Her face is very red,' Becca remarked with painful
honesty.

Louisa touched both of her cheeks with her gloved
hands. They did feel hot—but then so did the rest of
her. Oh, how she wished she were a polished and accomplished young lady.

'All right, Wick. I suppose we can play some *Specula-
tion*,' Helen said, the last word dripping with innuendo.

All the Stringhams laughed—even Wick. The three
sisters moved to the round table on the other side of the
room and sat down. Mrs May brought them a pack of
cards but did not join their game.

Wick grinned at Louisa and her heart jumped inside
her chest. Her pulse felt erratic, and even the blood in
her veins seemed to heat under his scrutiny.

'There's no need to be nervous,' he said, with a smile
that melted away what was left of her sense. 'I don't
bite…despite what my sisters say.'

But Louisa had already been bitten. This young, handsome, loving, kind and perfectly wonderful marquess had
quite captured her heart. But Aunt Rockingham had been
right. Such a man would not be interested in her roman-
tically. Not even her fortune would tempt him.

Her eyes fell to her borrowed slippers. 'I don't want to disgrace you or myself in public.'

He shook his head, giving her the same sweet, tender look he gave his little sisters. 'You couldn't. You're every inch a lady.'

Louisa released a shuddering breath, daring to move her gaze from her feet to his boots. 'I've been dreaming of having a London season since I was a little girl. My mother died when I was seven years old, and my strongest memory of her is the story she told me of her presentation to the Queen.'

'I take it the event was memorable?'

She managed a small smile as she touched the back of her neck. 'Queen Charlotte had a strong reaction to my mother's perfume…it caused her to sneeze. And, according to my mother, her second sneeze was so strong that it blew off one of the feathers in Mama's hair. The Lord Chamberlain had to fetch it for her. Mama said that she was so embarrassed, but Queen Charlotte smiled at her and said, *"Well, I shan't forget you."* And she didn't. When Mama married Papa she was presented again, as the Countess of Rockingham. Queen Charlotte gave her another rare smile and told Papa that they were old acquaintances. When I was little, my mother would put a feather in my hair and we would pretend that I was being introduced to the Queen.'

'I am afraid that Queen Charlotte is not quite as fond of our family,' Wick said with a smirk. 'She and the King did not get on very well with their eldest son and heir, the Prince Regent, even before King George III went mad. And, like I told you, my mama is a great friend of the Regent's…despite their different views on almost every political subject.'

Louisa couldn't help but meet his gaze, leaning closer to him. 'Really?'

He took a few steps towards her, closing the distance between them. 'I can tell you from first-hand experience that I have never met a more personable man than the Prince Regent—nor a more juvenile one. But he's an odd mixture of parts and will probably make a terrible king.'

Louisa gasped at his honesty and covered her mouth with one shaking hand. He was standing close enough that she could smell him: a musky mixture of vanilla and vetiver. His nearness filled all her senses.

Wick laughed and rendered her breathless by gently tucking a curl behind Louisa's ear. 'I wouldn't say so to my mother, of course.'

He had touched her!

Gloved... But still, he had *touched* her.

'Never,' she whispered.

He stepped back and bowed to her again.

Without thinking, Louisa curtsied in return.

Wick took her hand and pressed a soft kiss to the back of her glove. She could have happily died on the spot.

'Perfect,' he said. 'All you needed was a little distraction to settle your nerves. Now you'll be the most elegant lady at all the *ton* parties.'

Her chest swelled with pride. She had done it. The gawky girl without a proper governess had managed a curtsy worthy of a lady. If only Aunt Rockingham could see her now. But she would still probably find something about Louisa to criticise.

Glancing over her shoulder, she asked, 'Should we join your sisters at cards?'

'Oh, please, no. They are not currently arguing, and I would hate to interrupt a perfectly harmonious game.'

Louisa couldn't help but giggle. She was relieved that he wanted to stay with her. She doubted that she would ever tire of his conversation or company.

Wick gestured with his hand to the sofa nearest the fire. 'Shall we sit? We can talk…or I can fetch a couple of books.'

'I should l-like to talk,' she managed to say, before sitting down. She knew it was foolish, but she wanted to get to know him better.

He sat down beside her, not quite touching her leg, but close enough for her to enjoy his masculine scent again. Louisa's breathing was irregular and her face felt hot again. She needed to focus on something else—anything else but him.

Leaning down, she pulled the needle out of the inside of her hem. 'Would you mind if I finished embroidering these handkerchiefs while we converse?'

'Not at all,' he said, grinning at her. 'Do you always keep a needle in the hem of your gown?'

Louisa threaded the needle and pulled the first stitch through. The steady tension of the thread helped calm her racing pulse, but her hands were still shaking from his nearness.

'I was always mending at Greystone Hall…it seemed wise to have my favourite needle handy.'

'To make a plain cloth beautiful or to mend something that is torn is truly a wonderful gift. Few people have the ability to repair what is wrong in the world.'

She kept her head lowered, unable to look him in the face. 'You give my skill too much credit.'

'Or perhaps you give yourself too little,' he said, bumping his knee with hers.

It felt warm and hard. She wished he would rest his knee against hers.

'Besides, we are all more than the measure of our talents. How we treat others... Who we are kind to... How we fulfil our responsibilities to those who depend upon us... My parents taught me that those are truly the things that must be measured.'

'You are clearly not a seamstress,' Louisa said, glancing up at him with a half-smile. 'For everything must be measured precisely if a garment is to fit properly.'

Wick laughed. It was a deep but soft sound. It made her heartbeat quicken and the blood pump through her body. She wished again for the impossible...

Focusing on her sewing, Louisa pulled another stitch through. 'But I believe you are right,' she said. 'What is truly important about a person's soul cannot be measured... But I have never heard of a gentleman being introduced with a list of his accomplishments. Only ladies.'

Interlocking his fingers, he stretched out his arms. 'It's because our accomplishments aren't quite as impressive or presentable as those of the fairer sex.'

Louisa toyed with her needle between two fingers. 'Nonsense. I daresay that your talents could take up a whole page.'

'At least my good intentions.'

Louisa chuckled, and he grinned back at her. His face was close enough that if she leaned forward a little her lips would brush his. Blushing, she realised that she wasn't the only one looking at lips. Wick's eyes were lowered and he was gazing at her mouth as if there was nothing else in the room.

How badly she wanted him to kiss her! It would be even more wonderful in reality than it was in her dreams.

But he could hardly do so with his three little sisters and Mrs May in the room. Even though the girls were now yelling at each other on the other side. Their harmonious card game had not lasted long.

Shakily, she got to her feet, clutching her embroidery. 'I think I shall retire to bed. It has been a long day and I know we make an early start in the morning.'

Wick stood up and bowed to her. 'Of course. Sleep well.'

Louisa took only one step away from him, but it already felt too far. She bade goodnight to Mrs May and the Stringham sisters and made her way up the candlelit staircase to her room.

Alone.

It reminded her that she wasn't truly a part of their family. She was only a temporary guest.

Chapter Thirteen

Wick rode beside the carriage on their way to London the next morning, after ensuring that his little sisters had not brought with them any reptiles or vermin. He had handed all the extra pets to Harper before they'd departed—Helen had another 'new' snake and Becca a mouse—and he even had the forethought to check their trunks. Happily, there were no stowaways there.

He had let them bring their kittens, because Frederica had told him that the dear creatures would be full-grown cats by the time they returned to the castle. Wick sincerely hoped that he wouldn't have charge of his three little sisters and their three kittens in London for *that* long. He planned to conclude Louisa's business in less than a week and interview governesses from a respectable agency.

They stopped at an inn for a midday meal, and then continued the long drive to London. Both Wick's backside and his temper were in need of a rest by the time they reached his sister's townhouse in Mayfair. Servants streamed out through the front doors to meet the carriage, followed by his sister Mantheria and his nephew Andrew. His brother-in-law was strangely absent.

The three-year-old squirmed out of his mother's arms and ran down the stairs towards his uncle and aunts. Wick and all three of his sisters had their arms outstretched to the little boy with wild black curls. All competing for his favour, begging him to come to them first.

Andrew launched himself at his uncle. Wick grabbed him by the waist and swung him round. He couldn't miss his words.

'I want an ice!'

His bribery was working well.

'And Uncle Wick will take you to Gunter's to get one.'

His adorable nephew reached out his chubby little arms to Frederica and Wick reluctantly relinquished him. Andrew was his favourite member of the family. One he could love and spoil without having any responsibility over his health and happiness.

Andrew squeezed Helen and Becca, before hugging Louisa's legs. Then his little head tipped up and his blue eyes became wide circles. He let go of Louisa and pointed up at her. 'Who is she?'

Louisa touched the very noticeable red curls that had escaped from her bonnet and turned pink as she smiled. It wasn't an embarrassed blush, he thought, but rather a pleased one. He noticed that she often blushed—no doubt it was caused by her fair skin. But he had begun to recognise the different emotions behind her blushing. If her ears and neck were red, Louisa felt embarrassed. If her cheeks were pink, she was happy. And if her entire countenance was flushed, she was trying hard not to cry.

Life, it would seem, had not been kind to her since

her parents' deaths. It made his blood boil just thinking of the Rockinghams.

Becca knelt down next to their nephew. 'This is our new friend Louisa.'

Andrew pointed at Louisa. 'Loo-ee-*zah*!'

Becca clapped and hugged her nephew. 'That's right. You clever boy.'

Mantheria hugged all her sisters and Wick, before picking up her son and placing him on her hip. She bowed her head to Louisa. 'It's a pleasure to make your acquaintance, Lady Louisa.'

She gave Mantheria a shaky curtsy. Not at all like the graceful one she'd given Wick the night before. 'Thank you for letting me stay, Lady Glastonbury. I hope that it is not too great an imposition.'

'It is no imposition at all, and please call me Mantheria,' she said, waving her hand towards the house. 'Come inside, everyone. I've had my housekeeper prepare rooms for all of you—including you, Mrs May. I've chosen my very best…although Wick's letter said nothing about kittens.'

Wick ignored this sally, grateful that his sister was being so welcoming to Louisa.

Andrew reached out his hands towards Becca. 'Kitty!'

Becca grinned and handed over the black kitten to her nephew. Andrew cradled it like a baby. Helen handed Wick her kitten, the little orange ball of fur. Instinctively, he stroked the little animal's back.

'I want a kitty, Mama,' Andrew said.

Mantheria groaned. 'He's a Stringham through and through.'

Becca and Helen retrieved their kittens before dashing inside the house. Frederica linked arms with Louisa, leaving Wick and Mantheria, still carrying Andrew to take up the rear. His sister was six years younger than him, but in some ways she felt older. She was married with a child and ran several households of her own. Even though she was the same age as Louisa…only a few weeks younger.

When she had made her debut the *ton* had declared her 'a diamond of the first water'. And his sister *was* beautiful. Mantheria's person combined the best characteristics of his parents: Papa's blond, aristocratic features and complexion, and their mother's curvaceous figure.

'I hope Glastonbury doesn't mind our visit,' he said.

His sister glanced away from him as they entered her large and opulent home. 'Of course he doesn't mind. Alexander doesn't even know. He left three days ago for a house party in the company of Lady Dutton. I don't expect to see him for at least a fortnight—probably longer.'

Wick cursed underneath his breath. Mantheria had been too young to marry that lecherous old goat. Even if he *was* a duke. Lord Alexander Spooner, the Duke of Glastonbury, had been forty-five to his sister's seventeen years. Only among the *ton* could that sort of disparity in age be seen as acceptable. Or even desirable. When the Duke had married Mantheria the rumour had been that he wanted an heir. And he'd got one.

Wick felt a surge of protectiveness. 'Do you want me to have a talk with him?'

Mantheria set down Andrew, whose little legs were pumping before they even hit the marble floor. The lad was clearly anxious to catch up with his aunts.

Wick followed his sister into a parlour with dark maroon walls and matching furniture. She didn't sit down and so neither did he. They stood awkwardly next to each other. Their usual camaraderie gone.

'Do you think me a child?' she asked him. 'Incapable of handling my own affairs?'

He held up his hands. 'Of course not. I only thought to help. Forgive me for intruding where I am not wanted.'

His sister took his arm and rested her head on his shoulder. She had the same golden curls and blue eyes as their father and Matthew, also Charles, Helen and Elizabeth.

'I know you mean well, but I am not your responsibility any more. And I prefer things the way they are.'

Wick scoffed, shaking his head. 'You prefer your husband to be with another woman?'

She sighed, rubbing her face into his sleeve. 'Glastonbury's brief infatuation with me barely lasted past our wedding trip, when I became pregnant with Andrew. He has been with Lady Dutton ever since. Any jealousy I once felt is now long gone.'

Wick's fingers touched his parted lips. For over three years his sister had borne this terrible situation on her own. 'The villain!'

His sister's tense posture loosened and she let out a long breath. 'I do not hate him any more, but I cannot love him either, and I do not want him here. But at least he is good with Andrew. He positively dotes on him. And Lady Dutton is scarcely less friendly. She brings him a present every time she visits, and I know that Glastonbury takes Andrew to see her. He calls her Aunt Cressida.'

Wick's entire body stiffened. 'So you live together as strangers?'

'Glastonbury is always polite, and we tend to spend

very little time together outside of the London season,'
Mantheria said, her face pale. 'He is often at house parties or overseeing his other estates. He only visits to
spend time with Andrew.'

'Do Mama and Papa know? Did you tell them before
they left?'

'How can I tell them when they pushed for the match?
They thought I would grow to love Glastonbury, like
Mama did with Papa... And from a material point of
view I could not have done better. I am a duchess, and
one of the wealthiest women in England.'

Wick spoke between his clenched teeth. 'And the lone-
liest.'

He realised he did not want Louisa to make a similar
loveless match. She deserved a loving husband and family after all her suffering at the hands of her aunt and the
neglect of her uncle.

His sister forced a smile. 'Nonsense. How could anyone be lonely with Andrew around? And now that my
sisters, Mrs May and Lady Louisa have come to visit, I
am quite overburdened with company.'

'Does Glastonbury wish for more children?'

Wick knew that most peers wanted 'an heir and a
spare', just in case something happened to the firstborn
son.

Mantheria stepped away from him, a look of revulsion
on her face. 'Despite his many flaws, Alexander would
never force himself on me. He has an heir to his dukedom, and he knows that he will have no other children
from me.'

Wick picked up a figurine from the table and squeezed
it with all the anger he felt for his brother-in-law. A man
he'd once respected and admired. 'Would you consider

a divorce? It's common knowledge that he is unfaithful to you. It wouldn't be hard to prove.'

'A woman cannot obtain a divorce unless there is cruelty—which there has not been. Only a man can divorce for infidelity. Men are given all the privileges and never held to the same standards as women.'

'I could always shoot him.'

Mantheria burst into laughter, breaking the tense feeling in the room. 'Yes, but I wouldn't want you to hang.'

Wick huffed. 'In a proper duel—not in the middle of the street. I wouldn't hang.'

She lifted her hands and dropped them. 'What if you were the one who died? And anyway it's no matter. I could never deprive Andrew of his father. He adores Alexander and Andrew adores him… Now, let's focus on your own problems.'

'I need another governess.'

'Obviously—a lady who will get on well with Becca, Frederica and Helen. I'll ask around my friends to see if they know of any young woman who would suit our family. Someone who isn't averse to kittens, snakes or emus.'

Wick bit the side of his cheek. 'And I want Lady Louisa to be presented to Queen Charlotte and enjoy a London season. One of her only memories of her mother is being told about her presentation. Matthew and I will track down her trustees and sort out her finances.'

Mantheria laughed again, raising her eyebrows. 'You don't ask for much. Just a come-out wardrobe for a debutante, a royal presentation, and an introduction to the *ton* with absolutely no notice at all. It is something I cannot do on my own. In my husband's absence I will need a proper escort.'

A shiver of panic ran down his spine; he feared where

this conversation was heading. 'I hope you don't want *me* to accompany you to these society squeezes.'

His sister patted his arm. 'Yes, dearest brother. You must come to all the parties with us and lend our group your countenance.'

Wick stepped away from his sister and held up his hands as if he'd been waylaid by highwaymen. 'I will get eaten alive. The debutantes will swarm around me like killer bees. I will be of no use to you or Louisa.'

Mantheria lifted her chin. 'If you don't, then I won't.'

He was half tempted to test his sister's threats, but he'd promised Louisa that he would help her and he couldn't without Mantheria's assistance.

'You drive a harder bargain than Mama,' he said, putting down his hands. 'Fine. I will escort you to the presentation and to a couple of balls. But I won't dance. And you will have to help me find a new governess for the girls.'

His sister held out her hand. 'It's an agreement.'

'Agreement,' he echoed, shaking it and knowing that he would regret this pact.

Chapter Fourteen

Louisa had never been shopping before, so she didn't know what to expect. The stylish premises that Mantheria took her to the next day did not have any prices displayed. Nor any dresses. They were taken to a parlour with several chairs and given tea from a silver tea tray with small cakes. The modiste, a Madame Brunet, sat with them and chatted merrily about the weather with a pleasing French accent.

She was a petite, dark-haired beauty with an olive-skinned complexion. Her dress was cut fashionably, but sensibly. And nothing about her demeanour suggested that they were about to spend any money. Nor did Madame Brunet rush them at all. She waited for Louisa and Mantheria to finish their tea before she stood up.

'If you are ready, Your Grace?' Madame Brunet said, looking at Mantheria, who was the highest-ranking woman in the room. 'I shall have my assistants model the latest fashions from Paris. If any dress strikes your fancy, I can have it made up in the colour and material of your choice.'

Mantheria nodded and smiled at the other woman. 'Yes, Lady Louisa's colouring might prove a bit tricky on some of the shades. But I am sure that we can rely on your good taste to guide us to the best you have to offer. My mother would expect nothing less.'

'Of course, Your Grace,' said Madame Brunet, bowing. 'I am honoured by your family's custom.'

Louisa bit her lower lip. Mantheria wasn't asking for a price reduction. She was telling the modiste to show her only the most expensive wares. Louisa knew that Mantheria and her sisters were very wealthy, but she had no idea when she would be able to repay them for their kindness—nor for Parisian gowns. She prayed that Wick would be able to locate her trustees quickly.

She cleared her throat. 'May I speak alone with the Duchess?'

Madame Brunet curtsied. 'But of course, *mademoiselle*. I shall go and help my assistants prepare. *Au revoir*.'

Louisa waited until the modiste had left the room to open her mouth. Although they were the same age, she still felt nervous in Lady Glastonbury's company. She was afraid to disappoint the Duchess, as she had Aunt Rockingham and Aunt Laybourne. And she wanted so badly for them to be friends.

'I appreciate that you want the very finest for me... but the thing is...although I am an heiress...truly... I don't have any money yet, and I would hate to impose upon you further.'

Mantheria moved from her chair on the opposite side of the room to the one next to Louisa. She placed a lace-gloved hand on hers. 'My dear Louisa, I trust that you will repay me whenever you can. I am not in any hurry. Besides, the bills will be sent to my unfaithful husband, and nothing would please me more than to spend thousands of pounds in his name.'

It was an obvious question, but Louisa couldn't help but ask, 'You aren't happy in your marriage?'

The Duchess squeezed Louisa's wrist. 'Sometimes I forget that you haven't been a part of the family for long. My marriage to the Duke of Glastonbury is not a happy one. He spends his nights and most of his days with his mistress, Lady Dutton. And, like a good little wife, I am supposed to smile and pretend in front of society that I do not know that he is with Cressida. My marriage is an elegant lie.'

Louisa gulped, shaking her head in disbelief. 'His mistress couldn't possibly be more beautiful than you.'

Mantheria's grip on Louisa's wrist tightened until it hurt. It was clear that the Duchess had already known a great deal of pain in her marriage. The Duke's betrayal was even worse than her own aunt and uncle's treatment of her.

'Beauty has little to do with love.' Mantheria released her hold on Louisa. 'Do not be in too much of a hurry to marry, my dear. A lifetime can feel like an eternity with the wrong person at your side. Especially if your heart belongs to another.'

Louisa didn't know if Mantheria was referring to herself or to the Duke. She worried about her own choices. Would any man love her if she didn't have money or a title? She feared that Wick held more of her heart than was good for either of them. But he kept on making it abundantly clear that he would not be her suitor, and she couldn't let her feelings for him stop her from making a suitable match.

'I will do my best.'

Picking up the bell, Mantheria rang it. 'That is all you can do.'

Madame Brunet came into the room, followed by three women wearing the most delicate and beautiful ball gowns Louisa had ever seen. She couldn't stop herself from standing up and examining one more closely. The seams on the bodice of the gown formed a diamond shape in front. Walking behind the assistant, she saw that the sewing style made the back of the dress look very small, emphasising the oversleeves.

'It's called a tight back style,' Madame Brunet said.

Glancing over her shoulder, Louisa saw the modiste standing there.

'Do you sew, Lady Louisa?'

She bit her lower lip, nodding her head. 'But nothing as fine as this.'

Madame Brunet smiled. '*Non*. It is all in the pattern, my lady. I am sure you could sew something just as fine. You see the inverted pleats at the centre of the back? They give the dress shape and fullness to the skirt. Some ladies add a small roll or pad to create a subtle roundness, but with your lovely shape no such tricks are needed.'

Louisa blushed as she looked at the next model's gown. It was trimmed with festooned flounces and interspersed with puffs of net forming rosettes. The final assistant wore yellow crêpe embroidered with floral sprigs and applied shell designs that threw the hem into a three-dimensional relief. Every gown was a work of art. Louisa longed to run her fingers over the embroidery and the perfect little stitches. She wanted to untangle all the secrets of their sewing.

'One of each gown would be perfect,' Mantheria said from behind her, still sitting on her chair. 'But I don't think yellow would flatter Louisa. It would make her skin look rather sallow.'

Madame Brunet nodded her head vigorously. 'Yes, yes... Yellow would quite wash out her glorious colouring. But a bright green would look divine on the lady.'

'And blue,' Louisa added. 'Any shade.'

'One of her dresses must be white,' the young Duchess said. 'Every debutante has to have a white dress, and that won't clash with her red hair.'

Louisa would finally be a debutante. Something she'd always dreamed of being. She pinched herself to make sure that she was truly awake. She felt a brief stab of pain, but it was quickly replaced with pleasure. Wick would see her in these beautiful dresses. They might even dance. Her pulse quickened at the thought of being in his arms again.

'Why don't we get her light silk slips in white, pale blue and pink?' Mantheria said, fiddling with the braided lace. 'Then she can wear a white net gown or crêpe *lissé* over them for a new look each time.'

Louisa clapped her hands. 'Oh, I love that idea.'

She could mix and match and use her own skill with the needle to expand her wardrobe without costing the Duchess or her philandering husband any more money. She had no idea how long it would take for Wick to find her trustees, or for them to release to her the yearly allowance.

Mantheria cleared her throat. 'And any partially finished gown you have on hand that can be altered quickly and sent to my home would be much appreciated, *madame*. Lady Louisa needs a wardrobe immediately.'

'I am writing it down now, Your Grace,' Madame Brunet said, scribbling into a small book. 'I shall take down your entire order and then we can measure *ma-*

demoiselle to ensure that each piece of clothing fits her form perfectly.'

Mantheria smiled. 'Very good, Madame Brunet. Now, about a court gown… We will need it by the end of the week.'

The modiste shook her head. 'I am afraid that a court gown would take several weeks to complete, Your Grace. Even if my seamstresses sewed through the night we could not complete it in time.'

'Blast!' the Duchess said, and exhaled loudly. 'I have managed to weasel a spot at St James's on Thursday evening by calling in a favour. Is there nothing you can do?'

'Perhaps I could help? Another pair of hands?' Louisa said, holding her knees together, feeling the blood rush to her face. She felt awful, putting the unhappily married Duchess to more work.

Madame Brunet waved a hand. 'That will not be necessary. But your words do remind me that we have had a court gown returned because it did not meet Lady Rutledge's exacting approval. She is about the same size as Lady Louisa, and the gown could be altered in time. If my suggestion is not offensive?'

'We can hardly be particular,' Mantheria said, with a wink to Louisa. 'But we will be. Please show it to us, Madame Brunet. I am sure your work was exceptional. Lady Rutledge probably couldn't afford the bill for the gown—she runs through her quarterly allowance faster than a racehorse at Ascot.'

A few moments later the modiste returned with two seamstresses holding a dark green gown between them. It was the most ornate piece of clothing Louisa had ever seen. The train had to be at least eight feet long, and the skirt was wide, as if it had been made for an old-fashioned hoop. Flounces crisscrossed the skirts and were embellished by point lace.

Giggling, Mantheria gave Louisa a little push on her arm. 'You look overwhelmed by its sumptuousness, but I must assure you that this gown is quite perfect for a presentation to the Queen. The more ostentatious your dress is the better, and when in doubt you must add another flounce and two tassels.'

Louisa did feel overwhelmed—but by its beauty.

'It's magnificent,' she whispered. 'It must cost a fortune.'

'Three hundred pounds, my lady,' Madame Brunet said with another obsequious curtsy.

Louisa could only blink. She'd had no idea that one gown could cost so much. It was a small fortune!

But the Duchess of Glastonbury did not appear at all surprised by the price. 'We will take it. Now, Louisa, I'll wait here while you go with the seamstresses to be measured. And then we will be off to buy hats, gloves, slippers and everything else a debutante needs for the season.'

Louisa was in a daze as she followed the sewing women behind a curtain and they helped her out of her day dress. She felt embarrassed that her chemise did not even reach her knees and was practically threadbare. Madame Brunet did not mention it, but simply took out her tape measure and put it around Louisa's waist, chest and hips. She called out several numbers to one of her assistants.

Gulping, Louisa watched as the two seamstresses brought the beautiful gown towards her. 'Perhaps you will be so kind as to add underclothing to the order?' she said.

'Of course, my lady,' she said, squeezing Louisa's waist with her hands, 'and a hoop for your presentation gown.'

Glancing over her shoulder, Louisa saw another woman bringing a large hoop contraption to tie around her waist. She held herself still as the woman attached it with ties, letting the hoop fall almost to the floor. Then the two other seamstresses pulled the emerald gown over her head. It felt like a second skin as Madame Brunet did the buttons in the back.

'What do you think, Lady Louisa?'

The modiste gently turned Louisa's shoulders until she was looking into a mirror. She almost didn't recognise her own reflection.

'It's perfect,' she whispered. 'Perfect...'

If this was a dream, Louisa did not wish to wake up.

Chapter Fifteen

Wick knew better than to visit Mantheria before noon. His sister was not a morning person. She was positively prickly until she'd had her hot chocolate and read the morning news. He was reasonably sure that his three little sisters would be awake. But they couldn't get into too much mischief at Mantheria's townhouse, could they?

A cold sweat covered his forehead as he entered White's club. His younger sisters could and often did get into a great deal of mischief.

He allowed a footman to open the door to an adjacent room and ordered coffee. Sitting down, he was about to lean back in his chair when his best friend Lord Sunderland—'Sunny'—sat beside him.

'I didn't expect to see you in town again so soon. I thought you were rusticating in the country. Determined to avoid the desperate debs.'

Wick didn't bother covering his yawn. Sunny had been the one sent home to 'rusticate'. They'd been to Eton and then Oxford together, each staying at the other's homes during the summer holidays. Such old friends didn't need to stand on ceremony.

'My sisters need another governess.'

Sunny chortled. 'What does this make? Their seventh or eighth since the battle-axe Miss Nix retired? I'll say this for your old governess…she walloped just as hard as any man.'

Wick smiled wryly. Both he and Sunny had deserved the spanking she'd given them after letting out all the chickens. 'Only the sixth.'

'Give it time… I am sure there will be a seventh and eighth.'

He shook his head. 'Please don't talk about my sisters. They are Mantheria's problem for a few hours. I need a break from all the drama—just for a little while.'

Sunny grinned, emphasising his nose, slightly crooked above his straight white teeth. 'You have brought your little sisters to London? Surely there is more to this story.'

Wick closed his eyes, rubbing his temples. 'I couldn't leave them at home alone.'

'I should have thought Mrs May and Harper more than capable of containing them for a few days.'

Reluctantly, Wick dropped his hands and opened his eyes. 'Mrs May had to come to London.'

'Tell me the true reason why—and no more Banbury stories, Wick,' Sunny said. 'I am your oldest friend, and I can tell when you're lying or misdirecting.'

Huffing, Wick sat forward in his seat and said in a low whisper, 'The girls sent me on a wild goose chase in the wrong direction after their last governess and I happened upon another young lady and mistook her for the errant governess.'

Wincing, Sunny said, 'Oh, dear. You didn't try to kidnap the wrong woman, did you?'

'No! I mean, I did bring her home…but she was willing to come.'

'Of course she was.' His friend chuckled. 'When's the wedding?'

Wick's fingers clenched into fists. 'Don't make me break your nose again.'

Sunny held up his hands in surrender. 'Truce, old friend. Tell me the rest of your sad tale.'

'My sisters pointed out that she wasn't the governess, and then the blasted young lady wouldn't tell us her true name.'

'A lady? Wick, you *are* in the basket. Is she pretty, at least?'

'Ravishing,' he admitted, 'but I had the forethought to have Mrs May play chaperone, and when we discovered that she was Lady Louisa Bracken I tried to fob her off on her uncle, the Canon of Sherborne.'

Sunny clenched his teeth, shaking his head. 'Worse and worse.'

'The fellow wanted to send her back to the Rockinghams, who were treating her like a drudge, which I'd already promised her that I wouldn't do… When she ran away from her relatives her clothing was threadbare—and she's a blasted heiress. And she's twenty-one, so legally they are no longer her guardians. And all she wants is a proper season and to be given her yearly allowance.'

'Your soft heart is going to get you into trouble.'

'It already has,' Wick said.

Sunny shook his head. 'And Mantheria too. I take it you have dumped your mystery lady, Mrs May and your three little sisters on her doorstep?'

Wick felt the blood rush to his face. His friend was right. He'd literally dropped all his problems and responsibilities on his sister, who had enough on her plate with her own child and an unfaithful husband.

'I'm a wretch.'

'No, you're a softie, and all four of your sisters pull your heartstrings like a harp. You can't say no to any of them,' Sunny said. 'Except maybe Helen. I adore her bluntness. Did she bring her snake to London?'

'No.'

His friend grinned, then laughed. 'You know she'll just find another one. She's got a sixth sense about them.'

Wick dropped his head into his hands. 'Can you stop talking? Or at the very least change the subject?'

'What if I were to tell you there are a couple of prime 'uns at Tattersalls that you'll be interested in? I'd buy the chestnuts myself if I had a feather to fly with.'

'Are they beauties?'

'They prettiest set of goers I ever laid my eyes on,' his friend assured him. 'I think they could even beat your greys in a race.'

Wick's pair of matched greys were a splendid team, and he'd raced with them several times, never losing. But his father had purchased them when Wick was only eighteen, and the horses were growing older and slower. They still had several years in them, but their racing days were coming to an end.

'I'll go and give them a look later today.'

Sunny stood up and held out his hand. 'I'll come with you. I have nothing else to do except stop at Jem Belcher's. He's promised to show me how to block your bruising left hook.'

'Let's stop at Jem's first,' Wick said, getting to his feet. 'In my current mood I could pound even the champion into the wall.'

Sunny's upper lip curled. 'Jem's only let you hit him once.'

'He didn't *let* me.'

Sunny shook his head, linking his arm with Wick's. 'He did.'

They walked out of the room together, talking more loudly than they should in the gentlemen's club. Especially in the reading room, where they nearly ran into a gentleman with dark greying hair.

Wick was about to apologise when he saw the man's face. It was Alexander. Mantheria's husband. But no one in his family called the jackanapes by his first name any more. Only by his title—Glastonbury. His sister's unfaithful husband was supposed to be at a party in the country. He clearly was not. No doubt he hadn't left London at all, but had spent the last few days at Lady Dutton's townhouse. What Glastonbury saw in the woman Wick would never know. She had to be fifty, at least. And the widowed Lady Dutton couldn't be called pretty. At her age, handsome was the only epithet she could hope for. But, according to *ton* gossip, Glastonbury had loved her for thirty years—even before her husband had died.

The other man smiled, touching his hat. 'Wick, it is good to see you.'

Wick clenched his hands into fists. He wanted nothing more than to punch his brother-in-law in the face. To slap his glove across his cheek and demand the satisfaction of a duel. But Mantheria had told him not to, and he had to respect her wishes or he would be a villain like her husband.

'I take it that your house party broke up early, Glastonbury? Where was it again? Shropshire?'

A tinge of colour entered Alexander's cheeks. And

to think Wick had once idolised him. Envied him for being a notable whip and a renowned Corinthian. What a difference four years made—and it wasn't just the additional grey hairs on the man's head. Wick now knew that Glastonbury wasn't a man of honour, despite his friendly nature.

Four years ago Glastonbury had put Wick's name up at White's, Watier's, and even the Four Horse Club. With such a sponsor Wick had had no difficulty being accepted to any club in London. His own father didn't belong to any clubs. Nor was Papa at all interested in society.

Wick had been a young man, fresh out of university and looking for a mentor. He might have fallen prey to the sharks and hangers-on, but Glastonbury had taken him under his wing. Taught him how to race his greys. Which gaming hells to avoid. And once lent him money when he'd overrun his quarterly allowance. Wick had been eager to pay him back, but Glastonbury had refused to accept it. He'd become Mantheria's husband by then. Something that had made Wick feel proud.

Now he only felt shame for telling his sister what a great gun Alexander was and encouraging the match. He'd known about Lady Dutton—but many men about town had affairs. Particularly with willing widows. The *ton* usually closed its eyes to them. And so had Wick. He'd never thought that Glastonbury would be unfaithful to his beautiful sister. He'd let Mantheria down again.

Glastonbury cleared his throat. 'Yes. Well… It turned out that the daughter of the house caught the measles, and I felt it unwise to risk carrying them back to Andrew.'

'He dotes on you.'

The older man smiled slightly. 'I am very lucky to be his father.'

Sunny put on a fake smile. 'Glad I'm not a father—at least not that I am aware of.'

Wick should have passed by, but he couldn't leave without saying something more. 'You're very lucky that Andrew is too young to understand what kind of man you are. What kind of husband you truly are. But someday he will, and then your son will despise you as much as I do.'

Glastonbury flinched as if Wick had indeed struck him across the face with his glove.

Wick pulled his friend away from his brother-in-law. 'Come, Sunny, my fists are itching to hit something.'

'I hope you don't mean me,' Sunny said. 'You've already made my nose crooked.'

'You gave me a black eye first.'

His friend laughed. 'You're right. What was the fight over, anyway? I can't remember.'

They walked out of White's together.

Wick shook his head. 'A buxom barmaid in Eton, who was twice our age and considered us to be nothing but little schoolboys.'

Sunny grabbed his chest. 'I remember now. Molly was a tasty woman.'

'Whom neither of us tasted.'

His friend laughed loudly, and Wick couldn't help but join him. They didn't call for his carriage or hire a hack—instead they walked to Jem Belcher's boxing house.

The former champion met them at the door with a crooked smile.

Sunny waved to him. 'I'm here to learn that block against Wick's left hook. You promised me that you would teach me how to beat him.'

Jem shrugged, shaking his head. 'That will take a great many more lessons, my lord.'

Wick's friend was at least a head shorter and two stones lighter than him. Sunny had been taller than him at one time, but Wick had more than caught up. Wick laughed and went to change his clothes.

In a loose smock and breeches, he was able to land punches on his friend's stomach, shoulder, and even his chin.

Sunny touched his red jaw. 'Keep the punches lower, Wick. I've got to catch an heiress with this face.'

'*You're* participating in the season?'

'My mother insists upon it,' his friend said in a funerary tone. 'She says it's high time I found myself a wife and secured the family line by fathering sons. If only she had been kind enough to provide me with a brother, like yours did. Another heir…'

Sunny's father had died when he was only three years old, making him the Duke of Sunderland. Wick had only ever known him by his title. Now, at the age of six-and-twenty, Sunny was contemplating marriage and heirs. Wick would also inherit a dukedom—but *he* was in no hurry to produce offspring.

Chapter Sixteen

Louisa put on the dress of emerald velvet and wondered if it might be too elaborate. The style was not unlike her mother's own court gown, over twenty years before.

Mantheria assured her that it was how all court dresses looked, and that the Queen insisted on young women wearing the old-fashioned style. Their necks and shoulders had to be bare unless they had a doctor's certificate. Which she didn't. Even the corset was different. Instead of pushing up her breasts, it flattened them most uncomfortably.

Chandler, her new lady's maid, added another large white plume to her already enormous coiffure. Her head appeared to be twice its normal size because of all the ostrich feathers that were attached to lappets which hung below her shoulders.

Louisa made a face at herself in the mirror and thought perhaps her dress was too spectacular. 'I look like a prancing peacock showing off its fine feathers.'

'Peahen,' Becca corrected from behind her. 'Peacocks are the males of the breed. Peahens are the females, and their plumage aren't nearly as impressive.'

'But they're all fowl,' Helen said with a wink.

The sisters all laughed, but it took Louisa a moment or two to understand the play on words. 'I *feel* foul,' she said.

Frederica touched her shoulder. 'You look stunning.'

'And only a decade out of fashion,' Helen said.

'Don't be rude!' Mantheria scolded.

Her own dress was just as wide. The silk was a rather stunning shade of pink that set off her pale complexion. Even the ostrich feathers in her hair were dyed pink. The sleeves and underskirt were turquoise, and everything was trimmed in wide gold braid. She had tassels artistically draped around her artificially large hips.

'Now, *your* dress, Mantheria,' Helen said, 'looks two decades out of fashion. I daresay Mama had one just like it when she was first married.'

Mantheria dived for her sister. 'You little snake.'

Helen dodged out of her way. 'I take that as a compliment.'

'I think we've had enough compliments this evening,' Frederica said, handing Louisa a pair of lace gloves. 'Wick is already waiting for you two, and you know the Queen of England waits for no one.'

'Even those who wear flamingo-pink dresses,' Helen added, but wisely was already at the door, ready for her escape.

'Don't listen to her,' Becca said, touching her sister's puffed sleeve. 'It's more the soft pink of a newly born piglet.'

Louisa couldn't help but laugh. 'And my green dress?'

'The colour of an alligator or a crocodile,' Becca said, taking the question seriously. 'I can never remember the difference between the two creatures.'

'They both have sharp teeth—like Helen,' Mantheria said, offering her arm to Louisa, who took it. 'We shall have a marvellous time.'

Louisa's stomach roiled. 'What if I have to use the privy? I couldn't possibly, whilst wearing this gown.'

Mantheria wrinkled her nose. 'There are no privies at St James's court. If you need to relieve yourself, your maid will give you a sort of dish called a *bourdaloue* to put underneath your dress.'

Her insides clenched. 'I am supposed to relieve myself while standing?'

Colour stole into Mantheria's cheeks. 'Well, yes... Sometimes you must stand for hours at court before you are presented to the Queen.'

'I don't see what all the fuss is about,' Becca said. 'Animals relieve themselves standing. I cannot think of even one that sits to complete its business.'

Louisa watched Mantheria make a creditable effort at keeping in her laugh. Her face went red and her cheeks puffed out. Her lips were pinched together tightly.

'They don't even use a dish,' Becca added.

It was too much for the young Duchess. She burst into laughter. Louisa couldn't help but giggle with her. Wick's little sisters were positively incorrigible.

'Can we not discuss the habits of animals relieving themselves just now?' Mantheria said, but there was still a smile on her lips. 'Come, Louisa. Miss Chandler will bring the *bordaloue*, just in case... Most ladies try to drink and eat as little as possible at social events to avoid such a need.'

'I don't know why you're so missish about it, Mantheria,' Helen said, from the hall. ''Tis only a part of nature, and there will be a screen to go behind.'

The Duchess waddled towards Helen in her enormous dress, but Helen was easily able to escape her—not being hampered by hoops and trains.

Louisa followed behind Mantheria, and had to turn sideways to fit through the door frame. When she reached the front staircase she saw Wick, standing at the bottom. He was looking particularly handsome in knee breeches, an intricately tied cravat, a golden waistcoat and an embroidered green coat with long tails. The same colour as her own dress. She couldn't help but wonder if the choice had been intentional. She hoped so.

Wick smiled up at her as she walked carefully down each stair. 'Louisa, you are a vision of loveliness and sure to be this season's diamond of the first water.'

Louisa grinned back at him and decided that her gown was the perfect amount of sumptuousness. She hoped that if she looked pretty enough he would change his mind about courting her.

'And me, Wick?' Mantheria asked, holding up her fan as if it were a weapon. 'Where is *my* compliment?'

'It's still trying to find its way out of all that silk.'

Mantheria whacked him on the arm with her fan. 'You're as rude as Helen.'

'No one is as rude as Helen.'

Louisa saw his sister's head peek out from above the stair railings. 'I heard that!'

'Come,' Mantheria said, sweeping past him to the foyer. 'I daresay we are going to hurry to get there just to stand and wait. But that is the way of court.'

The butler opened the front door and Wick offered his arm to Louisa. She happily took it, but they were unable to walk together through the entrance. Her skirt was simply too wide. After their second failed attempt, Wick spun Louisa around and pulled her through after him.

He helped both Mantheria and Louisa into the carriage, but they had to sit on opposite seats because their dresses were simply too wide to accommodate a second lady. Wick was forced to lift up part of Mantheria's skirt in order to sit down beside her on the carriage seat.

'Ooh! I have found the compliment. You look as pretty and delectable as a French *macaron*… Also, you're the same colours.'

His sister tried to whack him again with her fan, but this time his hand came up to block it.

'And Louisa looks like a *langue de chat* dipped in green icing.'

'Oh, please stop talking about cakes,' Louisa said, clutching her rumbling middle. 'My stomach is already in knots and I feel rather sick.'

When they arrived at St James's Palace, a footman opened the door. Mantheria helped Louisa wrap her long train over her left arm, and then did the same with her own gown. They were led into the redbrick castle towards the drawing rooms, and then to a long gallery. Louisa was relieved to see that every young lady there—and some not so young—was wearing the same kind of ornate court dress.

Mantheria touched Louisa's cheek. 'You look beautiful. Now, all we can do is wait until you are summoned to the Presence Chamber. The Lord Chamberlain will announce your name. You will then enter the Queen's presence and make the deep curtsy that we have practised. Because you are the daughter of a peer, you do not kiss her hand. She will kiss your forehead. Then you may arise. Queen Charlotte may want to exchange pleasantries. But if she does not, you will curtsy deeply again and walk backwards slowly. You must never turn your back on a queen.'

Louisa looked down, once more clutching her rumbling tummy. 'I don't know if I can do this…'

'I know you can,' the young Duchess said with an encouraging look. 'You are one of the bravest people I know, Louisa. You left your home and your family, all on your own, and set off on an adventure to make your dreams come true. I am proud to consider you one of my friends.'

Louisa's eyes filled with tears, for this was what she had hoped for. Longed for. A friend of her own age. 'Truly? You consider me a friend?'

'Of course,' Mantheria said, leaning forward and kissing Louisa's cheek. 'I am so glad that Wick brought you to me.'

Wick cleared his throat and both Louisa and Mantheria turned their heads to see what he wanted to say. 'We are almost at the front of the gallery.'

Mantheria gave a small nod. 'Louisa, let go of your train.'

Louisa dropped the fabric in her left hand. Two footmen came forward and pulled the train gently to its full length. Then they did the same for Mantheria's pink silk robe. Even Wick straightened his coat. Louisa could barely breathe. She took quick, short gasps as her stomach continued to roil most uncomfortably. She longed to flee, but her feet would not move.

Wick took her arm and pulled her forward to the entrance of the Presence Chamber. Mantheria followed behind them, her fan around her wrist.

The Lord Chamberlain cleared his throat as they entered. 'May I present Lady Louisa Bracken, daughter of the late Earl of Rockingham?'

Wick dropped his arm and Louisa walked forward alone. The Queen sat on a throne at the front of the room. Her hair was white, but it might be a wig. Louisa knew that underneath her powder and cosmetics Queen Charlotte was in her sixties. Her expression was solemn, but not unkind.

Louisa continued to step forward, unsure of where she should stop and make her deep curtsy. Was she too far back? Or if she got closer would she be performing a solecism? Louisa took a few more short breaths and matching steps before sinking down into a deep curtsy. This at least she had practised several times with Mantheria and the girls. Becca tended to lose her balance and bring all of them to the floor like a row of dominoes.

Unconsciously, Louisa smiled at the memory.

She felt the brief contact of dry lips against her forehead. Then, still keeping her eyes to the floor, continued to stay in her low curtsy.

'You have the look of your mother,' Queen Charlotte said with a slight accent. 'But you don't make me sneeze.'

Louisa slowly came up to stand. Her eyes shone with unshed tears and her heart was full. If only her mother could see her now. If only her mother could have been with her to experience this day that they had practised for and dreamed of together. But she knew she was not alone. Wick and Mantheria were with her.

'Thank you, Your Majesty.'

Queen Charlotte gave her a benign smile, but she did not open her mouth again.

After a moment or two, Louisa realised that her audience was over. She swept into another deep curtsy before slowly backing away from the Queen.

Mantheria and Wick met her at the entrance and escorted her out of the Presence Chamber and through the long gallery to the drawing rooms. Wick stooped down and picked up both Louisa's and his sister's trains for them to put over their left arms. Louisa wondered why they couldn't hold them with their right, but did not ask. Court rules didn't seem to have much to do with logic.

Louisa exhaled slowly. 'I've waited for that presentation my whole life, and now I am so glad it is over.'

'Me too,' Wick said. 'My knees were knocking for you.'

Mantheria hit him on the back of the head with her fan. 'She was perfect.'

He raised his hand. 'If you touch me one more time with that accursed fan, I will snap it in two.'

'But it's made of mahogany.'

'I'll find a way.'

Louisa couldn't believe it, but felt a laugh bubble out of her. Wick gave her a slow smile and Louisa reached out to him with trembling hands. He held both of hers in his strong ones, squeezing them gently.

'You were marvellous.'

'And you didn't even need the *bourdaloue*,' Mantheria added from their side.

Wick blinked. 'What's a *bourdaloue*?'

Louisa gave another shaky laugh.

Chapter Seventeen

The next evening all four Stringham sisters watched Louisa as her maid, Chandler, pulled, laced, primped and then arranged her hair. Louisa couldn't help but be surprised at how well the white gown with the lace overlay fitted her. It had been a readymade garment that had been altered specifically for her frame. Madame Brunet and her assistants were truly talented with their needles.

'Isn't white the colour for young debutantes?' Louisa couldn't help but ask.

She didn't want to make any mistakes. She mustn't give society any reason to reject her as her own family had.

'We will be turning tradition on its head,' Mantheria assured her. 'With such stunning hair as yours, it would be a pity for any colour to compete with it.'

She watched Becca and Helen dig through a chest of jewellery that looked like a pirate's hoard, with many jewels of all colours set in different metals.

'Garnets?' Becca asked.

Helen shook her head. 'No, rubies. Nothing cheap for Louisa's first party.'

Frederica held out her hand. 'Give them to me.'

Louisa sat still while Frederica clasped a ruby neck-lace around her throat. One large ruby was surrounded by small diamonds and two more additional small rubies. It had to be worth at least a thousand pounds! The Stringhams didn't seem to notice or care for its value. Then Becca placed two ruby earrings in her hand, and with shaking fingers Louisa put them in her ears. Helen added two diamond combs to her red curls.

Chandler helped Louisa put on long, white satin gloves. Becca wrapped the lace shawl that Mrs Barker had given to her around her shoulders. It was the only item of clothing she had that was exquisite enough to go with the clothes the Duchess had bought her.

'One last touch,' Mantheria said, adding diamond bangles to Louisa's wrist.

Frederica smiled at her. 'You look stunning.'

Louisa glanced down at the bangles on her wrist and fiddled with one. She was not used to compliments and had to bite her lower lip to stop herself from decrying their kind words. How she loved being with them. It felt like belonging to a family.

Helen tugged the shawl into the right place. 'Beautiful.'

Becca gave her a tight hug around the waist. 'You'll dance wonderfully. Just remember everything we said and try to let the man lead. Even if he is dreadful at it like Helen.'

Dancing.

Louisa's growing confidence deflated like the flying balloon she'd once seen pictured in a book. 'But I've only had a few lessons with you and the dancing master. I can't possibly dance. I will make a fool of myself.'

'You can't waltz until an Almack's patroness gives you

permission, so don't worry about that,' Frederica said, hugging her with one arm around her shoulders. 'And you'll be fine during the country dances. Simply follow the lead of the person in front of you. No one will notice if you make a mistake on a figure.'

'We are already unconscionably late,' Mantheria said, pointing to a clock on the mantel. 'Come, Louisa, before my sisters overload you with more well-meaning advice that makes you feel quite ill.'

Louisa's heart beat against the rubies on her breast as she walked down the stairs with Mantheria. Wick was standing waiting at the bottom. She caught her breath. Everything about him seemed polished and sparkling. The brass buttons on his blue coat reflected the lamp-light. He wore the tails over knee breeches, which showed his defined calves to admiration. Even his brown hair seemed to glint and shine.

His coffee-coloured eyes stared at her intently. She could have happily lost herself inside them. His lips looked as if he'd just licked them. Blushing, she thought of how much *she* would like to lick his lips.

Wick bowed to them. 'My ladies, you both look too exquisite for mere words.'

Mantheria rapped his knuckles playfully with her fan and then linked her arm with his. He turned and offered his other elbow to Louisa. She placed her hand on his muscular forearm. She noticed that the dark blue coat fitted him so well that it looked a second skin.

Wick led them out to the carriage. They didn't speak much on the way to the ball. Louisa's throat felt too constricted for words. But once the vehicle stopped in front of a grey stone townhouse she found her tongue. 'What if they refuse me entry because I don't have an invitation?'

'I don't have one either,' Wick admitted. 'They will not ask for one at the door.'

'You are with me,' Mantheria said with a reassuring smile. 'And no one says no to a duchess.'

Wick took Louisa's hand and helped her out of the carriage. 'Not even our father.'

The young Duchess giggled behind her. 'Papa may be eccentric, but he isn't stupid.'

He assisted his sister out next, and escorted them both into Lady Dennard's home. Mantheria had been right. Lady Dennard didn't even raise an eyebrow at her extra lady guest, and her smile was all too wide when she saw Wick entering behind them.

'Lord Cheswick,' the lady said, fawning. 'I am deeply honoured that you have chosen to attend my small party. You are a rare guest at such events. This is quite a social coup for your hostess.'

Louisa almost laughed at the look of chagrin on Wick's face.

But he bowed over the lady's hand. 'I wouldn't have missed your party for the world.'

Lady Dennard tittered with laughter and they walked on. They were among the last guests to arrive, and it seemed to Louisa that an enormous number of aristocrats had been squeezed into several small rooms. Wick nodded to acquaintances as they weaved through the ballroom, which was as hot and crowded as a country fête.

'Oh, good,' Mantheria said. 'We've missed the first quadrille. It's such a long, slow dance.'

A fair gentleman walked up to them and bowed. He was the same height as Mantheria and had a pleasing countenance, a crooked nose and a winning smile. 'Lady

Glastonbury, may I have the pleasure of dancing the first waltz with you?'

Mantheria offered her hand and the man bowed over it, bringing it to his lips. 'I would be delighted to dance with you,' she said. 'Allow me to present my dear friend, Lady Louisa Bracken. Lady Louisa, this is Lord Sunderland. The best dancer in all of England.'

Louisa tentatively held out her hand and Lord Sunderland took it lightly, bending over it. 'Bracken? Any relation to Lord Barnabas?'

'He is my cousin,' she said, pulling her hand back. 'The current Earl of Rockingham is my uncle.'

'You poor thing.'

Louisa felt herself blushing with embarrassment. She had no idea how well her cousin or her uncle fitted into society. Would her connection with them hurt her own social standing?

Mantheria hit Lord Sunderland's shoulder with her fan and tipped her head towards Louisa.

Blinking, Lord Sunderland cleared his throat. 'Ah, Lady Louisa...might I reserve the set after next?'

Louisa looked at Wick, who gave her a slight nod. 'I should be pleased to accept, Your Grace.'

The music ended and the couples on the dance floor began to clap. Lord Sunderland held out his hand to Mantheria, who took it. Leaving Louisa alone with Wick in a room full of people, many of whom were openly staring at her.

Louisa touched the curls at her neck. 'Is something wrong with my face or my hair?'

Wick tweaked a red curl with two gloved fingers. 'You look beautiful. They are staring because you are the most arresting woman in the room.'

She couldn't stop her lips from forming a smile. If she hadn't been beautiful before, his words would have made her so.

Louisa felt herself beaming at him. 'Are you sure that they aren't looking at you? You are devastatingly handsome in evening clothes.'

'Oh, no!' Wick said, briefly touching his chest and turning his body towards her. He placed a hand over one side of his face, as if to hide his identity. 'They've spotted me. I am done for.'

'Who has spotted you?'

'Lady Ashton and Mrs Nells. Between them they have at least half a dozen daughters they're desperately trying to fob off on to any unsuspecting gentleman of means.'

She glanced over her shoulder and, sure enough, there were two matrons eyeing Wick as if he were a plum pudding at Christmas. 'Surely they can't make you ask their daughters to dance—let alone marry them.'

'You'd be surprised at how many tender young maidens hurt their ankles when I am near. Or drop their handkerchief or their fan.'

'Do you pick them up?'

He raised one eyebrow. 'The maidens or their fans?'

'Either?'

Wick took her arm and led her in the opposite direction from Lady Ashton and Mrs Nells. 'Neither. I walk by and pretend not to hear their calls for help. I have no intention of being trapped into marriage any time soon.'

Louisa's lips had quirked upwards at his jest, but his last words wiped the smile off her face. Wick did not want to get married. Perhaps that was why he refused to be her suitor. Maybe there was nothing too wrong with her after all.

Taking a deep breath, she tried to come up with a suitable sally. 'Then it appears that you have nothing to fear from being here.'

He shook his head, frowning. 'You're wrong. I have walked willingly into the lions' den. I will not escape without scratches and possibly a bite or two.'

'If you are to be bitten, I hope that it is at least by a pretty young lady and not by her mama.'

Wick groaned, but there was a smile in his eyes. 'I told Mantheria how it would be, but she insisted that I accompany you two.'

Her heart sank a little. He didn't want to be here. With her. She knew it, of course. Yet his words still stung like a wasp's sting.

'Cheswick, is that you? I thought you hibernated during the season with your father's beasts.'

Wick manoeuvred both himself and Louisa to face a man whose looks were arresting. His curly golden locks were longer than most men's. His eyes were a startling light blue in his slim, pale face. His suit was also golden, and he wore lace on his sleeves and around his throat. On his feet were golden heels with large brass buckles.

Louisa had never seen a more beautiful gentleman, or any person more sumptuously dressed. But he appeared fashionably bored and indolent.

The man held an ornate golden quizzing glass surrounded by diamonds and he brought up to his right eye and feigned surprise. When he spoke again his voice was surprisingly high and soft. 'It *is* you! I do believe you once told me at a curricle race that polite society was not your natural habitat.'

Louisa could feel the muscles in Wick's arms tighten underneath her fingers as he gave the man a painful smile that looked more like a grimace. He inclined his head slightly. 'Lord Norwich.'

The golden man dropped his quizzing glass. 'Would you do me the honour of presenting me to your companion? Word has spread quickly of her beauty and her identity. And how she was singled out by the Queen for conversation.'

Louisa couldn't help but look from the dazzling man to Wick and back again in surprise. Rumours about her were spreading through town! She wondered how long it would be until they reached her family.

Taking a step, Louisa moved closer to Wick.

Sighing, Wick gave another grimacing smile. 'Lady Louisa, may I present the Earl of Norwich?'

Louisa curtsied slightly and the golden man, with a speed belied by his previous indolence, took her free hand in his and gently kissed it. Her pulse quickened in fear or attraction—she was not sure which emotion.

'Lady Louisa, would you do me the honour of joining the set?'

She glanced at Wick and he gave her another sharp nod. Releasing her hold on his arm, she allowed Norwich to lead her away from him. She couldn't help stealing a glance over her shoulder to look back at Wick. He was no longer alone, but surrounded by a crowd of women. Some, she guessed, were the matchmaking mamas, and the others their daughters. A sharp pang of jealousy cut through her.

Turning back to her partner, she knew that she had no right to be jealous. Wick was not hers. And he never would be.

Lord Norwich led her to the dance floor and to their correct place. Louisa's pulse continued to race. She was finally dancing at a *ton* ball and she prayed that she wouldn't make a cake of herself. She saw that several eyes were upon them. She couldn't help but think it was her partner's elaborate suit in its shocking golden shade that made them look. But not all the eyes were female. Men of all ages were looking at them. At her.

Louisa's hands shook as she clasped hands with Lord Norwich for the first figure of the set. She tried to block out the people around her and focus solely on the music and the dancing. She desperately wished that she'd had more time with the dancing master Mantheria had employed to prepare her.

Taking another gentleman's hand, she glanced up to see that it was Wick.

He smiled at her, with no grimace. 'You're dancing superbly.'

But before she could answer he had moved to his next partner in the set and she was back with Lord Norwich. The look he gave her felt predatory... Shaking her head, she thought that perhaps she'd spent too much time with the younger Stringham sisters. She looked for Wick and saw that he was partnered with a pretty brunette with a heart-shaped face. The young woman was smiling, but Wick looked as if he'd had all his teeth pulled out.

'Would you be willing to indulge my curiosity, my lady?' Lord Norwich asked, his voice so soft that she could barely hear him over the lively music.

They spun together in a circle. 'I do not know, my lord. Ask your question and I will do my best to answer.'

Norwich laughed softly. It was more a breath of air than a sound. 'Despite having the countenance of an ingénue, you play the game like a dowager. Why were you not presented before now? You are older than most of the debutantes.'

Louisa was grateful that the figure caused them to separate at that moment, giving her time to come up with an answer. She could tell him the truth—but she did not wish to confide in him. Lord Norwich was certainly beautiful, yet he felt cold. Mocking. Indolent. None of the things that she hoped for in a suitor and a husband.

They clasped hands again. She gave him her most dazzling smile. 'I was thinking the same thing about you, my lord.'

One of his eyebrow's quirked up. 'I beg your pardon?'

'That you look older than most of the debutantes.'

Norwich gave another of his nearly soundless laughs. Louisa was glad that her sally had not insulted him.

The music ended and they bowed to each other. Lord Norwich took her hand and led her to the side of the room, where Mantheria was standing next to Lord Sunderland. He relinquished her hand and bowed to them both. Mantheria snapped her fan open to hide her face and Louisa guessed that she disliked the Earl.

Sunderland inclined his head. 'Norwich.'

The Earl took a deep breath before slowly picking up his quizzing glass and gazing at Mantheria and Lord Sunderland. 'Sunny…still pining for the one who got away?'

Louisa saw Mantheria's face pale at his insinuation, and Lord Sunderland's cheeks coloured. Louisa touched her throat and wondered if there was something between her friend and the young Duke who was most certainly *not* her husband.

'After another heiress, Norwich?' Sunderland said be-

tween clenched teeth. 'I suppose someone must pay for
your many tailors. Lady Louisa, shall we?'

Sunderland offered his hand to Louisa and she took
it. They returned to the dance floor and performed the
Roger de Coverley. The young Duke did not speak much,
for which Louisa was most grateful. It took all her concentration to follow the steps of the figures with only
occasional glances at Wick. His partner this time was
a small, beautiful blonde, with the sort of curvaceous
figure Louisa had always wished for. Instead, she was
a beanpole, with small breasts and not many curves to
speak of.

Wick, however, didn't seem too impressed by his
lovely partner. His expression was one of long suffering.

'I see I am not the only one besotted with a Stringham,' Sunderland said as they clasped arms. 'Happily,
not the same one. How awkward that would be.'

His words surprised Louisa into a laugh, and then she
blushed. She'd hoped that her feelings for Wick were not
too obvious.

'They're not,' he said, as if he were reading her
thoughts. 'I simply recognise the look of another suf-
ferer.'

Sunderland's eyes moved from her to Mantheria, who
was dancing with an older gentleman. 'Mayhap your
story will have a happier ending than mine. I can assure
you that I will do all in my power to assist you. Although
Wick is as stubborn as a mule and twice as stupid when
it comes to his heart.'

Louisa blinked at him, her own heart sinking a little.
'Lord Cheswick has made it very clear that he does not
wish to court me.'

'I did that to a lady once too—to my eternal regret.'

She was now sure that he was speaking of Mantheria, who had married another man. Another duke, even.

'Don't give in too easily,' Sunderland said, bowing over her hand at the end of the dance. 'Love is worth fighting for.'

The Duke led her to the opposite side of the room, where Wick was releasing the hand of the beautiful blonde.

Sunderland bowed to them. 'Wick, I have brought you your partner for the next dance. Lady Laetitia, would you do me the honour?'

The young Duke then placed Louisa's hand into Wick's and offered his arm to the young blonde. They walked away.

Louisa felt a burning heat where their fingers touched and it spread throughout her entire body. She glanced up at Wick, but his expression was unreadable. Perhaps he did not wish to be forced to dance with her by his friend. Embarrassed, Louisa tried to pull back her arm. She didn't want his pity.

Wick's larger hand tightened around hers. 'Shall we?'

She glanced down. 'Only if you wish to.'

'I'd rather dance with you than any other woman in the room.'

Shaking her head, she smiled, bemused. 'I am not sure that is a very high compliment, for I know that you do not wish to be here.'

His eyes met hers. 'I find that at this moment there is no other place I wish to be.'

Louisa pursed her lips and tried to swallow down her joy. She didn't want anyone besides Lord Sunderland to know of her *tendre* for Wick.

The country dance was a vigorous one. With lots of

hopping, clapping and spinning. And every time their
hands touched she felt as if she were on fire. A candle
burning brightly in the night. Hot and dangerous. When
his eyes met hers, she could almost imagine the sparks
between them.

The dance, like all perfect things, ended too quickly.
Although it had to have been at least a half an hour.

'What do you think of your first ball so far?' Wick
asked, leading her off the dance floor. 'You've already
surpassed every other lady here. You have danced with
the three highest-ranking gentlemen in the room.'

She fluttered her eyelashes in surprise. 'I did not think
you held Lord Norwich in high esteem?'

'The man is made by his tailors.'

'Is he what they call a Bond Street Beau?'

Wick snorted derisively. 'A more apt phrase would be
a Bond Street Buffoon.'

Louisa couldn't keep in a trill of laughter.

He glanced down at her, his lips twitching into an
almost-smile. Something intangible was still simmering
between them even now, after the dance was over. She
was certain that he felt it too.

Wick cleared his throat and turned his head away from
her. 'Come, let me escort you back to Mantheria, who
can find you more eligible partners before I am besieged
by the matchmaking mamas.'

Swallowing down her disappointment, Louisa managed to rally a little. 'Have you been scratched or bitten
by one of them yet?'

His lips twitched again, but she saw him suppress
the smile. He led her over to Mantheria, who was surrounded by gentlemen.

Wick bowed over her hand before letting her go. 'The only scratch I've received has been from you.'

Before Louisa could interpret the meaning of his words, Mantheria had linked arms with her.

'My dear Lady Louisa,' she said in a bright voice. 'All of these gentlemen are waiting eagerly to be introduced to the diamond of the season.'

She stopped watching Wick walk away from her and focused on the four gentlemen standing around her friend.

'Oh, dear,' Louisa said, shaking her head and touching her flaming red hair. 'I thought I was a ruby.'

The gentlemen laughed politely, and she tried not to feel too disappointed that Wick was not among them.

Chapter Eighteen

The next night, Wick groaned audibly and tried to shake Sunny's hand from his arm. But despite being smaller and lighter his friend had a surprisingly strong grip.

'Let go of me, you idiot.'

Sunny's fingers pinched into Wick's flesh further through his evening coat as they walked down the street, passing carriages waiting to unload their passengers.

'Mantheria asked me to make sure that you attended this ball.'

For the third night in a row, Wick would be stuck at a *ton* squeeze. A fate he did not feel he deserved. 'I suppose we could look into Lady Kensington's ball for a little while. I've agreed to go. Now let go of me—before I make your nose even more crooked than it already is.'

His friend released his arm. 'Just another street away.'

They walked a few more feet before Wick sighed and asked, 'Why are you so determined to get me to this ball?'

Sunny, whose countenance was usually as light and happy as his nickname suggested, looked grave and serious. 'I gave your sister my word.'

'She shouldn't have asked you to.'

'Mantheria could ask me anything and I would do it gladly.'

His friend's words caused him to stop in his tracks. 'What do you mean by that?'

Sunny took a deep breath and then exhaled. 'I never thought I would tell you this... I never thought I would want to. But when we were twenty-one and still at Oxford, do you remember, we went home to Hampford Castle for Christmas? Mantheria was only sixteen, but she was the most beautiful woman I had ever seen. So, being my stupid self, I tried to avoid her—but she caught me underneath the mistletoe and kissed me. There are only a handful of moments in my life that are transcending and that was one of mine. I promised to dance with her at her come-out ball in the spring, when she would turn seventeen and have her first season.'

Wick didn't know what to think or what to say. Despite being best friends for years, he and Sunny rarely spoke of their feelings. It was even more awkward to hear that Sunny seemed to harbour emotions for Wick's sister.

He shook his head. 'You didn't come to her ball.'

'I know. Mantheria cornered me the day after, wanting to know why,' Sunny said, bringing his hands to cover his eyes. 'I told her that I had no intention of getting married any time soon and therefore would not be attending *any* of the debutante balls. The expression on her face is one I will never forget. She didn't cry. She didn't try to argue with me. She simply became coldly polite. And three weeks later she was engaged to the Duke of Glastonbury—the greatest catch on the marriage mart with a fortune ten times the size of my own. I told myself that I was happy for her. I went to her blasted wedding and watched her walk away with another man. I thought it would break my heart, but I was still a young fool. My heart was only bruised. It wouldn't truly break until I saw how unhappy she was in her marriage and could do nothing about it. It was too late.'

Wick patted his friend on the shoulder awkwardly, attempting to show his compassion. 'I am sorry, Sunny, but I don't understand why you're telling me this now and on the way to a ball.'

He watched Sunny's gloved hands tighten into fists. 'I don't want to watch my best friend make the same mistake.'

'What do you mean?'

'Don't be obtuse, Wick. You care for Lady Louisa. I can see it. Your sisters can see it.'

Wick began to walk again and could hear Sunny's footfalls behind him. They passed several houses before he spoke. 'I am not ready for marriage yet.'

'I don't know any man who is. But believe me, you won't want to see her married to someone else. Someone like Lord Norwich.'

'Or Lord Glastonbury?'

Sunny nodded slowly.

Wick hadn't liked watching Norwich dance with Louisa. Or with Sunny for that matter. Or even the eligible and not so eligible gentlemen who had claimed her hand for a set the night before. It had been torture. But nothing like the pain of losing someone he loved. Of feeling partially responsible for their death.

'I am not interested in marriage.'

Sighing, Sunny bumped Wick's arm with his elbow. 'You've got to let them go, mate. It's been nearly ten years. You have to let your grief for Charles and Elizabeth stop dragging you down. There was nothing you could have done. Scarlet fever killed them—not you. And you're the reason your other five siblings are still alive. You rode to London and got a proper doctor to take care of them instead of a country quack.'

'It wasn't enough.'

What Wick was really saying was that *he* wasn't enough.

'You were only sixteen. Still a child. And, as much as I love your parents, they should never have asked you to bear such a heavy weight. You weren't ready for it then, but you are now. You're doing a bang-up job of taking care of your sisters.'

He huffed. 'I've already lost a governess and have yet to find a suitable replacement.'

'And your parents have lost five governesses—six if you count the old battle-axe Nix, who retired. Give yourself some credit… And sooner or later you'll have to settle down and make heirs. It might as well be with someone you love.'

Wick was saved from giving Sunny an answer because they had arrived in front of Lady Kensington's redbrick townhouse. Footmen lined the front façade and eagerly ran to open carriage doors and assist the guests into the well-lit house. Wick and Sunny passed two footmen on the way to the front door. They followed the line of guests into the hall, where Lord and Lady Kensington stood greeting them.

Lady Kensington's eyes widened, and she grinned when she saw the pair of them. She stepped towards them with her hands outstretched and squeezed each of their hands. 'Lord Sunderland… Lord Cheswick, how delighted I am that you were able to come. I am sure all the young ladies will be thrilled as well.'

'It is my pleasure,' Sunny said with his polished smile.

'Ah, Kensington, we have missed you the last few days at Parliament. Are you quite recovered from your cold?'

Wick didn't hear the lord's answer, because Lady Kensington had stepped in front of him. 'Rumour has it, Lord Cheswick, that you are here for the lovely Lady Louisa Bracken. The latest heiress who is strangely not in possession of her own fortune.'

His jaw clenched. 'No. It is in the control of her relatives, the Rockinghams.'

Lady Kensington gave him a glittering smile and nodded. 'Yes, your dear sister Lady Glastonbury asked me personally to invite them tonight. And Lady Cowper so dear Lady Louisa could get a voucher to Almack's and permission to waltz.'

Wick bowed, groaning inwardly. He fervently hoped his sister wasn't planning on creating a scene with the Rockinghams. 'I pray it has not been a great inconvenience?' he said.

'Nonsense. I am hedging my bets upon it making my party the most talked of event of the season.'

He gave her a perfunctory smile and walked past her husband to catch up with Sunny. They were among the last guests to arrive. The rooms were already so full that it was hard to walk to where Mantheria and Louisa were standing. Wick had to apologise more than once for bumping into a sir or a lord. Lady Kensington's party was truly deserving of the epithet 'a squeeze'.

Mantheria gave them both a glittering smile and Sunny a pointed look.

He nodded, and held out his hand to Louisa. 'May I have the first dance, my lady?'

Louisa's eyes were on Wick as she said, 'Yes.'

Sunny managed to lead her through the throng to the crowded dance floor. It was only then that Wick realised his friend usually danced first with Mantheria at every ball. He gazed at his sister and wondered if she returned Sunny's regard. Not that it mattered. She had a husband. A husband who was having an affair with another woman...

Mantheria gently tapped his arm with her fan. 'Thank you for coming, Wick. I should love to stand and chat, but I must go and procure more partners for Louisa.'

He grabbed at her hand to stop her. 'Wait, I need to tell you something.'

Mantheria turned on her heel to look at him. Her eyes were hooded. 'What?'

'Glastonbury isn't away in the country,' Wick said slowly. 'I ran into him at White's... He has never left London. I don't think you'll see him here tonight, at Lady Kensington's party, but just in case I don't want you to be surprised. Or embarrassed if someone mentions seeing him.'

'You're warning me not to give the excuse that my husband is out of town,' Mantheria said, waving her painted fan at him. 'But you needn't have bothered. For reasons unknown, the beau monde never minds if a man has an affair. They will not think less of me for coming alone to a party. Obedient wives are praised for their understanding natures. My popularity will only grow. There will not be a dance for which I won't have a partner.'

Wick took a deep breath. 'I'm sorry, Mantheria. I didn't call him out, but I did insult him. I couldn't help myself. I once idolised him, for goodness' sake. I even aped his ways...trying to flick my snuffbox open with only my thumb.'

She touched his shoulder. 'You don't even like snuff.'

'I was only pretending.'

'And so was I when I thought I could love him.'

He shook his head, clenching his teeth painfully together. 'But you have been faithful to him. You have done nothing wrong.'

Mantheria smiled sadly. 'Nor have I done much right in my marriage besides Andrew. You can ignore your feelings, like I did, but that will not make them go away. Be wiser with your heart than I have been, my dearest brother.'

Wick's heart already felt rather battered, and the pain didn't lessen as he watched Louisa dance with Sunny, Lord Carlisle, Mr Peterson and Lord Norwich. Despite being approached by several matrons who dropped extremely obvious hints, he did not dance.

He couldn't.

Standing at the side of the room, his eyes followed Louisa and Mantheria through the figures of the dance. His sister Helen had the same colouring as Mantheria and Elizabeth before she'd died, but if Lizzy had lived she would have matured like Mantheria and been a beauty in her own right. Would Elizabeth have wed and become a mother by now, too? Had she survived, would she have stopped Mantheria from marrying a man she didn't love? Would Elizabeth have seen past Glastonbury's wealth and title to his soul?

Elizabeth had been sensitive like that. She had sensed other people's emotions, and more than once soothed Wick's pride or bruised ego. How different all their lives might have been if she and Charles had lived. If he could have saved them both. Then maybe he could have courted Louisa. Loved her.

Instead, he watched her twirl around the dance floor with another man.

Chapter Nineteen

Despite wearing another beautiful new gown of celestial blue with a matching silk slip, Louisa felt rather flat. Wick had arrived late to the Kensington ball and he had not asked her to dance. It was some solace, but not much, that he had not asked any other young lady to dance either. He was making it clear to the world—and to Louisa—that he hated these things and everything to do with the marriage mart.

She needed to stop hoping for him to change. For him to love her. Besides, she was not worthy of his love. The gentlemen who had asked her to dance seemed to be fonder of her fortune than of her face. It was just as Aunt Rockingham had warned her. Without her title and her money, Louisa was nothing.

Her partner Mr Snow bowed to her and took her hand to lead her to the crowded side of the ballroom, where Mantheria stood next to two young gentlemen. Louisa assumed that they would be her next partners. The young and beautiful Duchess had made sure that Louisa had a partner for every set.

A step away from Mantheria, Louisa felt someone grab

her free arm and step on the hem of her gown. Louisa thought it might be Wick, but when she turned her head she saw that it was Cousin Barnabas. 'Louisa, what are you doing here?' he said, in a loud voice that caused several pairs of eyes to turn in their direction. 'Mother has been looking everywhere for you.'

'Let go of me!' she said, twisting out of his grip and tearing the flounce on her gown.

Barnabas reached for her arm again—but this time Wick stood between them. 'If you lay a finger on her I will knock you to the floor. Then beat you senseless.'

Her cousin blinked and his bulbous eyes focused on Wick's muscular arms. Louisa knew that it was no idle threat and felt her own confidence rising. She was no longer friendless and helpless. All the Stringhams had accepted her into their pack, and Wick's sisters would have fought for her as viciously as he did.

'Louisa!' Aunt Rockingham practically yelled from the other side of the dance floor and rushed towards her. The crowd parted to make way for her and all eyes fell on Louisa.

Her aunt tried to brush past Wick, but still he stood between them. 'No, Lady Rockingham. You are not to touch her.'

'She is my niece. I am her guardian.'

The once loud ballroom was now as silent as a church on a Thursday afternoon.

Louisa found her backbone and her tongue. 'I am of age, Aunt Rockingham. You have no further hold on me.'

Aunt Rockingham clutched at the diamonds around her neck. 'Is this how I am to be treated after taking care of you for over ten years? For loving and protecting you?

I would not have thought you so ungrateful as to run away with a stranger. I have been so worried.'

There were several gasps. Louisa glanced around the room and saw that the dancing had stopped. Everyone was watching the scene her cousin and her aunt were making as if they were in a play on the stage.

Wick stepped menacingly towards her relatives but Louisa placed a hand on his arm. The Stringham sisters didn't need anyone to stand up for them. They stood up for themselves and she could do that too. She stepped forward to challenge them head-on.

'I was tired of being your servant, Aunt Rockingham,' Louisa said loudly. 'I was weary of wearing rags while you were dressed in diamonds. You claimed that my allowance would not cover better clothing, or even boots that did not pinch. You said that you could not afford to bring me to London for my debut. If that is the case, then you need not worry about spending another farthing on me. I have friends who do not begrudge me the basic necessities of life, and they treat me with the honour that I should have received in my own home, as befits my birth and station in life.'

'How dare you speak to my mother that way?' Barnabas said, raising his hand as if to slap her.

Louisa briefly closed her eyes, but the blow did not fall. Instead, she saw Wick standing over her cousin, who was flat on his back on the floor. Wick delivered another punch to Barnabas's face and then grabbed his coat collar, dragging him across the ballroom floor and out of the room. The expression on his countenance was murderous. She almost felt sorry for her cousin. *Almost.*

'This is not over,' Aunt Rockingham said.

'I should think not,' Mantheria said, linking her arm

with Louisa's. 'You will be hearing from my lawyers to-morrow about the misappropriation of your ward's funds. I suggest that you contact your own solicitors.'

For the first time in Louisa's life she thought she saw fear on her aunt's face. The woman's left eye twitched and her mouth was set in a grim line.

'You will regret this, Louisa.'

'The only regret that *I* have, Lady Rockingham,' Mantheria said loftily, 'is wasting even a minute in your tedious company. Come, Lady Louisa, there are more important people to speak with.'

Louisa's heart raced as she and Mantheria walked away from her livid aunt. She supposed that her aunt knew better than to cross swords with a duchess. Even one as young as her friend.

She exhaled slowly. 'I hope we haven't ruined Lady Kensington's ball.'

Mantheria laughed, patting Louisa's arm reassuringly. 'Oh, no, Louisa. If anything, we have made it the most talked about event of the season. She will be ecstatic—I promised her fireworks. Lady Kensington really ought to send us a thank-you note.'

A small, nervous giggle escaped Louisa's lips, but she sobered when she glanced down at the torn flounce that was dragging on the floor. 'I am afraid Barnabas stepped on my hem and tore it. Do you mind if I go to the retiring room and repair it quickly?'

'I shall come with you,' Mantheria said. 'But I must warn you that I have no skill with a needle. I am coming only to offer emotional support.'

Together they walked into the retiring room, and Louisa let go of her friend's arm to kneel down and reach the needle she had stuck inside her hem.

'You have brought your own needle?' the Duchess said with a little laugh.

Louisa tied a knot in the end of the thread and poked the needle through the inside of her gown, to attach it to the torn flounce. 'I never go anywhere without one. You never know when you might need a needle.'

'I am duly chastened,' Mantheria said solemnly, but her eyes danced with laughter. 'However, I would more likely prick my thumb than actually accomplish anything if I carried a needle around. My old governess, Miss Nix, was always saying, "Don't bleed on the cloth." She was always more concerned for the material than for my poor injuries.'

Louisa made several tight little stitches to secure the flounce to her gown. She made one last loop and knotted it. 'Then perhaps it is best that you don't carry anything sharp.'

Mantheria let out a trill of laughter and Louisa found herself smiling, despite everything.

She poked the needle through her hem and stood up. 'I am ready.'

'To be the belle of the ball?'

'Yes.'

Mantheria looped her arm with Louisa's. 'Good. For you deserve to be, my friend.'

They left the retiring room just as the musicians began to play a new tune, and Mantheria took her to where Lord Sunderland stood.

He bowed to her. 'My lady... Shall we dance? Or would you prefer I fetch you a glass of punch after that unfortunate ordeal?'

Louisa would have loved a drink, but she had waited

her whole life to go to parties and dance. Holding out her hand, she smiled. 'Dance, please.'

Lord Sunderland led her to the front of the dance floor, the most prominent position. He was a duke, after all, and for the first time she saw his countenance wore a hauteur equal to his rank. He stared down several matrons, and even a lord. Louisa might have lost a little of her heart to him if she hadn't known that he was doing it all for Mantheria. The woman he loved and could never have.

He put his hand on her waist and then they twirled together. 'I'd say our plan is working extraordinarily well. It is obvious that Wick cares for you. He has never made a public scene before, and he's now nursing his dignity out on the terrace.'

'Lord Sunderland—'

'Sunny, please.'

They switched hands in the dance. 'Sunny, just because Wick cares for me, it doesn't mean that he's ready for marriage.'

'Don't give up on him yet. I haven't. You should ask him about his brother and sister.'

Louisa didn't know to which sister Sunny was referring. Frederica? Helen? Becca? It seemed odd for him to tell her to ask him about his brother Matthew, whom she had never had the pleasure of meeting. Mantheria said he avoided society balls even more assiduously than Wick.

After the dance ended he returned her to Mantheria, who kissed both of Louisa's cheeks. 'You were marvellous and so self-possessed. You are the envy of every lady in the room. Let me find you another partner. It would be quite a different sort of scandal if Sunny danced with you three times.'

Louisa held up her hand to stop her well-meaning

friend. 'I am very thirsty and quite out of breath. I think I shall go to the refreshment table and rest for this set.'

Mantheria smiled. 'I will come with you.'

'Oh, no you don't,' Sunny said, possessing himself of Mantheria's hand. 'I have danced with every single lady you have told me to. Now it is my choice and I choose you.'

A pretty pink stole into Mantheria's cheeks as she allowed Sunny to escort her away from Louisa. How she wished her friend could have the happy ending she so richly deserved! But Louisa knew from her own experience that life was not fair. And happy endings were rare.

Several people openly ogled her as she made her way to the refreshment table. A few ladies even looked at her and talked behind their hands. Sighing, she picked up a ladle and poured some lemonade into a glass tumbler. Her throat felt rather dry and scratchy. She had not been fibbing to Mantheria when she'd said that she was out of breath. Louisa was not used to dancing vigorously for several hours at a time.

After draining her cup, she immediately refilled it.

'I see that you are fond of lemonade.'

She didn't have to look up to know that voice—it was Wick's. He was standing near her, the ladle now in his hand as he poured himself a drink.

Louisa knew that several eyes were on them, but she couldn't quite keep in her smile. 'As are you.'

Wick took a sip of the sour concoction and made a face. 'I would infinitely prefer something stronger.'

Sipping, she nodded slightly. 'So should I after that awful scene with my family... I feel I am constantly thanking you, but please accept my gratitude for protecting me from my cousin. He's never tried to hit me before.'

'You've never defied him before.'

Louisa didn't know how Wick knew that, but it was accurate. She'd been nothing but a doormat for her relatives to wipe their feet on. 'I wish it had been me who had punched him.'

Wick lifted his glass to his lips. 'He's not worth bloodying your knuckles over.'

Her eyes went to his white gloves as he took a drink and she saw that they were discoloured around his knuckles. 'Oh, dear. I didn't know that you had been hurt. I am so terribly sorry.'

He drained the rest of his lemonade in one big gulp. 'Don't be. My fists have been itching to hit your cousin's face ever since I learned your true name. I haven't felt this good in weeks. The only thing that would make my night better would be to dance with you.'

Louisa's heart expanded in her chest in forlorn hope. His eyes were gazing intensely into hers; she could have happily lost herself in them. Then Wick leaned slightly towards her and she revelled in his scent—spicy and masculine with a hint of vanilla. His gaze dropped to her lips, and she couldn't help but lick them. How she longed to be kissed by him!

But Wick shook his head and stepped back. 'It is best not to. I have no wish to cause further scandal, and the entire *ton* is now aware that you are not in possession of your fortune. I will go and see my grandfather first thing on Monday, and discover if he has learned who your trustees are. There's not a better businessman in all of England. Your inheritance will be yours soon, and you will need have no further connection or communication with your tedious relatives.'

Louisa brought the tumbler to her lips and choked down

a little lemonade. Wick was back to keeping her at arm's length.

'Ah, there you are, Lady Louisa,' a soft voice droned.

Wick jerked his head and gave the man a sharp bow. 'Norwich.'

The Earl of Norwich was not dressed in gold tonight, but in a stunning shade of salmon. Louisa was certain that no other gentleman could have worn such a suit of clothing and still appeared handsome. No, that wasn't a strong enough word: he was beautiful.

Louisa curtsied. 'My lord.'

'Lady Glastonbury assures me that you would be in raptures to dance with me again,' he said, with a slight sneer on his lips, as if he were addressing the question to Wick instead of herself. 'Unless you are already claimed…for this next set?'

The meaning behind Norwich's pause had to be as obvious to Wick as it was to Louisa. She stole a glance at him. Wick was wearing his grimacing grin that looked more painful than joyful.

'Happily, she is not.'

He took the glass from her hands and the hope from her heart.

Taking a deep breath, she put on her own grin. Louisa held out her hand for Lord Norwich to take. 'I *am* in raptures, my lord. Thank you for your kindness.'

Lord Norwich took her fingers and lifted them to his lips, placing a lingering kiss on top of her hand.

Louisa heard Wick groan, but he said nothing.

Did nothing.

As another man led her away from him.

Chapter Twenty

On Monday morning, Wick drove his phaeton to pick Matthew up at his rooms. His brother was waiting on the steps of the building. He resembled Papa, with blond hair and blue eyes, and it irked him to admit that his little brother was four inches taller than him and considered to be the handsomer of the two. Despite being the Duke's 'spare' heir, Matthew was chased by matchmaking mamas even more than Wick was. Probably because he rarely left London.

Climbing into the phaeton, his brother smiled mischievously. 'I hear that you attended two balls last week—and a presentation at St James's Court.'

Wick flicked the reins. 'Yes.'

His brother elbowed him in the side. 'You went to the marriage mart...on purpose?'

'I escorted our sister and Lady Louisa to a couple of balls,' Wick said stiffly. 'Nothing more.'

'Did you dance?'

He was not about to give his little brother ammunition with which to tease him. He was almost as bad as his sisters. So Wick played the dunce. 'Is *that* what you're supposed to do at a ball? I am so glad somebody has told me.'

Matthew chortled merrily. 'If only I had seen you before Saturday. It is said that you didn't dance even once at Lady Kensington's ball. Although that might have been awkward for your partner after you'd bloodied your gloves on Lord Barnabas's face.'

Tightening his hold on the reins, Wick forced himself not to rise to his brother's baiting. 'I have been wanting to punch him in the nose since Eton.'

'You *did* punch him in the nose at Eton. I was there.'

A reluctant smile formed on his lips. Wick had forgotten that episode, having endured—and fought—several bullies while at school. Lord Barnabas was one of many who had picked a fight with him. If only Wick had broken his nose like he had Sunny's.

'I did hear that you danced with several eligible young ladies at Lady Dennard's ball,' said Matthew. 'But none so beautiful as a certain runaway heiress.'

Wick turned the corner quickly, causing his brother to hold on to the side of the phaeton. 'Say another word and I will flatten your nose next.'

Matthew only laughed.

They arrived at their Grandfather Stubbs's business premises and a groom took the horse's reins. Wick and Matthew entered his office. The old man sat behind his desk, his cane leaning against his chair. His white hair obscured his face as he studied the document in front of him. He didn't look up as they entered. Wick watched his maternal grandfather read for several more minutes before the man glanced up at them.

'You only visit me when you need something, Wick.'

He flushed, pulling at his collar. 'That's not true, Grandfather.'

'Your grandmother and I haven't seen hide nor hair of you in two months.'

Wick took off his hat and hung it on the rack. 'I've been busy trying to take care of my little sisters. They cannot seem to stay out of trouble for longer than a day. Not even that.'

'I hear they are in need of a governess *again*.'

He shrugged his shoulders and sighed. 'It would appear so.'

'Your Grandmother Stubbs thinks that one of her great-nieces might be of use.'

Wick cleared his throat. Anyone his starchy step-grandmother might select would not approve of his wild sisters, nor their pets. 'As much as I appreciate Grandmother Stubbs's offer, Mantheria is already handling it.'

Matthew laughed. 'Anyone want to lay odds on how long the new governess will last? I'll give you ten to one that she doesn't last a full day. Twenty to one she doesn't last more than three hours.'

Wick gave his brother a blistering glare, which only caused him to laugh harder. Even Grandfather Stubbs guffawed. Wick's lips quirked up of their own volition.

'Well, since you've brought the girls to London,' Grandfather Stubbs said, 'don't forget to bring them to visit us. I'd like to hear first-hand about their latest mischief. Frederica is the best storyteller of them all.'

'You'll need to reserve an entire afternoon,' Wick said dryly. 'Possibly two.'

'I wouldn't be averse to meeting your Lady Louisa, either. Rumour has it that she is a very lovely young woman.'

Matthew tried to elbow Wick again, but this time he wasn't driving his carriage. He grabbed his brother's elbow and twisted his arm behind his brother's back, pushing his face against the wall. 'Not another word from you.'

'No fisticuffs in the office, boys,' their grandfather said, as if they were still children.

Wick released Matthew's arm and they sat down in chairs set on opposite sides of the room.

Grandfather Stubbs held up the document on his desk. 'I am particularly good friends with the head of Fordham's Bank…' he said. In other words, the man was terrified of his grandfather. 'He has been kind enough to send me a copy of the late Earl of Rockingham's will. I'll have my solicitors comb over it later, but it is straightforward. The late Earl's wife left her personal fortune of one hundred and fifty thousand pounds to her only daughter, Lady Louisa Bracken.'

Matthew let out a low whistle. 'You really do know how to choose them.'

Wick was scarcely less surprised. He'd thought Barnabas was exaggerating when he'd said that his cousin was set to inherit such a large fortune.

'She was meant to receive a yearly allowance of seventy-five hundred pounds for her maintenance While she was left in the guardianship of her uncle, the new Earl of Rockingham. Over the last ten years the amount would have come to seventy-five thousand pounds.'

Wick clenched his hands into fists. Her aunt and the current Earl had been stealing her allowance. 'The way Lady Rockingham has treated Louisa is robbery. She must have used the funds to support her own family and lifestyle, while keeping her niece in penury.'

Grandfather Stubbs set down the paper. 'Unfortunately, I don't think we will ever be able to recover those funds. The late Earl didn't seem to realise that his brother and sister-in-law would treat his daughter poorly. He must have known that they were not good with money, for he appointed three trustees to invest her fortune: Mr Pickett, Lord Waller and Mr Biggs. As far as I can tell, they have done a bang-up job. Lady Louisa's fortune has grown under their management to one hundred and eighty thousand pounds.'

This time Wick whistled. 'No wonder Lady Rockingham wanted to keep Louisa in the family—or at least her fortune.'

'Yes,' Grandfather Stubbs said, rubbing the end of his beard. 'According to the will, Lady Louisa's fortune becomes her own when she reaches five-and-twenty years of age or when she marries someone of whom her guardians approves.'

'What can we do?'

Matthew cleared his throat. 'Nothing until she is married. The will is quite clear that she is to have no control over her fortune before her marriage or until she is five-and-twenty. I have sent letters to all three of Lady Louisa's trustees. Mr Biggs has already responded by sending a note with his servant. From what he says, that they will agree not to send this quarter of her yearly allowance to the Rockinghams, but they will not allow her to touch a penny of her fortune until there is a ring on her finger.'

Wick's hands curled into fists. This was not the answer he'd hoped for. Wick had wanted Louisa to be in full control of her fortune immediately. He didn't wish her to have to marry a rotter like Lord Norwich to receive her inheritance.

'At least the Rockinghams won't get their grimy fingers on another shilling of her fortune,' he said.

Matthew slumped in his chair. 'It might turn into a nasty scandal. I've heard rumours of the Rockinghams' financial difficulties in certain less respectable quarters. The Earl's heir seems to be drowning in gambling loans. He's tangled with a particularly villainous moneylender named Marcus Sullivan. If Lord Barnabas isn't careful, he'll end up being murdered and thrown into the Thames.'

Wick's grandfather grunted. 'The head of Fordham's also hinted that the Earl of Rockingham is in debt. He would not tell me how much. I could put pressure on him to do so…'

Wick shook his head. 'It doesn't matter. Perhaps it is best for Louisa to make a clean break from them.'

Matthew tapped his fingers on the wooden armrest of his chair. 'I wouldn't want to let them off that easily… We could threaten legal action if Lord Rockingham refuses to approve of the man Lady Louisa wishes to marry.'

Wick knew they meant *him*.

Grandfather Stubbs smiled and Matthew smirked.

He blushed like a blasted debutante at her first ball. 'I have no intention of marrying Lady Louisa. Of marrying anyone.'

'Then you haven't asked her yet?' his grandfather asked.

'Wick has always been a bit slow.'

He jumped out of his chair and charged at his annoying little brother. Matthew might be taller, but Wick was broader and stronger. His brother tried to push Wick off as he got to his feet. But Wick wrapped his arms around Matthew and, after receiving a few hits to the shoulder and face, soon had him in a choke hold.

Matthew tapped the arm that was around his neck. 'Give!'

Wick released his brother. They were both breathing hard. Grandfather Stubbs chuckled. Matthew shrugged and then laughed, clapping Wick on the back.

And then Wick couldn't hold it in any longer—he laughed too.

Chapter Twenty-One

Wick wished that he had better news to bring to Louisa and his sisters. In fact, he would have preferred to break the news of the conditions in her father's will to only Louisa and Mantheria. But Becca, Helen and Frederica would not leave the room without bodily violence. And, while he was more than happy to wrestle Matthew, he wasn't about to give his little sisters the same treatment. Especially since he knew that they fought with their fingernails.

Clearing his throat, he forced himself to look at Louisa. She was looking a little pale. There were shadows underneath her luminous green eyes. He wished the words that he was about to speak were better tidings.

'My grandfather has procured a copy of your father's will, Louisa, and he has been in touch with all three of your trustees.'

Becca clapped her hands. 'I knew he could do it!'

Helen hushed her, and then Mantheria hushed them both.

Louisa's gaze never left his face.

'Unfortunately, the late Earl's will specifically states

that Louisa is not to have control of her mother's fortune until her five-and-twentieth birthday or until she is—'

'Married.' Louisa finished the phrase for him.

'What rot!' Frederica said, grinding her teeth.

For once, Wick was entirely in agreement with his most wilful sister. But it didn't change the facts.

'My grandfather is certain he will be able to convince the trustees not to issue any more of Louisa's yearly allowance to the Rockinghams. So at least they will no longer profit from their exploitation of her and treating her like a servant in her own home.'

Louisa leaned forward, and it was as if her eyes were devouring him whole. 'And the money they've already taken from me?'

Sighing, he admitted, 'It is lost. There was nothing in your father's will to stipulate exactly how the yearly allowance for your maintenance should be spent by his brother and his wife.'

All his sisters were talking at once. Wick couldn't follow all the conversations, but the expressions on his sisters' faces were murderous.

He held up both of his hands. 'Quiet!'

One by one his sisters stopped talking and looked at him.

'I know that this is not the news any of us hoped for, but Grandfather and Matthew are still working on it. And if anyone can twist a situation to his advantage, it's Matt. Now, we can stay here, arguing over what cannot be currently changed, or I can take you all for ices.'

His nephew Andrew had been playing in the corner of the room with his boat, but at the sound of the word 'ices' he dropped the wooden toy. 'I would like an ice!'

'I'll call for Mantheria's barouche,' said Wick, eager

to leave the room and no longer be followed by Louisa's disappointed eyes.

All six of them squashed into the large carriage, and none of his little sisters argued on the way. A rare trip.

When they arrived at Gunter's, Wick ordered Andrew's raspberry ice first. Then ordered for all his sisters. He would have given Louisa the next choice, but she was still trying to decide on the flavour, and whether she wanted a sweet or a savoury one. Wick ordered both: one parmesan ice and one strawberry ice—his personal favourite.

They all sat down at a table in the centre of the room. Every eye was on them. His family drew attention wherever they went. They were infamously wealthy, and notorious for not caring about the *ton*'s rules.

Andrew's ice came first, and his nephew did not wait for the others to receive their own treats before he began spooning it into his mouth. Wick was the last to receive his strawberry ice, but he didn't mind. He was enjoying himself watching Louisa.

'Try the strawberry one first,' he told her.

She dipped her spoon into the pink ice and took a very small bite. He watched her touch the spoon to her lips. How he burned to touch those lips with his fingers. His mouth. His tongue. Louisa licked her lips and her eyes were on his. She took another small bite, this time of the parmesan ice. Never before had Wick thought that the eating of an ice could be seductive. But it was when Louisa used both her lips and her tongue to take such a small bite off the spoon.

'Why aren't you eating, Uncle Wick?' Andrew asked.

Wick had been so absorbed in watching Louisa that he had not started on his own ice. Feeling the blood rush to his face, he picked up his spoon and took a large cooling bite. The ice made his tongue cold, but the rest of his body was still on fire. Longing for Louisa. Wanting to kiss her over and over again.

Mantheria smiled with knowing eyes at both of them. 'Louisa, what do you think of your first ices? Do you prefer sweet or savoury?'

Louisa lowered her eyes, her cheeks turning a pretty shade of pink. 'The sweet—but the parmesan is also nice, and an unexpected taste.'

'It was our brother Charles's favourite.'

Wick choked on the ice in his mouth, feeling cold all over.

'Charles was our third brother,' Mantheria explained. 'Just two years older than myself and my twin sister.'

Louisa set down her spoon. 'I am sorry. I did not know that you had a twin…or a brother named Charles.'

Wick's sisters rarely talked about Charles and Elizabeth around him. They knew how painful he found it. But Mantheria seemed determined to open that old wound today.

'I don't remember them very well,' Becca admitted, her lips drooping. 'I was only three when they died.'

Mantheria's eyes were full of unshed tears, but she smiled. 'Oh, they would not wish for you to be sad that they are gone. Both Charles and Elizabeth were the happiest children I ever knew. Charles was so sweet, and he loved animals—just like you and Helen. He taught Sadie the elephant all her parlour tricks—like putting on her own cloak and kneeling to allow rides. And he didn't like sweet foods at all. Not even fruits. That is why the parmesan ice was his favourite.'

'Charles was usually good-natured,' Wick said. 'But

Papa called him Char Bear, because occasionally you'd poke him and he'd get really angry, like a bear. I was teasing him one night at dinner and he picked up his plate and pushed it into my face. There were carrots in my hair and gravy on my nose.'

'And mashed potatoes in Wick's eyebrows,' Mantheria added.

Helen put her elbows on the table and leaned forward. 'What did Mama and Papa do?'

Wick shook his head. 'Nothing.'

'Nothing?' Becca repeated.

Wick couldn't help but smile at the memory. 'Mama said that justice had been served and told Harper to bring me another plate. We continued eating dinner as if nothing were amiss.'

Helen shook her head. 'And you say *we* are wild animals!'

'What about Elizabeth?' Becca asked eagerly, her ice quite forgotten.

'Elizabeth loved sweet things,' Frederica said, sniffing. 'She was the only one who could steal biscuits from the kitchens without getting into trouble. Papa said that her tongue was sweeter than sugar. No one could stay cross with her for long.'

'She was very slight…bordering on frail,' Wick found himself saying. 'Cook was always trying to fatten her up. It wouldn't surprise me if Cook had brought her the biscuits.'

'Or Mrs May!' Mantheria said with a little laugh. 'They both doted on her. She was the good twin and I was the naughty one.'

'That hasn't changed,' Helen said, giggling.

But it had. Wick had been the only one old enough

at the time to see it. Mantheria had changed after Elizabeth's death. She had become serious, obedient and eager
to please, as if trying to take the place of her twin in
the family. She had carried a heavy burden as the oldest daughter.

Wick's eyes filled with tears and he got to his feet
abruptly. 'Come with me, Andrew. I'll buy you another
ice. Yours is all gone.'

His sticky nephew dropped his spoon on the table
with a clatter and eagerly placed his hand in Wick's.
They walked away from their seats, but he could still
hear his sisters' voices.

'Wick blames himself for their deaths,' Mantheria
said. 'He was the oldest, and our parents were away in
Africa when scarlet fever hit the family. He rode all night
to London, to fetch a specialist for Charles, but it was too
late. The fever had taken his strength and his heart. Wick
stayed up with both of them, night after night. Charles
died a few days later and Elizabeth did not outlast him
by more than an hour... I know it sounds strange, but I
was glad of that. I had always been with Elizabeth, and
I was happy to know that neither of them was alone—
even in heaven.'

'Mama and Papa didn't blame Wick,' Frederica said.
'They blamed themselves for leaving us. I suppose we
all feel the guilt of surviving when they didn't.'

Unconsciously, Wick tightened his hold on Andrew's
wrist. His sisters had put his feelings into words that he
never could. As he'd held Charles's slender hand in those
final hours, he had prayed that God would take his life
instead. But his prayers had not been answered.

'Too tight, Uncle Wick!' Andrew protested, yanking his hand away.

'Sorry,' he said with a sniff.

Wick would always be sorry.

Chapter Twenty-Two

~~~~~~~~~~

They finished their ices and Mantheria suggested they stroll in the park before heading back home. Louisa was grateful for the extra time with a certain marquess, and the younger Stringham sisters also took up this suggestion with enthusiasm.

Once they reached the park, they began running along the path. Andrew tried to keep up with them, and Mantheria followed her son. Louisa slowly walked behind them and found Wick by her side. The familiar thrill of his nearness caused her pulse to quicken and her mind to reel. She wished she knew what to say to him. How to comfort so great a loss.

Wick cleared his throat. 'I suppose I won't see you again until tomorrow night at Sunny's ball. He's promised actual fireworks, after I assured him that we were not going to offer another free drama or more fighting for his guests. He confessed his keen disappointment, but still wishes us to come.'

A smile played on his lips and made him look breathtakingly handsome. Wick was so dear to her. Too dear, perhaps.

'How forbearing of him,' she teased gently. 'Who is hostess for the ball? A gentleman doesn't host a party alone, I believe?'

He nodded. 'Sunny's mother, the Dowager Duchess of Sunderland, will be the formal hostess, but I can assure you that Sunny, or at least his secretary, has done all the work. The Dowager has spent the last twenty-three years making mourning a profession. She wears only black, and often a veil over her face. The clocks in Sunderland House have not been set since the death of the late Duke, and she keeps black curtains on all the windows. She only bestirs herself from her coffin-like house during the season, when she half-heartedly tries to marry Sunny off to an heiress.'

Louisa felt a pang of sympathy for Sunny; her own father had not been the same after her mother had died. It had been as if he were a shell of the person he once was. He'd no longer read to her or played with her. She had felt as if he'd died three years before he actually had.

'I suppose she'll like me, then,' she said with a forced laugh. 'My title and my money are quite the best things about me.'

Wick stopped walking and touched her arm. 'I know she will like you—and not just because you are an heiress. Your fortune is the least interesting thing about you.'

She sighed ruefully. 'Or lack thereof. I am probably the only penniless heiress. I hate it that I have imposed so much upon Mantheria. It makes me want to accept the first offer of marriage I receive so that I will be able to repay her.'

His hand tightened on her arm. 'Do not rush into a marriage that you may some day regret. If you're worried about the bills, *I* will repay her.'

'I am not your responsibility either. You have quite enough of that, with your little sisters, and in my humble opinion you are doing a wonderful job. You clearly love them, and you listen to them. I know that you have their best interests at heart and will find the perfect governess for them.'

Wick dropped his hand. 'I do love them dearly, and I wish that I could protect them from all the dangers in the world.'

Louisa shook her head. 'You cannot protect them, but you can prepare them...and catch them when they fall.'

Wick's brown eyes gazed intently into hers. 'Who catches you, Louisa?'

You, she thought.

That day on the road, when he'd mistaken her for the governess and brought her to Hampford Castle with his sisters, he had saved her from a life of not knowing a loving family or a happy home. An existence without friends her own age. Wick had made her dreams of being presented to the Queen and having a London season come true—everything her mother had planned for her.

She spun her parasol. 'Your sisters,' she said. 'Becca, I would say, caught me first, when she begged you to let me stay, but no doubt Frederica and Helen would argue that it was them. And I don't know what I would do without Mantheria. She is like the sister I always wanted but never had.'

Louisa had tried to lighten the mood, but Wick continued to frown, his countenance serious. Blushing, she wondered if he thought she was trying to take Elizabeth's place in Mantheria's life. Her words had been so thoughtless!

'Not that I am her real sister,' she said. 'I could never

be that. And I would never presume to fill the void left by her twin… I only meant to convey that Mantheria has treated me better than anyone of my own family and I will never be able to repay her goodness to me.'

Wick shook his head. 'I do not think you are being presumptuous. If I appear stern, it has nothing to do with you. It is the weight of loss and guilt. Because I didn't realise how much Mantheria has had to bear on her own. I thought… I thought I was shouldering the burden. I didn't know how much responsibility she was taking. If you are providing her with a confidante and friend of her own age, I can only be grateful to you. She needs one now more than ever, with her philandering husband.'

'Must you carry your burden alone?' Louisa whispered. 'My housekeeper, Mrs Barker, always said that we share our burdens so that they may be lighter. I know that each of your sisters would happily share yours with you, and I would help you in any way that I can. When you carry your burden alone, it makes you lonely.'

He turned his head away from her. 'Why should they have to carry the burden of my guilt when it wasn't their fault? They were only children. Becca and Helen don't even remember the night Charles and Elizabeth died. But it's emblazoned in my memory. I have never felt more helpless in my life. I knew that I had let them down, but I didn't know what else to do. I didn't— I couldn't—'

Wick stopped mid-sentence, his voice choked with emotion.

Louisa longed to throw her arms around him. To hold him. To comfort him. To share the burden that caused him to push her and everyone he loved away. But he wouldn't let her.

Clearing his throat, Wick offered his arm. 'Shall we

catch up with my sisters? I can't have them falling into any scrapes before we return to Hampford Castle at the end of the week.'

Louisa gently placed her hand in the crook of his elbow and they continued walking. She felt more sorrowful with every step. He was leaving.

'Have you found a governess yet?' she asked.

'No,' he said. 'I will be interviewing several candidates tomorrow, that Mantheria has found from an agency. I am hopeful that one of them will be good enough.'

Taking a deep breath, Louisa couldn't help but give him some unwanted advice. 'You should ask Mantheria and Mrs May to go with you for the interviews. Mantheria will know who will prepare the girls best for society. Mrs May can get the girls to look after Andrew.'

Wick didn't say anything, so Louisa tumbled on in her speech, 'After we arrived home from my Uncle Laybourne's, Helen asked Mrs May where her new snake was, and your housekeeper pretended that she didn't know what your sister was talking about. But I knew she did. She had let the snake out in my aunt's best parlour. I realised then and there that Mrs May doesn't let your sisters flummery her, and that she has a great affection for them. I know that she is not their mother, but I think if you asked her she would help. With a governess, of course. She already has her duties as housekeeper. Then you'd be free to conduct your business affairs.'

'I appreciate your suggestion,' he said in a low voice. 'I shall ask them both if they'd be willing to attend the interviews with me.'

Louisa couldn't help but smile. He was taking *her* advice. He was going to let others help carry the burden of his little sisters' care whilst his parents were away. Maybe, just maybe, he would let her help carry the burden of his grief. The loss of his two younger siblings. She would happily share in any of his burdens if only he would open his heart to her.

A phaeton stopped by them on the path and she saw it was the Earl of Norwich. Today he was dressed in an exquisite crimson driving coat with no less than fifteen capes. Louisa counted. His tall beaver hat shone in the light and his hessian boots sparkled as if they'd just been buffed.

Lord Norwich's lips curved into his usual sneering smile. 'Lord Cheswick, Lady Louisa…what a pleasure, seeing you here.'

Wick gave the man a curt nod.

Louisa curtsied deeply, still holding on to the support of Wick's strong arm. 'Lord Norwich, shall you be at Lord Sunderland's ball tomorrow?'

Norwich switched the reins from one gloved hand to the other. 'I shall indeed, my lady. And, if I may be so bold, might I request from you the first two dances?'

She glanced at Wick's profile, but it was as if his face had been carved from granite. There was no emotion there. Nothing to show that he cared for her or that he had any intention of dancing with her at the ball at all.

'I should be pleased to reserve them for you, my lord.'

The Earl touched his hat. 'Until then.'

Louisa watched the Earl urge his team of horses forward and pass by. He gave her one last wave. Wick took no notice of it, or of her. He started walking again at a quick pace and Louisa trailed along at his side like a rag doll.

'Should I not have said yes?' she said breathlessly. 'Your sisters have said that a lady is not supposed to say no when a gentleman asks her to dance at a ball. I did not know how to refuse politely.'

'You needn't refuse Norwich. He's not a bad match, as long as you don't mind that he will love his clothes more than you.'

Wick's curt words cut at her heart. Did he not care for her at all?

She swallowed. 'Then you approve of Lord Norwich as a suitor for me?'

His jaw clenched, but he didn't look her in the eye. 'There's only one better catch this season on the marriage market, and that is Sunny.'

Louisa's lips drooped. 'I do not think Sunny is truly on the market. He's only playing at it. His heart has already been taken.'

'Regret is a cold bedfellow.'

Wick's tone was harsh and she knew he was speaking from his own experience. Louisa's soul ached for the pain she knew Wick had felt and would always feel about the loss of Charles and Elizabeth. She understood now why he wasn't interested in marriage. He did not want to love another person he could lose. He didn't wish to feel helpless again.

But Louisa had felt helpless her entire life until leaving Greystone Hall, and at this moment she was hopeless. Wick was not ready for her love. And she was tired of loving those who did not love her back. Like her Aunt and Uncle Rockingham. Her cousins.

And now Wick.

She would not give her heart to anyone who did not love her in return.

Chapter Twenty-Three

Louisa and Mantheria sat in the elegant barouche on their way to Lord Sunderland's ball. They looked like opposites.

Mantheria wore a black gown, low-cut, with scalloped sleeves and several flounces on the skirt. Her silver necklace held three large black diamonds with matching earbobs, and in her hair were tall black feathers that contrasted greatly with her yellow curls.

Louisa's dress was simpler, with no ornamentation besides a lace overlay of creamy white. Her neckline was also higher, and around her throat was a set of three rows of pearls on loan from the young Duchess. Louisa's hair did not have any feathers, but Chandler had woven in baby's breath from the bouquet Wick had sent for her.

Mantheria took Louisa's hand and they intertwined gloved fingers like the keys of a piano. 'How were the girls today?' she asked.

Louisa snorted, and then laughed. 'Becca rescued a mouse from her kitten and I think she believes it is her newest pet.'

The Duchess closed her eyes and shook her head. 'No

doubt she'll cause an infestation in my house before they leave for Hampford.'

'Did you find a new governess?'

'They were all awful,' Mantheria said with a sigh. 'Even Wick thought so. The first one, a Miss Thornburgh, flinched whenever we spoke to her. Can you imagine how she would handle the girls? Let alone the animals in the menagerie?'

Louisa giggled, covering her mouth with one hand. 'They would frighten her to death.'

'My sisters or the animals?'

'Your sisters.'

They laughed together until tears started falling out of Mantheria's eyes and she shook her head. 'Then a Miss Meadows talked of using the strap as if it were some great personal pleasure.'

Louisa shuddered. 'Oh, no!'

'Don't worry, Wick would never let anyone beat our sisters. The next candidate from the agency was a lady in her sixties, clearly not in good health. Mrs May didn't think she would have the stamina to keep up with them.'

Louisa found herself nodding in agreement. The Stringham sisters needed someone young and vibrant.

'And the last, a Miss Tucker, positively frightened me during the interview. I sat up so straight that my neck still hurts.'

'Perhaps she would be better suited as a drill sergeant rather than a governess.'

Mantheria shrugged, slumping a little in her seat. 'None of them will do.'

Trying to appear nonchalant, Louisa asked, 'And what did Wick say? Will he stay in London longer? Until he finds the right one?'

'He swears that he won't stay even one extra day,' his

sister said with a harrumph. 'He is more stubborn than any animal Papa has ever owned.'

Louisa bit her lower lip to stop it from trembling. She had hoped that Wick would be near her longer. But he was determined to leave.

A footman opened the door of the carriage and escorted them into a beautiful grey stone London mansion with countless candelabra lit, making it appear almost as bright as day. Lord Sunderland's blond locks looked golden in the candlelight, and he beamed when he saw them. Or rather when he saw Mantheria. His eyes seemed to eat her whole.

Louisa wondered, if she married another, whether her traitorous heart would continue to long for Wick. But it didn't matter. Without her fortune she had no money and nowhere to go, and the only way to receive her inheritance early was for her to marry. She could not continue to take advantage of Mantheria's charity and wait for a man who had openly refused her.

A woman stood next to Sunny. She was a petite little thing, whose head did not even reach his shoulder. She was dressed in black bombazine—a material known for not reflecting the light. Her face was covered by a black lace veil, as if she were attending a funeral.

'Lady Glastonbury… Lady Louisa,' Sunny said, showing his usual endearing smile beneath his crooked nose. 'Now my ball can begin. But where is Wick? He said that he would be escorting you.'

Louisa's eyes darted to Mantheria, whose cheeks had turned a pretty pink as Sunny took her hand and lifted it to his lips. 'I am sure he is coming. Perhaps he is late. We had a rather dismal afternoon interviewing for a new governess.'

The Dowager Lady Sunderland removed her veil to

show a surprisingly young-looking face. Her skin was smooth, except for the fine lines around her mouth and eyes. She pointed a black gloved finger at him. 'Lord Cheswick should be interviewing candidates for a wife. He's not getting any younger and neither are you, Alphonse.'

Sunny's given name was Alphonse. The nickname fitted him much better, Louisa thought.

Sunny's smile turned rather hard. 'That is why I am here, Mama. But let us not hold up the line any longer. Lady Glastonbury, will you please save me the supper waltz?'

Before Mantheria could answer, Lady Sunderland spoke again. 'There's no point in asking *her*—she's already married. You ought to have asked Lady Louisa. Not a bad-looking girl, even with the freckles, and she has a fortune besides.'

Louisa could have happily sunk down to the floor at the Dowager's words.

Mantheria linked her arms with Louisa's. 'Alas, Lady Louisa, you are too late for the supper waltz, for I accept your offer, Lord Sunderland. But perhaps you might want to reserve another dance with our fair Louisa?'

Sunny took Louisa's hand briefly, bowing over it before letting go. 'Shall we say the first set?'

Louisa felt the blood rush to her face as she answered, 'The first two dances are already claimed, my lord.'

'The third, then?' he said, his eyes bright.

'Very good.'

'Phew. I am glad I got in early.'

Mantheria gave a little laugh and guided Louisa away from the receiving line. 'Oh, please tell me that my brother has reserved those dances.'

Louisa swallowed and shook her head. 'Alas, no. They were reserved by Lord Norwich.'

Her friend appeared almost as disappointed as Louisa. 'Perhaps Wick, like Sunny, wants to save his dances for the supper waltz. That way he will also be able to escort you to dinner and sit by you during it.'

'I don't think he intends to dance with me at all.'

Mantheria sniffed, shaking her head. 'That will not do. He is not going to spend another ball skulking around the sides and snubbing every young lady here. My mother would not have stood for it and neither will I.'

Louisa's eyes filled with tears and she cursed her uncontrollable emotions. 'Please do not ask Wick to dance with me. I shall die of shame on the spot if you do.'

The young Duchess stuck out her chin. 'Very well. There are plenty of handsome young men who would happily queue up to dance with a beautiful young lady like you.'

Louisa wiped away an errant tear from her cheek and attempted a small joke. 'According to Lady Sunderland, I am not a bad-looking girl. Even with my freckles.'

'Don't listen to that old prune! You are gorgeous.'

'I'm skinny and freckled.'

'Your figure is willowy—which is the prevailing style, I'll have you know. And your skin is perfectly lovely. Your freckles give your face character.'

Louisa glanced down. 'My Aunt Rockingham always said that they made me ugly.'

Mantheria's hand touched Louisa's cheek. 'Nothing could make you ugly, my friend. You have the purest heart and the kindest soul I have ever known. And they shine through your eyes.'

Louisa's eyes threatened to fill with tears again, but

she shook her head. 'What do you think of the Earl of Norwich?'

Mantheria gave a little gurgle of laughter. 'Oh, I never think about men who are prettier than me. How lowering it is!'

Louisa felt her lips tug upwards into a smile. 'Lord Norwich is very beautiful.'

'And dresses like a god. Beau Brummell mocks his flamboyant style, but I think it suits Norwich down to his high-heeled boots.'

'Yes!'

Mantheria's smile slipped for a minute, but then it was back on her face. 'He has a lovely estate in Norwich, and two smaller ones, I believe. One near Bath and the other near Brighton. The *on dit* is that he's in debt because of gambling with the Duke of York. But that was last year. I have not once seen him at a card table this season. Perhaps he has learned the lesson that fortunes are only lost at gaming and never won. I start to break out into a cold sweat if my losses rise above fifty guineas.'

'I've never gambled before.'

'*Life* is a gamble, my dear Louisa, and you don't always get to choose the cards you are dealt,' Mantheria said, and then curtsied to Lord Norwich. 'Ah, you are here to steal our lovely Lady Louisa away for a dance.'

The Earl wore an intricately embroidered silver suit that gleamed in the light like freshly polished silver. He looked cold and perfect enough to be a marble statue. 'How clever of you, Lady Glastonbury, for I do indeed intend to steal Lady Louisa—and her heart.'

He offered Louisa his hand and she placed hers inside it. How different it felt from Wick's. Lord Norwich's fingers were long and slender. They lacked the size and strength of Wick's. And the warmth.

They spoke very little during the quadrille—the dance most fashionable balls started with. She found Lord Norwich to be an excellent dancer and a thoughtful partner. He was always where he should be, and more than once helped her through a mistake in the figure without bringing attention to it.

The next dance was a country jig. Louisa was a little breathless as she hopped about, but words spilled from her mouth when he took her hands. 'Are you interested in my heart or my inheritance?'

Lord Norwich's perpetual sneer turned into a grin. 'Oh, I do like you, Lady Louisa. Straight to the point.'

The figure caused them to part, but when they came back together, he answered, 'Both, I am afraid. Like yourself, I am in desperate need of funds. I believe you are currently living on the generosity of Lady Glastonbury and will not see your fortune until you are married?'

'I do not wish to be courted for my inheritance.'

'Nor do I for my title. But it is what people first notice.'

She turned away again and followed the line, his words sinking in with each step. She could not blame him for being interested in her money when she wanted a husband with an estate and home. Perhaps pecuniary reasons were not entirely wrong to consider in a marriage partner.

Lord Norwich held out his hands and she took them. 'You are wrong, Lord Norwich. It was not your title that first brought you to my notice, but your suit of clothes.'

He gave a soundless laugh as they twirled together in a circle. They returned to their own sides of the line and bowed to each other as the music ended.

Lord Norwich took her hand and began leading her back to Mantheria. 'A word of warning, my dear,' he whispered in a soft, cold voice. 'You are not the first woman to set your cap at Lord Cheswick, and nor will you be the last. But he has no need to marry. Do not turn down a real offer for a forlorn hope.'

He let go of her hand and Louisa gave a full-body shiver, despite feeling a little overheated. His words crawled down her spine. Had they been a threat? A warning? Or honest advice? Had she not told herself something similar?

Before she could confide in Mantheria, Sunny appeared at her elbow. 'This is our set, I believe, Lady Louisa?'

Mantheria blew them a kiss—or perhaps just Sunny. His jaw was tight and his usual smile absent. The set was a waltz (which she could now participate in after receiving Lady Cowper's permission), and Louisa thought it was like dancing with a stranger. Sunny appeared to be in a grim mood. She wondered if it was his mother's words about Mantheria or his own misery.

'My housekeeper always said that misery loves company,' Louisa said quietly. 'If you need company in your misery, I am here.'

Sunny took a deep breath and guided them around another couple. 'I do not want company in my misery. Yet I fear my bloody idiot of a best friend will soon be joining me, because he is too stubborn and stupid to allow himself to be happy.'

Louisa knew that he was speaking of Wick. 'He's not coming, is he?'

He huffed, shaking his head. 'I don't know. He hates balls. He hates the season. But he came here for you—he even had Mantheria secure you a presentation with the Queen. I have never seen him bestir himself so much for a person who is not part of his family. I had hoped that he had finally forgiven himself for Charlie and Lizzy's deaths, but the fool seems determined to live in his own personal purgatory.'

His words ought to have stung, but rather they were a balm to her battered heart. She, Louisa Bracken, was not the problem. She was not unworthy of love. Undeserving of happiness. She was none of the awful things her Aunt and Uncle Rockingham had told her that she was as a child and a young woman. And believing those lies was keeping her in her own personal purgatory. She could not save Wick, but she could save herself.

'I am sorry if I have put Lord Cheswick to so much effort,' she said, her voice a little shaky. 'I can only promise that I will not be a burden upon him for much longer.'

The music stopped and Sunny faced her. 'You were never a burden, Louisa. You are his salvation. If only he is not too blind to see it.'

Louisa did not know what to say, so she didn't say anything at all.

When Sunny returned her to Mantheria her friend had already lined up several more partners for her: Mr Beesley, Lord Thorley and Mr King. She noticed that Mantheria had not found her a partner for the supper dance.

Mantheria briefly squeezed Louisa's hand. 'I am sorry, Louisa. I thought he would be here by now.'

She didn't need to ask who her friend meant.

She watched Sunny lead Mantheria away and then waltz with her. Their dancing together was so beautiful that it brought tears to her eyes again. She could see that they loved each other. Every movement was a graceful give and take...a stolen happiness that would end with the music.

Then Louisa felt a hand on her lower back and turned to find herself in Wick's arms. His usually perfectly tamed locks were dishevelled. His cheeks were red and his breath smelled of spirits. His always intricately tied cravat was rumpled. His other hand took hers and he started waltzing with her before they had even reached the dance floor. Over his shoulder, Louisa could see several eyes upon them.

'Are you intoxicated?' she asked.

He closed his eyes and then opened them again. 'Completely foxed.'

'Should you be dancing?'

'Probably not,' he said, pulling her closer to him. 'Perhaps you could steer?'

Louisa was tired of him toying with her emotions. Pulling her to him and then pushing her away. 'I am not sailing a boat.'

Wick's hand pressed into her back until their bodies were touching. He gazed intensely into her eyes. 'No, you're my Louisa, with hundreds of sweet freckles, and I want to kiss every single one. I'd start with the one just above the curve of your lips.'

Despite her best intentions, she melted in his arms. His words soothed a thousand of her Aunt Rockingham's slights about her looks. The spots on her skin weren't blemishes—they were sweet freckles. She felt her temperature rise at the thought of Wick's lips on every single one of them.

Then he twirled her around and Louisa quite forgot everyone else. He was uncharacteristically silent, but she didn't mind. She lost herself in the pleasure of waltzing with the man she loved. In the thrill of his hand on her back. The scent of vanilla and leather that characterised his person. There was nowhere in the world that she'd rather be.

The waltz ended all too soon, and Louisa was afraid

that Wick was going to pass her off to another man to dance with.

'Shall I fetch you a drink?' he asked.

Louisa touched one of her hot cheeks. 'Perhaps a little fresh air?'

Wick offered her his arm and they wove through the room. She watched him nod at several acquaintances, almost challenging them to give him the social cut. But none did. Maybe because some day he would be a duke.

He led her out to a small garden lit by hanging lanterns. Louisa had thought that there couldn't be anything more romantic and lovely than a ballroom, but she'd been wrong. This little garden smelled of roses and mint. The warm lights of the lanterns transformed it into a fairyland, like in one of the stories her governess had told her before she'd been dismissed.

Louisa's knees were shaking and so were her hands. Her heartbeat felt loud in her ears. If it hadn't been for his firm hold on her elbow she would probably have fallen to the ground.

Wick released her. Louisa felt unbalanced and fell forward against his hard chest. Her arms naturally wrapped around his neck. She heard the thunderous sound of his heartbeat.

Wick's hands clutched her waist, pressing her even closer to his body. Louisa felt his sweet breath on her lips. Tilting her head back, she offered her mouth in open invitation. Wick did not keep her waiting long. His soft lips first brushed that freckle above her mouth, and then her lips. Over. And over. And over again. Then he increased the pressure of his mouth against hers and Louisa tightened her arms around him. She didn't want this kiss to end. Or *kisses*, as he continued to explore the shape of her mouth.

Then she felt something wet and soft against her mouth. His tongue. He was licking her lips! Louisa opened her mouth in surprise and felt his tongue slip between her lips. She felt hot all over and a growing need deep in her belly. Wick deepened the kiss, and Louisa was sure that there could be no greater pleasure in the world than kissing. She gasped, and he pressed his tongue farther inside her mouth. It felt wanton and wickedly wonderful. She opened her lips wider and felt his tongue teasingly touching all over her mouth, sending sparks of pleasure through her entire body.

Taking a breath, Wick kissed her again and nuzzled her neck. Louisa clung to him, knowing she would fall without his touch. He raised his eyes to look at her, but Louisa didn't wish to talk. She pressed her lips to his mouth and then licked his lips to make him open them. Capturing his bottom lip with her teeth, she tugged on it gently. Then she released it and opened her mouth for another decadent kiss. She felt Wick's tongue enter again and she could not resist sucking on it.

She felt his body stiffen against hers.

He released her and stepped back.

Louisa touched her hot neck, unsteady on her feet. 'Did I do something wrong?'

Wick shook his head and brought his hands to his face. 'No. You could never do anything wrong. The fault is all mine. I should not have brought you out here. I should not have kissed you. You deserve so much better. Someone who is worthy of you.'

She reached out her hand to touch him, but he flinched and she dropped it to her side. 'You are the worthiest man I have ever met...'

'I'm a wreck, Louisa... A wreck held together by responsibilities and mostly good intentions,' he said, turning his back to her. 'I am not the man for you. For anyone.'

Every word was like a needle-prick on her sore soul. Unbidden, her eyes filled with tears and her throat felt full of emotion. She swallowed it down.

'We are all wrecks, Wick. Ships beaten about by the storms of our past. Every single one of us. My parents died. My aunt and uncle stole my fortune and my self-esteem. I was a complete and total wreck. Then you picked me up off the road and took me home to your sisters. And I learned that even wrecks can be worthy of love. That a person can be imperfect and still cherished. I learned that from you. From the way you treated your wild, flawed and entirely loveable little sisters. To be loved by you would be the greatest gift in all the world.'

Wick took another step back from her. 'I just can't...'

Sniffing, she wiped the tears from her cheeks. 'Fine. Stay in your personal purgatory and may your regrets keep you company—for I will no longer.'

Her legs shook as she walked away from him, back inside the house. Wick did not follow her.

Louisa swallowed her sadness and slipped into the crowd heading to the supper room, her heart shattered.

Chapter Twenty-Four

Wick waited a few minutes after Louisa went inside. His mind was still a little fuzzy, but kissing Louisa had sobered him. He knew that it would be a bad idea to walk back into the room at the same time as her. People would think that he had done exactly what he had—kissed her. Some members of the *ton* would even think that he'd compromised her.

Fustian!

He raked his hands through his hair. What a mess he'd made of his life—and of hers. He oughtn't have come to London and attended these balls. He wasn't interested in marriage. Not yet. Maybe not ever. His brother Matthew could inherit the dukedom for all he cared. He'd never wanted the responsibility of being the head of the family. The oldest. The one in charge when something went terribly wrong.

Charles and Elizabeth's deaths would always haunt him. He'd spend the rest of his life wondering whether, if he'd done something different, they would have lived. Elizabeth should have been at this ball with Mantheria. She should have danced every single dance. Maybe she would even have been married, with a child of her own. Charles should have been in Africa with their parents, learning more about the animals that they all loved. He would have been old enough now to sail all over the world, looking for new specimens. He should have been making a name for himself as a naturalist.

Oh, how Wick wished things had turned out differently. Wished that he could have been the sort of free man who could give his heart to Louisa and take responsibility for a wife and a family of his own.

Shaking his head, Wick knew in his heart that he was not good enough for her. Louisa deserved to be loved by someone whole. Someone who could give her the family and home she'd lost when her parents had died.

The sound of footsteps on the gravel behind him caused him to turn. Even in the dim fairy lights of the garden he easily recognised the features of his best friend.

'Getting some air?' Sunny asked.

Wick gave him a jerky nod.

'You're higher than a kite.'

He took a deep breath. 'Just a little in the wind.'

'What's wrong, old friend?' Sunny said in a low voice. 'It's not like you to get blind drunk, let alone arrive in that state at a ball.'

Wick blinked at Sunny. He didn't know what had come over his best friend lately. He'd shared his personal feelings and wanted Wick to talk about his. That was not how Englishmen behaved. They punched their friends and were polite to their enemies. They were stoic and strong and didn't cry in public. Not even when they wanted to. And they most certainly did not confide in other men.

'I'm fine.'

'You look terrible,' Sunny said, pointing at him. 'Your appearance would make your valet weep. Your hair is a mess and your clothes are rumpled.'

Wick snorted. 'If my appearance offends you, then I shall leave.'

He spun on his foot to go, and nearly lost his balance on the loose gravel.

'You can't just waltz with her once and leave,' Sunny said, grabbing Wick's shoulder and forcing him to face him. 'You'll have every tabby coupling your names together. You need to dance with other ladies.'

'I don't want to,' Wick said, sounding like a child even to his own ears.

Sunny's free hand went to Wick's other shoulder. 'I don't care what you want, you idiot. I care about Lady Louisa's reputation—which is already a little shaky, thanks to her horrid relations. You will make her the talk of the town. You waltzed with her as if she was a serving wench you could hold as close to you as you liked. Then you escorted her out of the ballroom. Many a matron will be expecting an engagement announcement in the *Gazette* tomorrow.'

Swallowing heavily, Wick shook his head. 'I can't. I can't marry her. It's too much—*too much.*'

His friend huffed in frustration. 'Well, if you won't marry Lady Louisa, then you will restore her reputation, and yours, by dancing every set until this cursed ball ends.'

'You said I look a fright.'

'Oh, you do,' Sunny said sharply. 'But after my valet has had you for a half an hour I expect you to return to the ballroom as fresh as a daisy and ready to dance. Am I clear?'

'Yes.'

Sunny moved his hands from Wick's shoulders and grabbed him by the elbow. He hauled him through the back of the house and went with him up the servants' staircase—which wasn't necessary because Wick knew his friend's house as if it were his own. Then Sunny opened the door to his bedchamber and shoved Wick inside. He stumbled a few steps, still trying to clear his foggy, pounding head.

If Mr Mayhew was surprised to see either lord during the middle of a ball, he gave no such sign. He was a young man about their own age. Slim, pale and unassuming, with light brown hair and a hooked nose.

He bowed. 'May I be of assistance, Your Grace?'

'Tidy his clothes and his hair and sober him up, if you please, Mayhew,' Sunny said. 'I don't expect a miracle—just do your best. Then escort him back to the ballroom.'

Wick sighed. 'I know the way.'

'You know nothing,' Sunny said, shutting the door behind him.

Mayhew came up to Wick. 'Why don't you take a seat, my lord? I'll find you a drink that will help clear your mind, and then we can tidy up your appearance.'

Unsteady on his feet, Wick was grateful for the chance to sit down. The valet led him to a chair and Wick closed his eyes. He must have dozed off, for suddenly Mayhew shook his shoulder roughly.

'Lord Cheswick, here is your drink.'

His eyes flickered open and he accepted the glass from the man. Lifting it to his nostrils, he winced. It smelled horrendous. 'What's in this thing?'

''Tis best if you don't know,' Mayhew said, with a faint look of amusement on his face. 'Just swallow the whole thing down as quickly as possible.'

Wick followed his directions, and the concoction tasted even worse than it smelled. For a few moments he feared that he would be sick all over his shoes. But slowly the fog in his brain began to clear, leaving only a pounding headache and a heart full of regret.

Sunny had been right. Drunk or sober, Wick's behaviour at the ball towards Louisa was unpardonable.

He allowed Mayhew to comb his hair and replace his crumpled cravat with a new one belonging to Sunny. Wick usually tied his own cravat, but his hands were shaking too much for him to do a creditable job. Mayhew confided that Sunny never tied his own cravat, and carefully folded Wick's into the mathematical style. Then the valet brushed out the wrinkles in his coat and polished his shoes.

Finally Mayhew helped him to his feet and escorted him down the main staircase and back to the public rooms. Wick wanted to wish the fellow to the devil, but on the stairs he was grateful for his steadying hand underneath his elbow. The valet took him all the way to Sunny, who was standing in the doorway to the ballroom.

'Thank you, Mayhew,' he said with a nod. 'Cheswick, you have arrived at the most opportune time. I was just telling Lady Ashton how eager you are to dance.'

Wick groaned, and Sunny elbowed him sharply in the ribs. Lady Ashton had three unmarried daughters who were all out at the same time, and she was desperately trying to fob them off upon any unsuspecting gentlemen of means. As the wealthy heir to a dukedom, Wick was well worth pursuing.

He glanced at the matron and, sure enough, she was grinning at him. Behind her were three young women who all had blonde hair and willowy figures.

Wick bowed stiffly, still unsteady on his feet. 'Lady Ashton, it is always a pleasure to see you. And you too, Lady Nancy, Lady Eliza and Lady Caroline. Now I have the delightful dilemma of choosing which young lady to lead out first.'

Lady Ashton grabbed the eldest daughter's arm and all but shoved her at him. 'Nancy is particularly fond of the waltz.'

Sunny gave him a little push and Wick held out his hand to Lady Nancy, who accepted it. He led her to the dance floor and took her into his arms. She was pretty enough, but she kept giggling. Waltzing with her felt nothing like dancing with Louisa. It was a slow march of death and he could barely wait for the end of the tune to arrive. Especially when he eyed Louisa waltzing with Lord Fulton. She was giggling too. How he *hated* that perfect dandy.

The tune finally ended, but Wick was only granted a brief reprieve before he had to dance the Roger de Coverley with Lady Eliza. His only solace was that Lady Eliza did not laugh. If anything, she looked disappointed to be stuck with him as a partner. He tried more than once to make eye contact with Louisa, who was now dancing with Mr Beesley. He was a second son, with a respectable reputation and even more respectable fortune. Louisa determinedly wouldn't look in his direction, even when they touched hands in the dance.

But that was what he had wanted—for her to marry someone else. Someone worthy of her.

Wasn't it?

Chapter Twenty-Five

A man was standing near Mantheria when Louisa came into the breakfast room the following morning. His hair was silvered at the sides and his countenance handsome, if a bit wrinkled around his eyes and forehead. Mantheria wore a frown and appeared pale. Even her usually pink lips were devoid of all colour.

She held out her hand to Louisa. 'You've finally awoken, sleepyhead. Allow me to introduce my husband to you. Lord Glastonbury, this is my dear friend Lady Louisa, who is staying with us for the season.'

Louisa took Mantheria's hand and was not sure which of them required the most support from the connection. She was certainly glad to be holding her friend's hand.

Louisa bowed her head. 'It is a pleasure to make your acquaintance, Your Grace.'

Lord Glastonbury bowed to her, but he looked stern. Disapproving. 'I have received a visit from the Earl of Rockingham, my lady. He was most distressed to learn from his wife that you had fled your family home and were in London without the protection of your guardians.'

Louisa could feel the blood drain from her face, and was certain that she was just as pale as the young Duchess. 'Lady Glastonbury has been so very good to me—unlike my own family, who have treated me as if I were a servant in my own home.'

The Duke gave an impatient sigh. 'Be that as it may, it is not proper for my wife—'

'To have not introduced you to our *dearest* friend Lady Dutton.' Mantheria cut him off. 'Something that will have to be remedied immediately. But first, Andrew and my sisters are waiting to go on a walk with us to the park. We must bid you a brief farewell, my dear husband.'

Louisa stood stunned. She knew from Mantheria that Lady Dutton was her husband's long-time mistress. She feared her presence in their home was causing more problems in Mantheria's already troubled marriage.

Still holding her hand, Mantheria dragged Louisa from the room. Louisa wanted to beg for her forgiveness, but they were met in the hall by Andrew, who hugged Mantheria and then Louisa around the legs. The small embrace filled her heart. The little boy had accepted her into the family.

Andrew tugged on her hand. 'You said we were going to the park!'

Mantheria smiled down at her son. 'And we shall. Let us fetch our hats and wraps and we can be on our way.'

They met the other Stringham sisters in the hall. They were already dressed for their walk to Hyde Park. The butler must have been expecting them, for he held both Mantheria's wrap and her own. Their hats were on the table beside him.

Louisa's hands were shaking as she tied the ribbon of her bonnet. She couldn't...*wouldn't* go back to

Greystone Hall and her Aunt and Uncle Rockingham. Her soul could not bear such an existence again. But it appeared that she could not rest on Mantheria's kindness for much longer.

Her only option was to marry—and soon. She needed to repay her friend for the expensive wardrobe they had purchased together. But how could she accept an offer of marriage when she loved Wick? And would her Uncle Rockingham even approve of any of her suitors after she had abandoned her family's home and protection?

'You have all been so very good to me,' Louisa said as they entered the park, chewing on her lower lip. 'I do not know how I will ever repay you.'

Frederica smiled. 'I suggest gold sovereigns.'

'I'll take an exotic snake from South America,' Helen said. 'And I don't mind if it's poisonous. I'd actually prefer it if it was.'

Becca grinned and wiggled her fingers. 'Diamonds. Only diamonds.'

Mantheria laughed. 'I hope you know we are jesting. There is no repayment for friendship, and you needn't feel any rush to pay for your clothing. The money I used was my own, not my husband's. He cannot protest at how I spend my allowance.'

The young Duchess briefly touched Louisa's arm, but it did not make her feel any better. She felt worse to have taken Mantheria's money. She would have much preferred to have borrowed from her unfaithful husband.

Several people waved at them. A few carriages wound their way through the park, and several ladies and gentlemen were on horseback. One of the riders was Sunny, who tipped his hat to them.

He focused on Mantheria's pale countenance. 'Are

you quite well this morning, Your Grace?' he asked so-licitously.

'Why are you being so stuffy this morning, Sunny?' Frederica asked. 'You never call Mantheria by her title.'

'Hush,' Mantheria said, giving her sister a little shove on the shoulder. 'We're in public and he's addressing me correctly.'

'You may call me *Lady* Helen, then,' her other little sister said with a cheeky grin.

Becca giggled. 'Yes, and I am *Lady* Rebecca. You are only a duke after all, Sunny. You mustn't get above your-self.'

Louisa found herself laughing, despite her worries.

Sunny winked at the girl, and said solemnly, 'Thank you for the reminder—Lady Rebecca.'

His eyes went back to Mantheria. Louisa saw her friend's cheeks turn a pretty pink.

'Glastonbury is at home,' she told him. 'One can only pray that he will be invited to another house party soon.'

All the light faded from Sunny's face and Louisa mourned for both of them. For the impossibility of their love.

Touching his hat, Sunny said, 'You may be assured of my support should you ever require it, Your Grace.'

He didn't wait for her answer, but turned his horse and cantered away.

Frederica furrowed her brow. 'What was he talking about, Mantheria?'

But her elder sister only said, 'Hush.'

A carriage pulled up beside them. A woman with dark curls and a pretty face looked at them with interest. Be-side her sat an older female companion.

'Lady Glastonbury, what a delight to have run into you this morning.'

'Lady Jersey.' Mantheria nodded like a queen, her face as pale as marble again. 'Allow me to introduce you to my new friend, Lady Louisa Bracken.'

Louisa kept her eyes up and performed a small curtsy.

The woman smiled at them, her eyes positively sparkling with interest. 'Yes. I have heard *everything* about you, my dear young lady. The reports do not do your beauty justice.'

'Thank you, my lady,' Louisa said breathlessly, a little surprised that such a fashionable lady should take an interest in her.

Mantheria gestured with one hand. 'And these are my sisters, Lady Frederica, Lady Helen, Lady Rebecca, and my son Viscount Chambers.'

Andrew beamed up at the woman and pointed at himself. 'I'm going to be a dook.'

'Of course you are,' Lady Jersey said with a winning smile. 'I know your papa—and I knew yours too, Lady Louisa. He was a fine man.'

Louisa's eyes watered. 'That he was.'

Lady Jersey's gaze moved back to Mantheria. 'I shall send Lady Louisa a voucher for Almack's.'

Mantheria bowed her head again, a hint of a smile on her lips. 'You are too kind, Sally. But also too late. Emily has already sent Louisa one and given her permission to waltz.'

Lady Jersey nodded and said her goodbyes. Her driver urged the horses on.

Becca waited until they were out of earshot to ask, 'What is Almack's and why does Louisa need a voucher?'

'The Almack's Assembly Rooms is only the most exclusive club in London,' Frederica said excitedly. 'And only the *crème de la crème* of society are allowed to attend.'

Helen beamed at her. 'Seven lady patrons decide who is admitted, and they only give those people vouchers.'

Mantheria patted Louisa's arm. 'It is quite a compliment to you that Lady Jersey has singled you out. Usually one asks for a voucher. It is rarely offered without being requested.'

Louisa couldn't help but puff her chest out a little bit. Her Aunt Rockingham had been entirely wrong. Louisa was not ill-favoured and floundering in society. She was being included by the highest sticklers.

Helen squealed. 'You are going to be the toast of London society.'

Becca's stomach grumbled. 'Must you mention food? I am starving.'

Frederica poked her. 'We have only just eaten breakfast.'

Louisa's own stomach turned, but it had nothing to do with hunger. More with anticipation for her long wished-for London season.

Becca grabbed her sister's finger and was twisting it when another carriage pulled up. The Stringham sisters released each other and smiled, as if they hadn't been fighting moments before.

'Viscount Duncannon… Viscountess Duncannon,' Mantheria said with a deferential nod.

'Lady Glastonbury—and your sisters,' a vivacious lady said, looking at them all with great interest. 'Your parents are still in Africa, I believe?'

'Yes,' Mantheria said. 'Mama is hoping to find new plants for her perfumes.'

'Next time you write to her, be sure to mention that I asked after her.'

'I will.'

As they drove away, Frederica whispered. 'Lady Duncannon is Lady Jersey's sister. She is still angling for Mama to make her a scent of her very own.'

'Mama only gives them to her *particular* friends,' Becca explained with a sniff. 'It's quite a social coup to have a perfume made specifically for you.'

The wind picked up and Andrew's little hat flew off his head. It tumbled along the grass towards the Serpentine. Instinctively, Louisa ran after the errant hat. She ducked down to grab it, but the wind took it away again. Holding on to her own bonnet, she chased Andrew's to the rocky shore of the lake. She stepped on it with one foot, before reaching down to pick it up.

She waved the hat. 'I've got it!'

Before she could walk back to Mantheria and the girls, a man wearing black rode his horse in front of her. With one strong hand he hauled her onto his lap. His arm was around her neck, making it hard to breathe.

She dropped Andrew's hat as she tried to scream and kick to free herself. Faintly, she heard the shouts of the Stringham sisters, but the horse's rider urged his steed forward, away from her friends. Twisting to see his face, she saw that it was masked. Whoever it was, he clearly meant her harm.

Using the last of her strength, she jabbed her elbow between the man's legs. He gasped and released his hold on her. Louisa slid off the horse and hit the ground hard, knocking the wind out of her body.

The masked man stopped his horse and turned the animal around, ready to come back for her. Louisa forced herself to her feet and began to run back towards her friends. The sound of the horse's hooves caused her pulse to beat frantically.

She took two more steps before she felt a stunning blow to the back of her head—and then she knew no more.

Chapter Twenty-Six

Wick didn't expect Mantheria's house to be quiet when he arrived. That would be too much to hope for. But he certainly didn't expect to enter a room where Andrew was sobbing and clutching his hat while Mantheria held him, hyperventilating. Frederica was stamping on the floor. Helen was sniffling, tears running freely down her cheeks as her fingers tapped the side of her chair. And Becca held a pencil and paper and was sketching as if her life depended on it. She was a good caricaturist—accurate and unflattering.

'What in heaven's name is the matter?'

Mantheria handed Andrew to his nurse and came towards Wick, taking his hands. 'Louisa's been abducted!'

He squeezed his eyelids shut, shaking his head. 'That's ridiculous. Such things only happen in trashy novels. There must be a logical reason for her disappearance. Perhaps she is visiting a friend.'

Frederica snorted. 'A man dressed in black and on a horse grabbed her right in the middle of Hyde Park.'

Becca set down her pencil. 'She put up a fight and was able to escape his first attempt, but the villain knocked her out cold and carried her off.'

Wick blinked, trying to make sense of their outrageous story. 'In broad daylight?'

'Yes!' all four of his sisters yelled.

Stumbling to a chair, Wick sat down, still trying to process their words. 'Why didn't anyone help her?'

He blinked rapidly, trying to understand who would abduct Lady Louisa and why. And then he remembered his grandfather's words... The current Lord and Lady Rockingham were in debt and Louisa would inherit a fortune. Of course they wouldn't want to let her go. But would they go to such lengths to secure her money?

Helen stopped tapping the chair and put a gentle hand on his forearm. 'We were nearly twenty feet away. Louisa had gone to chase Andrew's hat. It had flown off in the wind. We ran to reach them, but the villain had already got away with Louisa.'

'What are we going to do, Wick?' Mantheria asked.

It was just him and his sisters. He wished his parents weren't on another continent. He would have valued both their experience and their wisdom at this moment.

Wick wet his lips, feeling more vulnerable than he had before in his entire life. Louisa had stolen his heart and now she'd been stolen. It was the thing he'd feared most—losing another person he loved. If only he had accompanied his sisters to the park. He might have stopped the assailant. He was sure of it. Instead, he'd been nursing a hangover. Again, he'd let down someone who trusted him and he cared for.

'You are all going to stay here,' he said, getting to his feet. 'I'll go and speak to Lord and Lady Rockingham and see if they know anything about where Louisa has been taken.'

Mantheria released a long breath. 'That is a prudent place to start.'

'Take my sketch.'

Becca held out her drawing: it was of a man on a horse. The man's face was obscured by a mask, but she had captured with her pencil-tip the horse's bald face and the white mark that reached past its eyes. One of the horse's legs had a white sock.

'You can show my sketch to people and ask if they've seen this horse or this man.'

Mantheria pulled the cord for a servant. 'Please have a carriage brought round immediately for myself and my brother.'

The butler bowed. 'Very good, Your Grace.'

Wick raked his hands through his hair. 'I don't need you to come with me and hold my hand, Mantheria.'

'Good, for I have no intention of holding your hand. I am coming as a chaperone for Louisa. She is my friend, and she will need me to preserve her reputation.'

Chagrined, Wick muttered, 'Sorry.' He hadn't thought about the propriety of being alone with Louisa after she'd been rescued.

'But why would they abduct Louisa?' Helen asked.

Wick was about to answer, but Frederica beat him to it. 'It's obvious to anyone who reads gothic fiction. Clearly they want to force her to marry their horrendous son, so that they'll be able to keep her fortune. A woman's inheritance becomes her husband's upon marriage.'

'That's true,' said Wick, rubbing his chin. 'But what I cannot understand is why an abduction? Unless Lord Barnabas and his parents plan to travel to Scotland a marriage in England takes several weeks to arrange. The banns must be called, or a special licence obtained. But they can hardly extract a special licence for an unwilling bride. The Archbishop of Canterbury would not countenance such a thing.'

'Scotland is an awfully long way away…' Mantheria said dubiously, wrapping the string of her reticule over her wrist. 'The journey there would take a week, even with fast horses and dry roads. It would be hard to transport a prisoner that far without being seen or questioned by local innkeepers.'

Becca leaned forward, her eyes wide. 'Maybe the villain isn't trying to marry her, but to compromise her. So that she *must* marry him.'

Wick's jaw dropped. If Lord Barnabas or any other villain tried to force himself upon Louisa, he would tear them into pieces as a lion ripped apart its prey.

'You don't even know what that means,' Helen said haughtily.

His youngest sister sniffed. 'I asked Frederica, and she explained to me that if a young woman of reputation is alone with a man it is believed that they have behaved like a married couple. And the only way to preserve her good name is for them to marry.'

Frederica rested her chin on her elbow. 'Becca has a point. It would certainly be cheaper, and they would not have to travel as far. And if the man has a cottage or a house within a few hours' ride, then it would be harder for us to track them. The great north road to Scotland is infamous, and a lady without baggage would be memorable. And Louisa's red hair is very noticeable. Every innkeeper on the way would recall her.'

Wick ran his hands through his hair. His sisters were hardly comforting him, but they did make some very good points. And if…no, *when* he found Louisa, at least *he* would not be compromising her by being alone with her. As much as he wanted to.

The door opened and the butler intoned, 'The carriage is ready, Your Grace.'

Wick stood up and Becca launched herself into his arms. Followed by Frederica, Helen and Mantheria. They all piled into the embrace, squeezing the life out of him.

Becca stepped back first. 'Whoever did this is going to regret tangling with the Stringhams.'

Wick could only blink at his sisters. All four of them. Foolishly, he had thought to bear all his grief and problems on his own. But he needn't. In fact, they wouldn't let him. Just as Louisa had told him, his sisters were eager to share his burdens. To lighten them. If only he would let them. Let *her*.

'Forgive me for entering unannounced,' Sunny said, walking through the door. He was still wearing his blue riding coat, but took off his hat. 'I saw what happened at the park. I was too far away to stop the villain, but I chased after him. I watched him put Louisa into a carriage and four that was waiting for them just outside the park. He took off his mask. It was Lord Barnabas Bracken. I followed for several miles, but my horse was already spent. They were headed east, on the road to Windsor and Slough. I decided it was best to come back and get you. But you weren't in your rooms, so I came here.'

Wick stepped forward and hugged his friend. He didn't know which of them was the more surprised by his action. He let go.

'Sunny, I don't know how to—'

'No need, old friend,' Sunny said, clapping a hand on his shoulder. 'I will always be here for you.'

Mantheria touched Sunny's arm and Wick saw the searing look that they shared.

'Will you go and notify Matthew and Grandfather Stubbs about what has happened?' she asked. 'Perhaps they can go and speak to Lord and Lady Rockingham instead of us.'

Sunny nodded. 'As you wish.'

His sister let go of Sunny and Wick almost thought he must have imagined the intense connection between them, but then he saw Mantheria's eyes, full of unshed tears. How would he feel if Louisa was married to another man? The thought made him see red.

'Come, Wick,' Mantheria said, tugging on his arm.

He glanced over his shoulder at his three other sisters. 'But the girls…?'

Mrs May stood at the door. 'Do not worry, my lord. I'll watch over them and keep them out of mischief.'

'Thank you, Mrs May,' Mantheria said. 'You're a treasure.'

Wick could only nod in agreement as he followed his sister out of her house. When they reached the carriage door, he gave the driver instructions to take them to Slough, a village over five-and-twenty miles west of London. There, they would try to discover in which direction the hired carriage had gone.

He thought his heart would explode from his chest before they reached there. He couldn't endure the possibility that her cousin had violated Louisa. Hurt her. If Barnabas had so much as laid a finger on her, Wick would kill him. With or without a duel.

Chapter Twenty-Seven

Louisa opened her eyes, but all she could see was blackness. Had she lost her eyesight from the terrible blow she'd received to the back of her head? Tentatively, she touched the bump with her fingertips and gasped in pain. Her head was aching. She wanted to scream for help—or simply just to scream.

Covering her mouth with her hands, Louisa forced herself to breathe slowly through her nose. She couldn't allow whoever had kidnapped her to know that she was awake. Even though she could not see, she could feel. Her hands and her feet were not bound, nor her mouth. Wherever the man had taken her must be remote, for he did not care if she cried out.

She felt around with her hands, down to her knees and the edge of her gown, pricking her finger on the needle in her hem. It was small and sharp. Hardly a weapon. But it was all she had. She touched the floor; it was made of earth. She reached out her hands around her and felt a couple of wooden barrels and some sort of leafy vegetable in a basket. She closed her fingers on what felt like a carrot.

Her stomach grumbled. Her mouth and throat were dry and sore. She hadn't eaten since breakfast, and she felt positively famished. Wiping the unknown vegetable on her dress, she brought it to her mouth and took a bite. It was indeed a carrot, and even raw it tasted delicious. Louisa chewed as quietly as she could, not wanting to alert her attacker.

Once she had finished the carrot, she felt for the wall and managed to get to her feet. Touching the wall, she followed it until her knee hit some wooden stairs. She cursed beneath her breath and grabbed her sore leg.

'What did you bring your fancy piece here for?' a woman's shrill voice demanded. 'Aren't I enough for you?'

''Course you are, Belinda,' a man said.

Louisa recognised her Cousin Barnabas's voice. She gave a full-body shiver. *The rogue!* She should have known it was him from the start.

'Then why did you bring her to my house?' the woman asked. 'I thought you loved me. *Only* me.'

'I do. I swear it,' he said. 'My cousin is a freckled, ugly woman, and if I didn't need her money she wouldn't be here. But I do. Without Louisa I could not have paid for your cottage or for your fine dresses.'

Louisa gritted her teeth. Her allowance had been used to pay for Barnabas's mistress to wear fine clothes and jewels, whilst Louisa had been given rags. If she hadn't already disliked and distrusted her cousin, she would have hated him now. And she was sure her aunt had known it and not cared. Her villainy seemed to know no bounds.

She blushed as she heard the unmistakable sound of

kissing above her. She supposed that Belinda had forgiven Barnabas for bringing Louisa to her house.

Pressing her ear to the wall, she waited to hear more
words instead of amorous embraces.

'What do you mean to do with her?'

Barnabas cleared his throat; the sound caused Louisa
to shiver again.

'I will have to make it so she must marry me.'

'No, sir. I won't allow a woman to be taken against
her will in my house. Even *I* have morals.'

At least that was something to be thankful for. Louisa would rather die than allow her cousin to touch her.
Kissing Wick had felt beautiful. Pleasurable. The thought
of Barnabas's hands on her filled her mouth with bile.

'I won't lay a finger on her—I swear it,' he said. 'All
I have to do is spend the night in the same house as
her alone and her reputation will be ruined. Louisa will
have no choice but to marry me, and when she does
all of her money will become mine. I need that money,
Belinda—desperately. I have borrowed from a particularly nasty moneylender named Marcus Sullivan, and he
says that if I don't give him what he's owed by the end
of the month he'll murder me. And he ain't the sort of
chap to make idle threats.'

Louisa covered her mouth with her hands to stifle a
gasp. Barnabas would not let her go because his life depended on it.

Louisa heard a few footsteps come closer to where
she stood in the cellar.

'I can't say that I approve, my lord,' the woman named
Belinda said. 'But I suppose it won't do her no harm to
stay a night in my cellar... I've never had a real diamond
necklace, afore... I daresay you'll want to show me how

grateful ye are after I helps you to a fortune and saves your life.'

'I'll buy you a dozen jewels once she is my wife.'

Holding her breath, Louisa tried to keep in her tears. But it was no use. Barnabas was right. He didn't have to touch her to ruin her. Merely the hint of scandal would be enough to have Louisa expelled from society and spurned by the *ton*.

Wiping her running nose with the back of her hand, Louisa knew she would never meet the Queen again.

And Wick.

Just thinking of him made her silently sob harder. She loved him. *Loved* him. And she was pretty sure that he cared for her as well. If only he would allow himself to be happy.

But they would never marry now.

With one blow to her head, Barnabas had dashed all hope of that. Even though it was not her fault Louisa would be ruined. Her reputation would be in tatters. Lady Jersey, Viscountess Duncannon and several other fashionable people had seen her being taken by a man in the middle of Hyde Park. There was no way she could quash the rumours or hope that it would be forgotten. Mantheria had told her that Lady Jersey's nickname was 'Silence' because she could not stop talking. The woman had probably already told people about Louisa's kidnapping...

And even if Wick was willing to believe that nothing had happened, her reputation would be irrevocably ruined. If he married her, Wick would be ruined too. Even his sisters: Mantheria, Frederica, Helen and Becca. All who had treated her with such love and kindness would be tarnished by association. They had become the family she had lost. The friends she had longed for. She couldn't possibly injure them so deeply after all they had done for her.

Louisa laid her head in her lap and cried until there were no more tears inside her. And no hope.

Chapter Twenty-Eight

Several hours in a carriage had not improved Wick's temper. He wished that he had ridden his horse, and knew that he could have made better time without his meddling sister. But she had proved helpful in the search. More helpful than he liked to admit.

It was Mantheria who had learned from another lady in the posting inn where they had stopped that Lord Barnabas's carriage had taken the road to Cookham. Wick nearly exploded with impatience as they waited for a change of horses. Mantheria insisted that he drink something. She drank milk, but he had ale.

Once the horses had been changed, they set off at a spanking pace towards Cookham. Wick told Mantheria's driver to spring the horses. If they needed to get a new set at the next posting inn, then so be it.

If he'd been feeling better, he might have appreciated the quaint Tudor village, with its beautiful redbrick buildings and beam work. The tallest building was Cookham Church, a grey stone edifice that resembled a castle from another era. It sat near a river.

Mantheria pointed out of the window. 'Oh, look, there's

an inn called the Crown. I dare say it is large enough to
have a private parlour for refreshments.'

Wick opened the carriage window. 'Stop at the Crown.'
He closed it with a loud snap. 'You can rest safely in a
private parlour and I'll continue my search alone.'

'I'm not giving up on the search, ninny,' his sister said
indignantly. 'Who better than the proprietor of a coaching in to know if Lord Barnabas has passed through? Or
if he has any haunts nearby.'

The driver opened the door of the carriage and Wick
reluctantly followed his sister out and into the Tudor-style
inn. The first floor was made from redbrick and the second was whitewashed, with triangular wooden beams,
three gables and windows. A short man who was nearly
as broad as he was tall bowed to them. He had a head full
of black hair and a beard that reached past his stomach.

'Can I offer you a private parlour, my lord?' he asked.
'I can tell that you and the lady are members of the quality.'

'Have you seen a carriage and four come through your
town this afternoon?' Mantheria asked.

The innkeeper stroked his beard, shaking his head.
'They didn't stop here if they did...'

What if they had already passed them? What if Louisa
was in mortal danger and he had gone the wrong way?

Wick's muscles were strained and his neck stiff as he
pulled Becca's sketch from his pocket. 'Have you seen
this man or his horse? The horse is brown with a bald
face and a white sock.'

He stroked his beard again. 'I reckon I have, my lord.
It belongs to a gentleman by the name of Mr Barnabas
Brecks, who keeps a cottage with a woman of dubious

morals. He often stops at the Crown when he visits the village.'

So Lord Barnabas had been clever enough not to use his real name or his title.

Wick felt his hands clenching into fists again. 'Have you seen him today?'

The innkeeper shook his head. 'Haven't seen Mr Brecks in a fortnight.'

The villain had not been foolish enough to be seen with Louisa in the village. Lord Barnabas was proving to be not as stupid as Wick had always taken him for. But he was twice as dastardly.

'Where is his cottage?' Mantheria asked.

'I don't rightly know, my lady,' said the innkeeper, shaking his head. 'Somewhere on the opposite side of the river. It's not my business to be nosy.'

'Mr Brecks has abducted a young lady,' Wick said, stepping closer to the innkeeper. 'It is everyone's business to stop him and to rescue her from his clutches.'

The innkeeper's breath hitched. 'But I thought he was a proper toff.'

Mantheria scoffed. 'There's nothing "proper" about him. A true villain he is.'

The short man exhaled slowly and twirled the bottom of his beard around his index finger. 'I don't know where he lives, truly. But there's someone who might.'

'Who?' his sister asked, before Wick could.

'I'd ask at the vicarage.'

Wick rubbed his tired eyes. 'The vicar?'

The innkeeper barked a laugh. 'Nah. Old Reverend Perkins can't see past the end of his nose. But his wife, Mrs Perkins, is the greatest gossip in the county. Nought happens within a ten-mile radius of Cookham that she don't know.'

'Where is the vicarage?' Wick demanded.

The older man pointed down the road towards the church. 'The house next to the church, my lord.'

Wick turned to the door. He had to find Louisa. Every moment counted. She might not have been violated yet. He could still save her.

'You go on foot,' Mantheria said. 'I'll wait with the coachman for the carriage to get a new team of horses and then follow you.'

Wick walked as quickly as he could without running. His heart was pounding and sweat poured down his face by the time he knocked on the door of the stone house next to the church. Taking out a handkerchief from his pocket, he wiped at his face.

A middle-aged woman answered the door. He took off his hat. 'Mrs Perkins?'

The woman shook her head. 'I am the housekeeper, Mrs Daily.'

Reaching into his pocket again, Wick pulled out a bent calling card. 'I am Lord Cheswick and I wish to see Mrs Perkins immediately.'

His title did the trick, and he was ushered into the front parlour.

'I'll go and fetch Mrs Perkins, my lord.'

Wick did not sit down. He could not stop himself from pacing back and forth through the room.

A young woman opened the door, carrying a book in her hands. She appeared to be reading as she walked. Her hair was light brown, and a delicate pair of spectacles were perched at the end of her nose. She had a pretty face with large brown eyes, a petite nose and a prim mouth.

'Forgive me, sir. I did not know that we had company.'

'Then you are not Mrs Perkins?'

'She is my mother. I am Miss Perkins.' The young woman held out her left hand, showing a slim gold band around her third finger. 'But I will be Mrs Wallace in a year or two. Once my fiancé has his own living.'

Wick could not care less about the woman, or her fiancé. 'I wish to speak to your mother about a serious matter. The man known to your village as Mr Brecks is truly Lord Barnabas Bracken, and he has abducted his cousin, Lady Louisa.'

She dropped the book in her hands. 'Good saints!'

An older woman stepped through the open door. 'What is this about Mr Brecks?'

The woman had the same brown hair, and a matching pair of spectacles, but there were lines around her eyes and mouth. She had to be Mrs Perkins.

'I believe that a man named Mr Brecks keeps a cottage near Cookham for a...' *could he say mistress in front of a vicar's wife?* '...a kept woman. I also believe that it is where he has taken his cousin, Lady Louisa, after abducting her in a London park.'

Mrs Perkins gasped and brought her hands to her chin. 'I always knew there was evil in that young man.' She curtsied to Wick. 'It is a great pleasure to make your acquaintance, Lord Cheswick.'

Wick didn't have time to be toad-eaten. He cleared his throat. 'Do you know where the cottage is?'

The vicar's wife moved her hand from her chin to her neck. 'Cross the bridge and head west for a mile. You'll see a road. No, it is barely more than a path... The path will lead you another two miles until you reach a white-washed cottage.'

Miss Perkins pushed her spectacles up her nose. 'I had better come with you. It is already getting dark. You'll never find the path on your own.'

Mrs Perkins nodded. 'Yes, daughter.'

Wick thanked them both profusely, wishing that they could leave that very second.

The sound of horses caused him to look out through the front window. By some miracle, Mantheria's carriage was in front of the vicarage.

'I'll grab my bonnet,' Miss Perkins said, dashing from the room.

Wick walked out of the house and opened the door to see the carriage was being drawn by a fresh team of horses. He opened the carriage door and saw Mantheria, sitting in the middle of the seat, eating a sprig of grapes.

'Would you like one? The innkeeper said I was looking peaky.'

Wick could only shake his head and turn back to the house as he heard Miss Perkins's footsteps. Her bonnet was already tied securely around her neck and there was a shawl around her shoulders. The young woman was certainly efficient.

'I shall ride with the driver,' she informed him. 'It will be impossible for me to see the way from inside the carriage.'

'Very well.'

Wick helped Miss Perkins up to the driver's perch and climbed into the carriage next to his sister. He opened the window so that he could hear the young woman's brisk voice, giving instructions to the driver.

Somehow it seemed that the last couple of miles of their trip were taking as long as their entire journey to Cookham.

Chapter Twenty-Nine

Belinda giggled loudly and Louisa stood up, covering her ears with her hands. She'd heard quite enough, and she had no intention of sitting in the cellar and waiting for Barnabas to fetch her in the morning. None of the Stringhams would sit and accept their fate. They would fight for what they wanted. And Louisa would too!

She'd found the stairs again. Once it was quiet above her, and she could be reasonably sure that it was night-time—it was impossible to tell in the dark—she would escape the cellar and make a run for it. Neither Barnabas, her aunt, nor her Uncle Rockingham were going to get another penny of her money. She was going to return to London. To her season. To the courtship she'd waited for her entire life. She wasn't going to let her aunt, her uncle or her cousin take another dream from her.

Never again.

Listening to her cousin and Belinda eat was making her stomach grumble. Louisa ate two more carrots, but they did not taste as nice. Delicious smells were wafting from the kitchen. Trust her cousin to choose a mistress who was as good in the kitchen as in the bedroom. She heard the scraping of forks and knives, but not their conversation. She did not think it was a great loss.

Leaning her head against a stair, she waited until there were no more sounds in the house. Then, crawling up the wooden stairs, she held a hand in front of her face so that she wouldn't hit her head on the cellar door. One more step up and she felt wood above her. Taking a deep breath, she pushed against the door. It didn't move at all. It must be locked.

Louisa used both hands to feel around the door for a lock. The wood was rough, and she felt more than one splinter enter her fingertips, but she did not stop until she felt metal. Touching it with her sore fingers, she found the keyhole. Obviously she didn't have a key. Or a weapon of any kind.

All she had was her needle. It would have to do.

One side of her mouth quirked up into a half-smile as she thought, *A lady doesn't need a sword as long as she has a sewing needle handy.*

Louisa pulled the needle out of her hem and carefully held the eye of it, while placing the sharp point into the lock. She stabbed and pressed with it. Nothing happened. Her eyes filled with tears and she longed to cry out her heart at the injustice of it all. She had finally reached London, had been presented to the Queen and attended *ton* parties. She had friends and fine gowns and handsome suitors...

Wick was unlike the men in her family in every way. He listened to and respected the women in his life. He bore his sisters' teasing and gave them their own back again. And he was thoughtful. She would never forget the soft expression on his face when he'd pulled out of his pockets the kittens for his little sisters. It was clear that he loved them just as they were. He didn't expect them to change into someone else to be worthy of being loved. Wick wanted the very best for them.

Oh, how Louisa longed to be loved by Wick too.

Blast Barnabas!

Louisa might be ruined, but she would not give him the satisfaction of marrying her for her money. If anyone would be buying jewels with her inheritance, it would be her. She was not the same docile creature who had left her aunt and uncle's home. Louisa felt strong and free. She would never cower before her relatives again, begging for a scrap of affection.

She pressed the needle into the lock once more. She felt it catch something. Pushing harder with the needle, she felt the eye stabbing at her finger, but she could not stop. Would not stop. At last, she heard a click. Louisa dropped the needle. There was no way to find it in the dark, so she didn't bother to try. She placed both hands on the cellar door and slowly lifted it up. The door was heavy, but she was determined. Louisa stepped on the highest stair and used her whole body's weight to push the door open. The hinges creaked loudly, and before Louisa could stop it the door fell backwards with a loud crash.

Blinking, she let her eyes adjust to the dim light. She wasn't blind. It was growing dark outside. She needed a weapon. Something to defend herself with. Louisa grabbed the kettle off the stove.

She ran across the kitchen towards the front door, but her cousin Barnabas was standing in front of it, wearing only his breeches. His bare stomach was hanging over his waistband. It was more of him than she'd ever wished to see.

He held a candle up to her face. 'How'd you get out?'

'It doesn't matter,' Louisa spat, holding the kettle like a cricket bat. 'I'd rather die than marry you, and I don't give a fig about my reputation.'

Barnabas sneered at her. 'No one will marry you after this. You're damaged goods now. Your only choice is to marry me. And don't worry—I'll leave you well enough alone. You can take care of Greystone Hall, as you have your whole life.'

'But will you leave me alone, cousin?' Louisa said loudly, so that his mistress would hear. 'Won't you need a son and heir for the earldom?'

'Shouldn't take too long. My aunt had you nine months after her marriage to my uncle.'

'A girl—not a son and heir. If you have any hope of continuing your line, you'll have to give up Belinda— and your other mistress who lives in Tunbridge Wells.'

The 'other mistress' was a fabrication, for Louisa had seen that Belinda now stood in the bedroom door. Happily, the woman was wearing more clothes than her cousin.

'You've got another girl in Tunbridge Wells?' Belinda said, throwing one of her boots at Barnabas's head. 'You gib-faced villain.'

The boot hit her cousin in the ear. Barnabas dropped the candle and covered his head with his arms. 'I never have, Belinda, love. She's lying to you.'

The mistress eyed Louisa with suspicion. Louisa held up the kettle. 'He's already planning to marry me— surely you don't think he'll stay faithful to you for long? Nor give you a diamond necklace? He'll pay off Mr Sullivan and leave you high and dry. I hope the deed to this cottage is in your name. Or he'll throw you out of it for his next mistress.'

Belinda hurled the second boot at Barnabas and it, too, caught him on his ear. The candle he'd dropped had now started a fire on the rug at his feet.

Louisa held up the kettle and advanced on her cousin. 'Let me out or I will strike you.'

Barnabas put a hand on each side of the door. 'I'll be dead before I let you out of my sight.'

'I will not marry you. *Ever!*'

'You have to. Mother says so,' he said. 'I owe over one hundred thousand pounds. Besides, you don't want the moneylender to kill me, do you? Your own cousin.'

Gaming. Her idiot cousin must have lost a fortune on cards and he'd been too stupid to stop after his staggering losses.

Louisa's swallowed. 'Your debts are not my responsibility.'

Her mind felt foggy…it was probably all the smoke in the room. The fire was growing. She had to do something.

Taking the kettle in her hands, she poured the contents onto the burning rug. It doused most of the flames, but didn't quite put them out. Then Louisa felt a strong arm push her away and saw Belinda throwing a blanket over the rug to smother the remaining flames. Belinda stamped on the blanket until Louisa was fairly certain that the fire was out.

'Some help you were, rum 'un!' Belinda yelled at Barnabas. 'Ye nearly burned down my cottage and did nothing to put the fire out.'

Barnabas opened his arms to his mistress. 'I swear,

I love none but you, my darling. But I had to guard the door. I couldn't let my cousin escape.'

Her cousin's broad form still blocked Louisa's way out as Belinda allowed him to put his arms around her. Then Louisa heard a clunk and a thud and her cousin's body hit the floor.

Belinda was holding the kettle. She must have struck Barnabas with it. He was sprawled out at her feet.

Louisa gulped, touching the column of her throat. 'Is he dead?'

Belinda pushed back her hair with her free hand. 'Nah… He'll wake with a bloody headache in a bit, and then I'll kick him out. I've got no need for a broke protector.'

Louisa's eyes stung from the smoke, and she couldn't quite believe what she saw. 'I am glad. He is quite odious, but I didn't want him dead.'

'Run for it, love,' Belinda said with a wink. 'Before he wakes up and tries to stop you. Thanks for saving my cottage. 'Tis bought and paid for in my name.'

Louisa didn't have to be told twice. She gave a thankful nod to Belinda and dashed out through the front door. Outside the cottage it was dark and wooded, and she didn't know which way to go. But the farther she was from her cousin when he woke up, the better.

She continued to run, her throat dry and her lungs burning.

Chapter Thirty

⁓⁓⁓∞⊙∞⁓⁓⁓

The sound of Mantheria's chewing grated on Wick's nerves. How could she eat at a time like this?

He kept glancing out of the window—not that it helped much. It was growing too dark to see anything more than the outlines of trees. He was glad that Miss Perkins had accompanied them. He doubted if Mantheria's driver would have been able to find a rarely used path at this time of night with only the light from the carriage lanterns.

Suddenly the carriage turned sharply and his sister gasped as they almost slid off the seat. The path seemed to be made of stones, for they all bumped up and down for a most uncomfortable mile or two.

Wick knew they must be close when he smelled smoke. When the vehicle came to a stop, he swung the door open and saw a cottage with its front door ajar and a lantern lit on the table. Pulling his pistol out, he cocked it. He rushed in to see Lord Barnabas on the floor and a pretty buxom woman sweeping up what appeared to be the remnants of a fire. Even with the door open, the smell of smoke was strong in the room.

'If you're looking for the lady,' the woman said, pointing, 'she dashed out five minutes ago. I told her to hop to it before he awoke.'

Wick swallowed; his mouth tasted of ash. 'Was she harmed in any way?'

The woman shook her head and leaned against her broom. 'A regular firecracker, that one. Escaped the cellar and stood up to His Lordship. Then the clunch dropped a candle and she helped put out the fire. So I knocked him out and told her to run for it. 'Twere the least I could do after she saved my cottage.'

Louisa had been locked up. Had she also been ravished? He had to find her.

Miss Perkins entered the cottage and pushed up her spectacles. 'Miss, do you know in which direction she went?'

'No.'

'Thank you,' Miss Perkins said, and then gestured to the prone Lord Barnabas on the floor. 'Do you require any assistance with Mr Brecks?'

The mistress snorted. 'Nah. I'll send him on his way as soon as he can stand upright. 'Tis my cottage, after all.'

Wick had no sympathy for an abductor and possible rapist. 'Thank you for your information, madam.'

The woman winked at him. 'It's *miss*.'

He could only nod and make good his escape from the smoky cottage.

Miss Perkins trailed behind him. The door to the carriage was still ajar and Mantheria was sitting on the edge of her seat.

'Where's Louisa?'

Wick took a deep breath, his chest swelling with pride. 'Escaped on her own.'

Mantheria clapped her hands. 'Bravo!'

'But we do not know where,' Miss Perkins reminded him.

He stretched out his hand to help his sister out of the carriage. 'Miss Perkins, may I introduce you to my sister, the Duchess of Glastonbury?'

Miss Perkins curtsied, but didn't appear overly awed by his sister's title. 'It appears that Lady Louisa has gone into the woods. I think it would be best if we were to go in pairs, taking the lanterns from the carriage, and spread out about twenty feet so that we may cover the largest amount of ground. Each group can take a pistol, and if one group locates her they can fire a shot in the air to let us all know to come back to the carriage.'

'Excellent,' Mantheria said. 'Miss Perkins, would you like to go with my brother or my driver?'

The young woman took a deep breath. 'Your coachman, Your Grace.'

Mantheria instructed her coachman to take down the lanterns and bring his pistol. Miss Perkins sent him and Mantheria in a north-western direction, whilst she and the driver went off in south-east. It was efficient and effective. Wick couldn't help but be impressed with her skills in managing a duchess and an irritable marquess.

Mantheria held the lantern in one hand and Wick's hand in the other. She squeezed it tightly as they stepped into the unfamiliar woods.

Wick cleared his throat. 'Louisa! Louisa!'

His sister's voice echoed his and she held up the lantern like a beacon. The forest was thick with trees, and Wick hoped that Louisa would see their light through them.

He called her name again, and then waited for a response.

Nothing.

Goosebumps formed on Wick's arms as he worried that she might have fallen and been hurt. That she wouldn't be able to see their light or hear their words. But then he remembered the saucy woman's words. Louisa had escaped the cellar *and* the cottage. She was strong.

'Louisa!' Mantheria yelled.

After a short pause, Wick heard a voice in the distance.

'I'm here.'

He dropped Mantheria's hand and cupped his fingers around his mouth. 'Keep talking so that we can find you,' he shouted.

Taking his sister's hand again, he followed Louisa's voice until he saw her sitting on the ground, leaning against a tree. The lantern's light shone on her face, which was dirty with soot and dust.

Louisa's hand was on her side and she was breathing heavily. 'I'm so thirsty. I haven't had anything to drink since before we went to the park.'

Wick stooped down beside her, desperate to touch her. Hold her. 'We will get you some water as soon as possible. Would you like me to carry you?'

Before Louisa could answer, he felt a tap on his shoulder. Glancing over, he saw Mantheria.

'Miss Perkins said we had to fire a shot when we found Louisa, so that the other search parties would know to return to the carriage.'

Again, he was amazed by how well thought-out Miss Perkins's plans were. Wick took the pistol out of his pocket and handed it to her. 'Care to do the honours?'

Mantheria nodded eagerly, setting down her lantern and taking the weapon from him. Like all his sisters, Mantheria knew how to handle a shooting piece. She cocked the hammer back and fired a shot in the air. The sound echoed in the night.

Louisa took a deep breath and then released it. 'Did Belinda tell you where I was?'

'Who is Belinda?' Mantheria asked.

Louisa took another breath before she answered. 'My cousin's mistress. Although I doubt she will be for much longer. He is in debt for over one hundred thousand pounds to a moneylender, and without coin Barnabas is of no interest to her.'

Wick let out a low whistle. He had known that Lord Barnabas played high; but he'd never have guessed his debts would amount to that.

'Shall I carry you?' he asked, for the second time.

She shook her head. 'I can walk, but I won't say no to leaning on your arm.'

Wick helped Louisa to her feet and she leaned heavily against him. Mantheria picked up the lantern and walked in front of them, back towards the cottage. He wrapped his arm around her waist, half carrying her. When they arrived at the carriage Miss Perkins and the driver had already returned.

Miss Perkins climbed up into the carriage seat. 'Hand her up to me.'

Wick did so, and Louisa leaned against the stranger.

Miss Perkins pointed to Mantheria. 'Do you have any water or wine?'

'In the basket on the seat behind you,' his sister said, climbing into the carriage to hold Louisa while the other woman uncorked the wine and placed it to Louisa's pale lips.

Wick was glad that she didn't force too much down Louisa's throat, only small sips.

'Shall we take her back to the Crown?' Mantheria asked him.

Wick said, 'Yes.'

Just as Miss Perkins said, 'No.'

'Excuse me, my lord,' she said, 'but I believe that there will be less talk if she spends the night at the vicarage rather than a coaching inn. Your sister as well. I promise that my mother and I will take care of them both.'

A surge of gratitude filled his heart. 'Thank you, Miss Perkins. You truly are an exemplar of Christian kindness. I'll give direction to the driver.'

He closed the door to the carriage and climbed up on the perch next to the coachman. 'The Cookham vicarage, if you please. And you can take it a little slower this time.'

The man touched his hat. 'Aye, my lord.'

The trip back to the vicarage passed by in a blur. Wick hoped—prayed—that Louisa had not been violated. That her injuries were only from her escape and the smoke and not from the body of her cousin. But even if she had been violated it would not change how he thought of her. Her virtue and her worth were not like chicken drumsticks, to be chewed up and discarded only once. Besides, his concern was not for her reputation, but for her heart. Her feelings. For the emotional scars that people could not see. Scars like the ones he possessed...

He climbed off the perch and opened the carriage door for Mantheria and Miss Perkins.

'Wick, stay with Louisa whilst we get her room ready,' his sister told him, and then followed Miss Perkins into the house.

Stepping into the carriage, he saw that Louisa was sitting up, but leaning against the squabs. 'I am quite fine, Wick. Only very dirty and very tired. The next time I escape I will make sure to drink some of the water from the kettle before I douse any fire.'

Wick sat beside her, his knee touching hers. 'I hope that there will never be a next time.'

Louisa bit her lower lip. 'I can't help but agree with you. Being abducted gives one a terrible headache.'

His hand gently touched her hair, caressing it lightly. 'I dare say you have a large bruise. My little sisters said that you were hit quite hard in the park.'

She inclined her head forward slightly and winced. 'Yes. Barnabas knocked me out. I didn't wake up until I was in the cellar.'

'Then he didn't—?'

'Oh, no. Belinda told Barnabas that she would not allow a woman to be taken against her will in her cottage. I find that I like her a great deal more than my cousin.'

Wick knew that Louisa was attempting to lighten the situation with humour, but it was too soon for him. His feelings were raw and his heart felt as if it had been scraped over a washboard.

'How did you escape from the knave?' he asked.

'With my sewing needle,' Louisa explained. 'Barnabas had planned to keep me in the cellar until morning and then claim to have compromised me. But I was able to use the needle from the hem of my dress to pick the lock. Except I made too much noise, and my cousin blocked the front door. I said some things to make his mistress jealous, and she threw her boots at him, causing him to drop a candle and set fire to a rug. But he still blocked the door, so I helped put out the fire. In gratitude for my efforts, Belinda knocked out my cousin and helped me escape.'

'She knew that he had locked you in the cellar?'

Louisa swallowed, her throat dry. 'Well, yes...'

'Then she is an accessory to the kidnapping,' Wick said. 'And should be reported to a justice of the peace.'

Louisa brought her hands together, wringing them. 'Oh, please don't. Belinda helped me, and Barnabas will get his comeuppance soon enough from his creditors.'

Wick only wished Barnabas's comeuppance could be at his own hands. Or rather fists.

'Louisa, I—I don't know how to express how sorry I am that this has happened. That I was not there for you. That I didn't protect you from your pernicious cousin.'

She placed her scratched and dirty hand on top of his. 'I protected myself, Wick—something I would not have dared to do if it hadn't been for you and your sisters. You showed me that I am strong. That I am capable. You need not feel any guilt on my account. You carry too much guilt already.'

Turning his hand so that his palm was underneath hers, he intertwined their fingers. 'I don't deserve your absolution. But I promise if you ever need me, I will come.'

'You have my absolution all the same,' she whispered. 'And I think both Charles and Elizabeth would give you theirs as well... I can tell when you speak of them how much you loved them, and I am sure they loved you too. They would want you to be happy, healthy—and whole. Yes, you should miss them, and mourn them. But you must let go of the guilt that is dragging you down. Live a life worthy of their love.'

Worthy.

Louisa had used that word again. She had said last night that he was worthy of her love, but the events of today proved that he wasn't.

'The room's ready, Wick,' Mantheria said from outside the carriage.

Wick half carried Louisa into the house and up to the room that Mrs Perkins and her daughter had prepared for her. He saw two female servants carrying buckets of water to Louisa's room for a bath. He would have been happy to help, but he was shown, politely, to the door.

He climbed back into the carriage alone and told the driver to take him to the Crown. Uncorking the wine, he took a long swig. Louisa had already spent most of her life unloved and neglected—he didn't want anything to hurt her again.

He should have protected her.

Wick had failed her as he had failed Charles and Elizabeth.

He was not in any way *worthy* of her.

Chapter Thirty-One

*N*ever *has a bath felt better,* Louisa thought, sinking underneath the hot water until it reached her nose.

Leaning her head back against the copper tub, she took a ragged breath. Her throat felt as if she had swallowed stones. She coughed, and the door to her room opened. The bespectacled young woman walked in with a glass of water.

The stranger gave Louisa a reassuring smile. 'I thought you might be thirsty.'

Louisa greedily accepted the glass, and quickly emptied the contents down her dry throat. She swallowed. 'I am afraid that we have not been properly introduced. Although it seems a little silly to have an introduction when I am in the bath. I am Lady Louisa Bracken—but you are welcome to call me Louisa.'

The pretty young woman pushed her spectacles up the bridge of her nose. 'I am Mary Perkins. I would be pleased if you would call me Mary. We might as well be on a Christian name basis, for you are about to wear one of my nightdresses.'

'We have both stolen Mary's clothes, I'm afraid,' Mantheria said from the door.

She came into the room, her long blonde hair in one plait over her shoulder. Her face was still pale in the candlelight. She was wearing a prim white nightgown that buttoned up to her neck. The hem of the gown reached the floor.

Mantheria pushed up the long white sleeves and knelt beside the copper tub. She picked up a sponge and set it in the soapy water.

'I can do that,' Louisa said, quickly. She was embarrassed to be waited upon by the Duchess and naked in front of a stranger.

Mantheria squeezed out the sponge. 'I'll have you know that Andrew gives me high marks for my scrubbing. Andrew is my son, Mary. Now, lean forward like a good girl and I'll scrub your back.'

Too tired to protest, Louisa leaned forward in the tub and allowed Mantheria to wash her neck, her back, her arms and even her hair. Then her friend handed her the sponge and Louisa washed the front of herself, before stepping out of the tub and into a robe held by Mary. Mantheria handed her a towel and Louisa dried herself as best as she could.

Both ladies helped her into a nightgown and tucked her into bed as if she were a small child like Andrew.

Louisa took both Mantheria's and Mary's hands. 'I cannot thank you enough for finding me and helping me.'

'It was my pleasure, my lady,' said Mary.

'Louisa.'

Mary curtsied to Mantheria and then pushed up her glasses with her free hand. 'Louisa. I will leave you two alone. I am sure you have much to discuss.'

She watched Mary walk to the door and quietly close it behind her.

Mantheria sat down on the edge of the bed, still lightly holding Louisa's hand. 'Of course I would come to find you. I am your chaperone, after all, and your friend. Although I seem to have been doing a poor job of being both. I should have protected you better. If only I had taken a footman with us to the park.'

Louisa shook her head against the pillow. 'Nonsense. Both you and your brother take too much responsibility upon yourselves and give yourselves too little credit in return. No one, especially myself, could blame you for my cousin's actions. And, as I have already told your brother, I was not ravished.'

A tear slid down Mantheria's cheek. 'I believe you, dearest Louisa, but that doesn't change the circumstances. Nor the rumours that will spread about your reputation.'

'You mean that I have been compromised?'

Sniffing, her friend nodded. 'The *ton* doesn't care about the truth—they only care about appearances. The only way to save your reputation and good name is to have the protection of a gentleman's name.'

Marriage.

But she didn't want a loveless marriage like Mantheria's. Nor did she wish to rely so heavily on her friend in the future. Louisa wanted to be independent. To forge her own destiny. She had finally awoken from the dream that was the Stringham clan. She loved them, but she would never be one of them. Not truly.

'I am so sorry if my presence in your home has caused more problems in your marriage,' Louisa said. 'What a poor way to repay your many kindnesses. I will find a new situation as soon as possible.'

Mantheria sniffed, shaking her head. 'Glastonbury and I were not arguing about you... I finally confronted him about Lady Dutton and asked if we could have a *divortium a mensa et thoro*.'

Louisa coughed. 'I don't know what that means.'

'It's Latin. Roughly translated, it means a separation of bed and board.'

Louisa brought a hand to cover her mouth. 'And what did he say?'

'Alexander told me the same thing my solicitors had— that we cannot have a legal separation because he has not beaten me nor treated me cruelly.'

Louisa knew all too well that words could inflict as much violence upon a person as fists. 'Flaunting his mistress in front of your face is cruelty enough.'

Mantheria held up a hand and Louisa closed her mouth.

'Glastonbury also does not want to cut me and Andrew off financially, which must be a part of an ecclesiastical separation. He suggested that instead we honour the spirit of the law. That he will find a separate living situation.'

'No doubt with Lady Dutton?'

'Most likely,' she said, exhaling. 'But he said that I can keep our London house for myself and Andrew, as well as use any of the Glastonbury estates. His only request was that he is to be able to visit Andrew frequently. Which I acceded to. He deserves to have his father in her life.'

Louisa thought of Sunny. 'And you deserve to have your own life.'

More tears fell down her cheeks. 'My life will have to be my son. Once my husband and I are separated, I will have to be more circumspect than ever in my social interactions in order to keep my position. I can't afford to give the gossips any reason to have my name on their lips.'

'I understand,' Louisa said, swallowing down a lump in her throat. 'I will not besmirch your name.'

Mantheria shook her head and tears fell on the coverlet. 'No, you do not understand. I meant Sunny, not you, Louisa. You are welcome to stay with us forever. Only, I am not sure how many invitations I will receive after the news of the breakdown of my marriage becomes known. Or if I will still be considered a proper chaperone for you.'

'Wherever I live, you must allow me to repay the monies you lent me,' Louisa said, sitting up. 'You shall need them now more than ever. And I will beg upon my knees to my trustees if I have to.'

Mantheria wiped her nose with her sleeve—very un-duchess-like. 'I don't think that will be necessary quite yet. After the behaviour of Lord Barnabas, I believe your trustees will see how unsuitable your Aunt and Uncle Rockingham have been as your guardians. I am sure my grandfather and Matthew will be able to wrest control of your fortune from them and pass it to you. No one is equal to my brother Matthew with a pen. If you gave him enough paper he could write the stars down from the sky and sell you the moon at a discount.'

Louisa forced herself to smile. 'I've always wanted the moon.'

'And I a bright and particular star,' Mantheria whispered, pressing her lips against Louisa's forehead before leaving the room with the candle.

Louisa leaned back against the pillow and closed her eyes. Sunny was Mantheria's bright particular star, yet they could never be together. Sunny had foolishly thought himself too young to court her, and Mantheria had married another. Despite being compromised, Louisa would not make the same mistake. For in her mind nothing could be worse than to be married to one gentleman and in love with another.

She would be much better off on her own. With or without proper society.

Chapter Thirty-Two

Wick's legs and arm muscles tightened, as if he were about to run. He took a deep, calming breath, reminding himself that Louisa was safe now. But still he only felt relief when the carriage ride was over and he stood in front of the vicarage. The housekeeper from the day before led him into a small parlour, where Mantheria sat with both Mrs and Miss Perkins.

'Where's Louisa?'

Mantheria stood up and offered her hands. 'Still sleeping.'

Wick squeezed her hands before letting go of them and recalling his manners. He bowed to the other ladies, who had also risen to their feet because of his entrance. 'I hope I haven't called at an inconvenient time.'

'Of course not, my lord,' Mrs Perkins said, giving him a friendly smile.

Miss Perkins pushed up her spectacles and gave him a wide-eyed stare. 'Perhaps we should go and check on Lady Louisa, Mama? I am sure Lord Cheswick would like to speak to his sister in private.'

Mrs Perkins touched her chest. 'Of course, my dear.

How thoughtful you are. And shall I call for some tea, my lord?'

Wick's stomach grumbled, but he didn't want tea. 'None for myself, thank you. But I am sure Lady Louisa would be glad of a cup.'

'Yes,' Miss Perkins said, and guided her mother out of the room by her elbow.

Once the door was closed, Wick sat down on the sofa next to Mantheria. She was wearing the same dress as the day before and it looked a little worse for wear. 'How is she truly?'

'Shaken, yet determined to assert her independence,' his sister said. 'One can hardly blame her with a family like the Rockinghams... But we both know that it will not do. There is no true independence for women in our society. She cannot remain unmarried long.'

Wick nodded his head gravely. 'I intend to propose to her. I will offer her the protection of my name.'

'I think Louisa would prefer the protection of your heart.'

His throat tightened. 'I cannot offer what I do not have.'

'A heart?' she said, shaking her head. 'Of course you do not have a heart—you've already given it to Louisa, if only you weren't too stubborn to see it.'

Wick scrambled to his feet and walked to the window. His feelings were too raw to be shared.

'And I have solved your other problem,' Mantheria continued. 'I think that Miss Perkins would be an ideal governess for our sisters. Mary—Miss Perkins—said something last night about having to wait a few years for marriage. I am sure that some additional income would be welcome before her wedding, and I am sure you would pay her well.'

Turning back to face his sister, he asked, 'Does she have any experience teaching?'

Mantheria waved that consideration aside with one hand. 'You don't need a scholar, Wick. You need someone to teach our sisters who doesn't go into hysterics over their pets or feel shocked over their behaviour... Miss Perkins didn't bat an eye over an abduction or a fire. She's perfect.'

'You have strange requirements in a governess,' Wick said, trying hard not to smile. 'No wonder none of the candidates from the agency fits the bill.'

Mantheria jumped to her feet. 'I had better ask Mary how she feels about snakes.'

'And elephants,' Wick added.

'Giraffes.'

'Bloodsucking ichneumons.'

Mantheria giggled and her shoulders shook. 'Kangaroos.'

'Cockatoos.'

'Ostriches and emus.'

'And don't forget the llama or the monkeys,' he said. 'If she is willing to put up with all the animals, we had better employ her on the spot.'

His sister threw back her head and laughed again, loudly. 'Little does the poor woman know that the animals are much better behaved than our sisters.'

The door opened again several minutes later, and Mrs and Miss Perkins came back into the room. Miss Perkins chose a seat next to her mother on the settee.

Wick cleared his throat. 'Miss Perkins, my sister and I have been impressed by your competence and character. We are wondering if you would be willing to accept as position as governess to my three little sisters, aged thirteen, fifteen and nearly seventeen.'

Mrs Perkins blinked and looked at her daughter. 'Governess?'

Miss Perkins didn't bat an eyelash. She sat perfectly still, as if considering his proposition.

Wick knew that a typical governess only received between ten and twenty pounds per annum. He would offer five times that.

'I should pay you the wage of one hundred pounds a year, in addition to your room and board. I am sure that such funds will be of use in your upcoming marriage.'

'I have never been a governess before,' Miss Perkins said. 'I fear, my lord, that my lack of experience would be a disappointment to you.'

Wick stood up taller. 'I don't give a fig about your experience. I am looking for someone who will have a degree of influence over my sisters. I know that they will never be controlled. It isn't their nature and I wouldn't want it to be. I only wish for a kind and well-mannered woman who can curb their more dangerous expeditions and will not have hysterics when they bring home snakes or other wild beasts.'

'I am not prone to hysterics.'

Mantheria smiled at the young woman. 'I noticed how calm and collected you were during last night's crisis. That is why I suggested the idea to my brother. I think you will be the perfect governess for my younger sisters.'

A little colour stole into Miss Perkins's cheeks and her glasses fogged up. 'I am well-versed in the Bible and English literature, but I do not speak French or Italian.

And, whilst I can play the pianoforte, I would not consider my skill anything worth mentioning.'

Wick waved his hand. 'Frederica already speaks both French and Italian, and she can play the pianoforte very well. You would only need to encourage her to practise. And Helen has no interest in music—she is a naturalist at heart. She would enjoy it most if you read the same books as her and collected insects. She doesn't believe in pinning them to boards, though. She thinks it's rather barbaric and so do I. And Becca... Well, my Becca is a sharp and talented young artist. But she has difficulty reading and she was teased at her former school. Her last governess called her slow.'

Mrs Perkins gasped, bringing her hands to her cheeks. 'The nerve of the woman, to speak to your sister that way. I hope that you sent her packing?'

'She left of her own accord,' he admitted. 'And she wasn't the first governess to find my sisters' strong natures too difficult to handle.'

'I do believe that I would be happy as their governess as long as you do not have any unrealistic expectations of my abilities,' Miss Perkins said slowly.

Mantheria clapped her hands. 'Hurrah!'

'And Becca?' he couldn't help but clarify. 'You'll be kind to her and help her with her reading?'

'I shall certainly never call her names,' Miss Perkins said, taking off her glasses and rubbing the lenses clean with her handkerchief. 'And I would be happy to help her with her reading. But I do not know that I will be any more successful at it than the previous governesses.'

He appreciated her honesty. 'Excellent—you shall be our new governess... Are you able to come to London with us today, or shall we send a carriage for you in a few days?'

Mrs Perkins stood up quickly. 'I shall go and have the servants prepare my daughter's trunk at once.'

She bustled out of the room and they could hear her voice in the hall, calling for a maid.

'I do not think we are in that great deal of a hurry, Mary,' Mantheria said with a little chuckle. 'We must wait for Louisa as well.'

But Miss Perkins had also got to her feet. 'Lady Glastonbury… Lord Cheswick, I should like to be ready to leave when you are. If you will excuse me? I must say my goodbyes to my father.'

Miss Perkins reached the door just as Louisa walked into the room. Wick did not recognise the gown she wore, and it looked as ill-fitting on her as Miss Young's dress had, that first night she'd arrived at Hampford Castle. It was tight on her shoulders and at least six inches too short on her legs. Her face, however, looked pink and fresh and healthy.

'I am afraid I was a bit of a slugabed this morning,' she said. 'Where are you off to, Mary?'

Miss Perkins pushed up her slipping spectacles with her index finger. 'Louisa, I have been offered the position of governess to the Stringham sisters.'

Louisa beamed at her. 'Oh, I am sure the girls will love you—and you them.'

Mantheria got to her feet as well, and walked to the door. 'I will help Miss Perkins pack.'

She closed the door behind her, leaving Louisa alone with Wick. Something that she had never done before, since she was supposed to be acting as her chaperone.

It took him only a few seconds to realise that his sister expected him to propose to Louisa right now.

Taking a deep breath, he wished he'd had a little more time to prepare. He walked back to the window and looked outside. What should he say? Should he kneel?

'Perhaps I should go and help Mary and Mantheria,' Louisa said, fidgeting with the material of her skirt. 'I'll leave you to your thoughts, Wick.'

Spinning on his foot, he held out his hand, although she was too far away for him to touch her. 'No. Don't go. Forgive me. I am trying to compose myself—words—speech...'

Louisa raised one eyebrow and it was as if her green eyes devoured him whole. Wick wished he was brave enough to offer his heart as well as his hand.

'The thing is... Well, you see... You can't go back to London. Or anywhere. Despite your bravery and your clever wielding of a needle, you have been compromised... And now I am making a total hash of my proposal...'

'Your what?'

Wick decided that he should kneel. Dropping to one knee, he said, 'Louisa, will you do me the honour of accepting my hand in marriage?'

Chapter Thirty-Three

Louisa's heart soared at his words. This was the happy ending that she had dared not even hope for. Wick was asking her to marry him! This handsome man whom she loved with all her heart. She would be a true member of the crazy and entirely loveable Stringham family. She and Mantheria would be real sisters. Her trustees would release her inheritance upon her marriage and she would pay back her dear friend, whose loveless marriage was ending.

Except…

Wick hadn't mentioned love.

He'd praised her bravery and her cleverness, but that wasn't enough. She had seen with her own two eyes the misery of being married to a person who didn't love you. She would rather live with the Rockinghams again than marry Wick without love.

'Dear friend, please stand up,' she whispered, not trusting her voice to be steady at a normal tone.

She watched him slowly get to his feet. His eyes were no longer meeting her own. He didn't wish to marry her. She was just another responsibility that he didn't want.

He was only proposing out of duty, because her reputation had been compromised.

'Did Mantheria tell you that she is separating from Lord Glastonbury?'

Wick shook his head.

'She will no longer stay in a loveless marriage,' Louisa said. 'And I will not settle for such a match either. I will wait as long as it takes, until I find a sensible, good man who can love me and I can love in return.'

'But your reputation has been ruined!'

'My reputation is not as important as my happiness.' Although speaking the words made Louisa feel as if her heart was breaking into little pieces too small to sew back together.

He finally lifted his eyes to meet hers. 'I've always wanted your happiness.'

Louisa nodded her head, knowing that if she tried to speak she would sob.

She turned and left the room. Like Mantheria, she was learning that independence came at a steep price.

Despite the excellent company of Mantheria and Mary on the way back to London, Louisa couldn't help but feel solemn. Wick rode beside them on a horse he'd hired from the innkeeper, claiming that the carriage was too full. But Louisa knew the real reason. He was avoiding her.

The carriage stopped first at Lady Glastonbury's house. Frederica ran out through the front door to meet them. 'Did you find Louisa?'

She was followed by Helen, Becca, Andrew and Mrs May.

'I am here,' Louisa said, leaning her head out of the carriage window.

The Stringham girls pulled her out of the carriage and surrounded her in a hug.

'I am so glad! I didn't sleep a wink. I have been worried sick,' Helen said.

'Me too,' Becca echoed.

Louisa felt another pang of regret that they would not be her sisters. Her new family.

Mantheria stepped out of the carriage and picked up her son. Andrew scrunched up his little nose and pointed a chubby finger at his uncle on the horse. 'You no get ices, Uncle Wick.'

He laughed.

Oh, how she loved that sound.

'I shall take you tomorrow, Andy. I promise,' Wick said. 'But today I need to go to my rooms and freshen up. I smell of horse.'

'I like horses,' Andrew said.

Louisa found her tongue. 'Before you go, Lord Cheswick, would you and Mantheria escort me to my Uncle and Aunt Rockingham's house? I have some unfinished business there.'

Mantheria set down her son with a kiss on top of his head. 'Andrew, can you keep an eye on your aunts whilst I am gone? And will you promise not to let them get into any mischief?'

The little boy sniggered, nodding. 'I will.'

'Oh, Mrs May, please allow me to introduce you to my new friend,' she said, as Mary got out of the carriage. 'This is Miss Perkins, and she will be the new governess. She likes snakes.'

Helen's eyes widened and she bounded towards Mary. 'Really? Which is your favourite type?'

'A grass snake.'

Frederica and Becca crowded around the new governess too, asking Mary questions faster than she could possibly answer them. Louisa saw that Andrew was in the capable hands of Mrs May.

Mantheria touched her elbow and a groom helped them back into the carriage. Louisa was sorry to ask her friend to travel farther, but she needed to confront her aunt and uncle once and for all.

Mantheria took Louisa's hand in hers. 'I know this interview will be unpleasant for you. If there is anything I can do or say to help you, please let me know.'

She squeezed her hand back. 'Thank you, dearest friend. Just having you there with me will make all the difference.'

And it was true. Mantheria held her hand until they arrived at her aunt and uncle's London house. Wick assisted them both out of the carriage and they were escorted into a parlour. Her aunt and uncle were both there. Her uncle was reading and her aunt was doing needlework.

Her Uncle Rockingham stood and walked towards her, hands outstretched, when she entered the room. 'My dear niece, you are safe. Lord Sunderland has been claiming the most outrageous things about my son abducting you. Has it all been an unfortunate misunderstanding?'

Louisa half wanted to say that it had. But Barnabas's actions had not been a misunderstanding. He had meant to force her into a hateful marriage.

'It has not. Barnabas hit me on the head in the park and dragged me all the way to Cookham, where he locked me in his mistress's cellar without food or water.'

Her uncle recoiled. 'It can't be true.'

'I wish it were not, Uncle,' Louisa said. 'However, from today I shall have nothing to do with any of you again—familial or financial. I won't sue you for the misspent funds of my allowance, but nor will I help you pay Barnabas's debts.'

'All we need is a brief loan to meet his most pressing creditors,' Uncle Rockingham said. 'We have cared for you for these last ten years, and I am sure your father would have wanted you to help his only brother.'

Wick grunted, but didn't say a word. Mantheria gritted her teeth. Louisa was in no doubt of their feelings on the matter.

Aunt Rockingham clasped her hands together beseechingly. 'How can you be so heartless to your own family? We will be ruined. Ruined!'

Louisa straightened to her full height. 'I *could* ruin you. I could press kidnapping charges against your son and have him hung or transported. But I will not. As long as you leave me alone. If you so much as speak to me again, I will be forced to take legal action… Come, Your Grace…my lord. It is time to leave.'

Louisa was grateful to be sandwiched between them as she left her aunt and uncle's house on her own two feet. For the first time she had no desire for their approval.

Chapter Thirty-Four

Wick could hardly believe that a week had passed since he'd left London for Hampford Castle with his little sisters and Miss Perkins. It had been the longest seven days of his life, and perhaps the most transformative. He felt like a new man. A lighter one.

One day, after his sisters' lessons, they had insisted he go with them to pick flowers and place them on Charles and Elizabeth's names in the crypt.

Wick had expected it to be a solemn outpouring of mutual grief.

It was not.

Somehow his little sisters had made it a celebration of their lost siblings' lives. They'd laughed, cried and shared stories. Frederica and Helen remembered things that he did not. Like the fact that Elizabeth had been a champion pincher and had been able to leave bruises. Or that it had been Charles and not Frederica who had broken a bottle of his mother's perfume in one his few temper tantrums. He'd felt so sorry that his little sister had happily taken the blame. Frederica had always been getting into trouble anyway.

Becca had asked Wick to tell the 'plate in the face' story again and he did, as well as sharing a dozen other reminiscences. Including one about a large swan that had chased poor Charles all around Animal Island, trying to peck him.

On the walk back to the castle Becca and Helen had each taken one of his hands, and Frederica had looped her arm to Helen's. And in that moment he couldn't help but think of Louisa and her wise words about sharing burdens to make them light.

Wick still experienced sadness over his siblings' deaths, but he no longer felt overwhelming grief. And after a few days of observing Miss Perkins with the girls, as well as noticing the benevolent hand of Mrs May over them all, he realised that his sisters didn't need him. Miss Perkins had a knack of making lessons fun and indulging them in their passions. Nearly half of every day was spent out of doors, and he noticed how the governess allowed his sisters to teach her too.

It had not taken Miss Perkins long to rise high—not only in his esteem, but his little sisters' too.

Wick went on long rides, overseeing the land, but also thinking. He missed Louisa with an ache as real as any ailment. She had refused his offer of marriage, but he still believed—hoped—that she loved him. The more he thought about it, the more he realised that Mantheria had been right. If he had offered Louisa his heart she would have accepted him. He would not wish for a loveless marriage based on duty either.

He told his sisters at dinner that night that he intended to go back to London to visit Sunny.

'You mean Louisa,' Frederica said, dropping her fork and grinning at him.

Helen folded her arms across her chest. 'Try to do a better job of your proposal this time.'

'Did you kneel?' Becca asked, spilling her drink in her apparent excitement. 'You should kneel and take her flowers. Lots of flowers. Miss Perkins, what flower means love?'

The governess didn't smile, but her spectacles fogged up a little as she said, 'Red roses.'

Becca beamed at him. 'Take vases of red roses.'

'How is he supposed to carry them?' Helen pointed out.

'While kneeling?' Mrs May said from the opposite end of the table, and they all chuckled.

Now, Wick couldn't help but smile as he remembered their well-meaning rose-laden advice as he rode to Hyde Park, hoping to see Sunny. He pulled his horse to a stop, and was looking around him when two riders approached: Sunny and Matthew.

'Oi!' his brother called out. 'The triumphant rescuer returns.'

Smirking, Wick shook his head.

'I assume you have heard?' Sunny said in a lower voice, as he pulled his horse to a stop next to Wick's.

He nodded. 'Mantheria has told me that she intends to separate from Glastonbury.'

'Yes, she already has,' Matthew said, waving a hand. 'But that's not what we're talking about.'

Wick didn't let his little brother change the subject. 'Do you think Papa and Mama will be disappointed?' he asked.

'In Mantheria's marriage dissolving?'

Wick felt a sinking feeling in his stomach. 'In me. Should I have perhaps done something more? Tried to

help patch it up instead of telling Mantheria that Glastonbury was not out of town as he had told her?'

Sunny turned his head away, his jaw clenched. He
knew his best friend had feelings for Mantheria, and that
he would not wish for her to stay in an unhappy relationship. But Matthew had no such bias, and even less tact.

'Our parents are never disappointed in you, Wick,'
Matthew said, without his usual mocking tone. 'You are
the ideal eldest son. A good property manager. Beloved
by all of your younger siblings. And you bear the responsibility well. Better than you know and better than I
would. I would have let the girls join a travelling perfor-
mance company and washed my hands of them. I would
not have crossed half of England trying to find them the
perfect governess.'

Wick's lips twitched, but he knew he could not allow
his brother to amuse him now. 'But—'

'No buts, Wick,' Matthew interrupted. 'Despite you
being annoyingly perfect, even *I* love you. And our parents and the rest of the motley Stringham crew don't
hold you responsible for our own choices. Mantheria is
a grown woman and a mother.'

Wick's entire body relaxed in the saddle. His brother's
words had relieved his worries regarding his care of the
family.

'Matthew was referring to Lady Louisa,' Sunny said
from his side. 'She has received a most flattering offer
of marriage from Norwich.'

Stiffening, Wick found it hard to breathe as he asked,
'And has she accepted him?'

Sunny shook his head. 'Not yet—but she might. She
fears that her presence in Mantheria's home is feeding the
unpleasant rumours regarding her separation. Not that

268 The Marquess and the Runaway Lady

Mantheria agrees with her, but they have both received letters withdrawing their invitations to parties and routs. They are social pariahs at the moment.'

Wick's hands tightened on the bridle.

'Poor Louisa was also feeling terribly guilty over borrowing money for her wardrobe from Mantheria,' Matthew said, riding up to Wick's other side. 'However, I have solved *that* particular difficulty. After the Rockinghams' bankruptcy was announced in the *London Gazette*, I paid a call to all three of her trustees and pointed out how they had failed in their fiduciary duties to protect Louisa's yearly allowance from her aunt and uncle. I may or may not have threatened legal action if they did not immediately release to Louisa control of her yearly allowance. Happily, they saw the weight of my arguments and I left with all the necessary legal documents in my hand. Louisa should no longer feel obliged to marry in order to repay her debt to Mantheria, but she might still feel obliged to marry a gentleman to restore her lost reputation.'

'Someone like Norwich,' Sunny added unhelpfully.

'Oh, dear me,' Matthew said in a light mocking voice, putting his free hand on his chest. 'Is that my sister's carriage near the Serpentine?'

'I believe it is,' Sunny said gravely, shading his eyes with one hand. 'And what luck! There is Lady Louisa inside it.'

Wick knew what his best friend and brother were doing, but he didn't need their urging. He knew now that he loved Louisa. That he had done for almost every moment they had been together since he had pulled her into his curricle after mistaking her for his sisters' governess. He'd first been bewitched by her beauty, and then he'd been pricked by her sewing needle, her intelligence and her kindness. He would do anything for her. She was everything he wanted in a wife and he wished to spend the rest of his life with her. To love her and cherish her. Protect her.

He didn't dare wait another moment; he spurred his horse forward.

Chapter Thirty-Five

Louisa made eye contact with Lady Jersey, who put a gloved hand in front of her mouth and whispered to the lady beside her in the carriage. The social cut. Blushing, Louisa glanced away. Why was she being punished for her cousin's actions? She had done nothing wrong. She was not ruined. Her worth did not depend upon one day or one event. Or one person's opinion and approval.

Tilting her chin up, Louisa determined to show the *ton* that she didn't care for their narrow minds, nor for their terrible treatment of women.

'It might not be you they're whispering about,' Mantheria said in an undertone. 'I am sure it is common gossip now that Glastonbury has moved out of the house… Perhaps we should have waited until next year before making our return to London society.'

Louisa could only be glad when Lady Jersey's carriage passed by them and moved out of sight. From the corner of her eye she saw Lord Norwich, driving his phaeton towards them. He was wearing the same elaborately caped driving coat as before. She hoped that he was not coming to ask for her answer. She wasn't quite ready to give it yet.

Only a week ago she had painfully refused Wick's offer of a marriage without love, so how could she accept another lord's proposal without love? The only difference in her mind was that she loved Wick and she did not love Norwich, although he was an amusing companion.

She couldn't decide what would be the worst torture: to be married to a man she loved who didn't love her back, or to be trapped in a marriage where neither person loved the other. Perhaps they would grow fond of each other? Or perhaps his gaming debts would swallow her fortune as well as his own? Norwich claimed to have learned his lesson at the tables, but Louisa didn't want to save her fortune from her cousin only to lose it to another gambler.

Lord Norwich's smart equipage pulled up beside their carriage and both vehicles came to a halt.

'Ladies,' he said, tipping his hat to them.

Louisa looked down at her hands in her lap.

She heard Mantheria clear her throat. 'Lord Norwich, what a pleasure it is to see you.'

Louisa stole a glance at the gentleman and saw his lips form their usual sneer. 'And to be seen by me… I fear many of our fond society matrons appear not to be able to see either you or your carriage.'

Mantheria gave a little laugh. 'Oh, and don't forget the horses and my driver.'

Lord Norwich gave his soundless laugh.

Louisa was all but certain she was going to refuse his offer, but she didn't wish to be a burden upon her friend. And she didn't want to spend the rest of her youth ostracised by the *ton* and unable to join the London season entertainments she'd always dreamed of.

'Lady Louisa, dare I ask if it is a pleasure for *you* to see me?' asked Lord Norwich.

She swallowed. Her answer to this question would be almost the same as accepting or rejecting his offer of marriage. She took a deep breath, trying to organise the chaos of her mind.

The sound of galloping hooves caused her eyes to turn. Mantheria had told her that no one was supposed to gallop in Hyde Park during the promenade—the fashionable hours of three to five o'clock. Yet this gentleman was openly disregarding the rules.

He lifted his face and she saw that it was Wick! Her heart skipped a beat. He was back. She hadn't thought that he would return to London for the rest of the season.

'Ah, I see that Lord Cheswick has returned, and it is certainly a pleasure for you to see *him*,' Lord Norwich said sardonically.

'Forgive me, my lord,' she said in a state of confusion, glancing back at him. 'I did not mean to offend.'

He gave her a rueful look. 'Sometimes being fashionably late is a liability; it appears your affections have already been engaged. I do wish you every happiness in proving me wrong about Cheswick. Now I shall bid you lovely ladies adieu. I have no wish to hinder the grand reunion. But please be assured of my continued friendship and support.'

Norwich lifted his whip and snapped it above his horses' heads as they cantered forward.

Louisa had never liked the Earl so well as in that moment.

'Against my will, I am growing fond of Lord Norwich,' Mantheria said with a half-smile.

Before Louisa could answer, Wick pulled his horse to a stop beside them. 'Louisa, may we go for a walk?'

Mantheria raised her eyebrows. 'But what of your horse, Wick?'

He swung out of the saddle, looking handsomer than ever. Grabbing the bridle, he tied it to the back of her carriage before opening the door.

Wick held out his hand to her. 'Shall we?'

'I should be pleased to walk with you,' Louisa said, in a breathy voice that was not quite her own.

She placed her hand in his and a sweet warmth flooded through her entire body. He helped her down from the carriage and then offered his arm. Louisa briefly placed her fingers on the crook of his elbow, and again she experienced a flushed heat and a feeling of rightness.

'You can walk down by the Serpentine,' Mantheria said. 'But stay in sight, Wick. I am her chaperone, after all. And Louisa—don't go too easy on him.'

Louisa had to bite her lower lip to keep in her grin.

Wick gave his sister a menacing glance before leading Louisa away from the carriage towards the glistening blue waters of the lake. They stepped on to the pebbled shore and he turned to look her in the eyes.

'Louisa, please say that I am not too late.'

'Too late for what?' she countered, hoping for but not daring to assume his renewed attentions.

'Too late to tell you—tell you how I feel. That I— That I love you and I have always loved you. And that I will do anything in my power to make myself worthy of you if you'll be my wife.'

Her eyes filled with tears. 'You are already worthy. You are the best man I have ever known.'

Wick stepped closer and gently brushed a curl back from her face and behind her ear. 'Does that mean yes?'

Louisa leaned towards him. 'Yes.'

She licked her lips in anticipation. He was so close to her she was sure that he would kiss her again. Waiting for his mouth to touch hers felt like an exquisite torture. Her gaze fell to his lips. Wick brought his gloved hand to her face, cupping her cheek. His eyes searched hers.

'I wish that I could kiss you again,' he whispered. 'But I suppose I will have to wait until we are married.'

Wick might be willing to wait, but Louisa was not.

Standing on her tiptoes, she gently pressed her lips to his. Lightly. Softly. She felt his other hand on her back, pressing her closer to him, against his muscular body. He moved the hand on her face to her neck, and then his fingers into her hair. Not once breaking the kiss. Gaining courage, Louisa wrapped her arms around his neck and pressed her lips harder to his. She heard him give a slight moan and felt her power over him. Wick wanted her as much as she wanted him.

His mouth moved over hers with more pressure. Louisa gasped, and she felt his mouth close over her lower lip and gently suck on it. She felt heat in her belly and her whole body tingled. Her eyes popped open and she saw his smiling face. Moving her hand from his neck, she traced his lips with her finger. He closed his eyes and made a sound not unlike his sister's kittens when they were being stroked. Wick clearly enjoyed her caresses as much as she had his kisses.

Leaning forward, she opened her mouth slightly as they kissed again. Wick responded in kind. She felt the heat from his mouth and the wetness of his lips. It was even more deliciously wicked and wonderful than their first kiss. She captured his lower lip between hers and sucked. He tasted sweet, like honey.

Reluctantly, she let his lip go. Wick did not move back from her, but returned his mouth to hers, deepening the kiss. His hands moved up and down her back and shoulders, overwhelming her senses and overturning her good manners. So much so that Louisa allowed one of her hands to drift from his neck down to his cravat, and then to the hardness of his chest.

Louisa felt Wick's hand cover hers. 'Perhaps we'd better stop giving the *ton* a show. I think there's been enough scandal for both our families already.'

The blood rushed to her face and she tried to pull her hand back, but Wick held it firmly.

'I didn't mean… I am sorry…'

'I hope that you *did* mean to kiss me and that you are *not* sorry,' he whispered, bringing her hand to his lips and kissing it. 'For this is the happiest day of my life.'

'You don't think I am too forward?'

He kissed her hand again. 'I think you are perfect just as you are. My only fear is that you have a sewing needle somewhere upon your person and that I am about to be pricked.'

Louisa giggled. 'You're quite safe. The needle is on the inside of my hem.'

'And you are inside my heart. Always.'

She couldn't help herself. Standing on her tiptoes, Louisa pressed a kiss to his cheek. 'And you are in mine.'

Epilogue

Wick walked into the dimly lit Hampford Chapel. He didn't think his body could take any more joy. Filling one side of the pews, he saw Mrs May, all the maids, the butler, the footmen, the grooms, the gardeners, the keepers and Merrell, the head animal keeper. They had all come to support him.

Wick's father didn't believe in making his employees attend church. He left the matter of their souls entirely to themselves. The fact that every single one of them had chosen to attend his wedding warmed his soul.

Vases of red roses lined the aisle and adorned the altar. His little sisters must have been hard at work all morning. He sincerely hoped that they didn't want him to kneel in front of Louisa now.

The other side of the chapel was more sparsely filled. Grandmother Stubbs sat in the front row with Andrew perched on her lap. Behind them were Helen and Becca, holding their kittens. Miss Perkins was handing Frederica a handkerchief. Wick was floored—he hadn't seen Frederica cry in years.

Matthew and Sunny stood at the front of the chapel

by the chaplain. They were both his best men. When he reached their side, they shook his hands. Mrs Berry, the chaplain's wife, began to play the organ.

Wick looked at his best friend and prayed that someday he too would have a happy ending with Mantheria, even if he didn't know how. But life was full of surprises and second chances, he'd discovered, and sometimes being a wreck brought you to the right shore.

Behind them was a large circular stained-glass window of the archangel Michael slaying the dragon. It wasn't the most romantic of illustrations for a wedding, but the soft coloured light that it shed into the chapel felt holy.

Then Louisa entered the chapel on his grandfather's arm and all other thoughts fled his mind. She followed Mantheria, her matron of honour, and she was holding a bouquet of red roses, but none were as bright and as brilliant as her own red curls. Her dress was seafoam-green, and on her shoulders was the delicate lace shawl that Mrs Barker had made for her.

Slowly, she came towards him, and with each step his heart grew fuller. When she reached him, Louisa let go of Grandfather Stubbs's arm. They turned to face each other and Wick couldn't help but smile at his beautiful bride. Louisa beamed back at him and she practically sparkled.

The Reverend Berry, the Duke's elderly personal chaplain, opened his book and began the ceremony. Wick heard maybe one word in ten. His eyes and concentration were on Louisa. He did, however, manage to say 'I will' at the appropriate moment, as did Louisa.

'I pronounce that they be man and wife together, in the name of the father, and of the son, and of the Holy Ghost. Amen,' Mr Berry said.

Wick could wait no longer. He swept Louisa into his arms and slanted his mouth towards hers. Louisa's lips were warm and insistent against his. The kiss ended to the sound of cheering.

Matthew clapped him on the back. 'Well done. But you'd better sign the register to make it all legal.'

Mantheria handed Wick a pen. He signed his name: *Lord Simon Anthony Peregrine Stringham, Marquess of Cheswick.*

'That's quite a mouthful,' Louisa teased, taking the pen and signing her own name beneath his. 'I think I shall stick to calling you Wick. But you can call me the Marchioness of Cheswick.'

'Or my wife.'

She beamed at him. 'That would be accurate too.'

They left the chapel arm in arm. Once out of the holy place his sisters descended upon both him and Louisa with hugs and kisses and kittens.

Andrew tugged on his knee breeches. 'Up, Uncle Wick.'

He laughed and swung the boy up to his shoulder.

Frederica punched his arm. 'I told you that Louisa was a lady. You should have trusted my instincts from the first.'

'Well, *I* thought she was a princess,' Helen said loftily, her long snake Theodosia curling around her right arm.

Becca smiled. 'And I thought she was beautiful.'

Wick kissed the top of his sister's head. 'Thank you, Becca, my heart.'

'I suppose Louisa is your heart now,' she said with a laugh, and followed Helen and Frederica to the Great Hall where a dessert table that had been set out.

Turning, he watched his grandmother kiss Louisa on both cheeks and his grandfather give her a bear hug.

His grandfather leaned heavily on his cane as he pulled a document out of his pocket.

'Wick wanted to ensure that your inheritance remained your own after your marriage,' he said in a gruff voice. 'And thanks to Matthew's devious talent with words it is thus. Louisa, your mother's money is still yours in a separate estate overseen by the Chancery Court.'

Louisa's green eyes widened and she looked at him. 'You have done that for me?'

Andrew pulled at his hair and Wick gave a painful gasp. 'Yes. Yes, I have. I want only you. Not your fortune.'

Grandfather Stubbs held out one hand to Andrew. 'Come here, Andy.'

His nephew managed to pull Wick's hair once more and kick his ear, before landing in his great-grandfather's strong arm.

'Shall we have some cake?' he asked the child.

Andrew giggled. 'And an ice!'

'Anything for you,' Grandfather Stubbs said, holding Andrew with one arm and his cane with the other.

Wick's little nephew had no idea that he was in the arms of one of the most powerful businessmen in England. One who could literally give him whatever he wished.

Wick felt Louisa's arms wrap around his waist. Smiling, he pulled her closer to him and rested his head on her hair. She fitted perfectly there.

Louisa snuggled her face against his chest. 'I can't imagine a more perfect day. Can you?'

'Actually, I can.'

She leaned back. 'What's wrong?'

He kissed her nose. 'This is only the beginning. I plan to keep you up for the rest of the day and most of the night.' Wick released his hold on his wife and held out his hand. 'Come, let's go.'

Louisa placed hers into his, but said, 'We cannot leave in the middle of the wedding party. Everyone will know why and what we are doing.'

Wick laughed wickedly. 'But they won't be able to find us.'

He pulled her out of the room, down to the hall and into the courtyard…stopping only once to give her a long, seeking kiss.

* * * * *

If you enjoyed this story, be sure to look out for more great books from Samantha Hastings, coming soon!

Get 4 FREE REWARDS!

We'll send you 2 FREE Books plus 2 FREE Mystery Gifts.

FREE
Value Over
$20

Both the **Harlequin® Historical** and **Harlequin® Romance** series feature
compelling novels filled with emotion and simmering romance.

HARLEQUIN
PLUS

Try the best multimedia
subscription service for romance
readers like you!

Read, Watch and Play.

Experience the easiest way to get
the romance content you crave.

Start your **FREE TRIAL** at
<u>www.harlequinplus.com/freetrial</u>.